OUTDRIVEN

OUTDRIVEN

Laurie Rogers

Matador
9 Priory Business Park,
Wistow Road, Kibworth Beauchamp,
Leicestershire. LE8 0RX
Tel: 0116 279 2299
Email: books@troubador.co.uk
Web: www.troubador.co.uk/matador
Twitter: @matadorbooks

ISBN 978 1800461 239

British Library Cataloguing in Publication Data.
A catalogue record for this book is available from the British Library.

Printed and bound in Great Britain by 4edge Limited
Typeset in 11pt Minion Pro by Troubador Publishing Ltd, Leicester, UK

Matador is an imprint of Troubador Publishing Ltd

This book would not have been possible without the support and encouragement of my wife, Sue, whose experiences as a lady golfer and running a golf business provided many of the ideas for this tale

1

Looking back years later I would say that was the moment it all started. Not that the event itself led to what happened. It wasn't even the catalyst. But it was the moment when the impossible suddenly seemed possible, when for once I had managed to achieve something that my late husband had never managed.

It wasn't as if there had been any build up to it. It was quite cold that October morning and the rain the previous day had made the fairways muddy. There were dead leaves everywhere, tumbling from the trees in the wind, floating on the puddles that had formed in the hollows on the fairways, clogging the ditches that criss-crossed the course. The trees were looking barer, like my life, I thought. The dead leaves signifying that life was over, rather like my own.

But trees don't die when they shed their leaves. They just shut down for a few months until the weather gets warmer and then they spring back to life, new leaves shoot, then branches spread further, their trunks get wider.

On the other hand, humans don't follow the same annual pattern. In my mind you grow up, you grow old and then you die. Regeneration is not an option. By 18 you've stopped growing upwards, even if your trunk expands in later years. Not that I had any morbid fascination with death. I quite expected to live for many more years. It was just that from now on it was all downhill. Things started to slow down. Things started to wear out. Things had to be replaced, but not renewed as a tree's leaves are. Hips, knees, they were the things that my friends were replacing. And there were the things that simply disappeared. Things like friends. Friends who one Spring Meeting were quite alright and by the next spring had succumbed to Alzheimer's or cancer. And it wasn't just friends, it was husbands too.

So there was no great expectation as I took out my five iron at the lake hole 12th. Just the usual fear. Fear that I would 'top' the ball and send it spinning into the lake.

I remember following the ball's flight as it rose up into the leaden sky. I remember the sense of relief that it was easily going to clear the lake.

"Lovely shot, Maggie." Rosemary always called the shot before it finished, usually short and in the bunker in my experience. But this time the ball kept travelling, its parabola taking it over the bunker and onto the green; not only onto the green but onwards towards the hole itself – nearer and nearer.

Oh no it can't. It can't, surely not? I thought. But it did. It slowed. It hesitated as if contemplating the depth of the cup to see if tumbling over the edge would hurt. Finally, with what I imagined was a shrug of its shoulders, the Pinnacle Lady golf ball disappeared into the hole.

"It's a hole in one, a hole in one!" Rosemary's voice rose to an even higher pitch than normal. She actually jumped up and down with excitement, letting go of her electric trolley in her excitement. We looked at each other, wide eyed, then turned to stare at the green as if waiting for the ball to suddenly pop back out of the hole. Rosemary's electric trolley purred its way slowly and determinedly towards the lake.

"Oh Frank would have been so proud of you!" said Rosemary as she recovered her clubs from the side of the lake where the trolley had come to rest, upside down.

Frank had been a great golfer; a winner of many of the Club's tournaments, head of the finance committee, the Club's authority on the rules of the ancient game. And a great provider for me. Yes, Frank would have been proud. But he wasn't around to see it. I felt strangely sad. A few months ago I would have been leaping for joy like Rosemary but all I could think of was Frank and how he would never know.

Frank had risen through the ranks at Reuters becoming head of the division that supplied brokers with their lifeblood – the city news as it happened; sometimes even before it happened. In fact knowing what was about to happen had made Frank a lot of money. Some very shrewd purchases of share options contracts had made him very wealthy. By the time he left Reuters he had bought our big house outside Sunningdale, a villa on the San Lourenco course in Portugal and a couple of powerful Mercedes. He had also managed to educate Hugh, Simone and Estelle privately, something of which his father would never had approved.

But he had never managed a hole in one.

Frank's ambition had always been to become Captain of West Downs Golf Club (founded in 1909). The pity was that three years before the Club's centenary he had parked his SL500 on the roundabout on the A30, upside down. Police, trying to console me, had assured me that death had been instantaneous and that the amount of alcohol in his blood would anyway surely have deadened any pain.

The result was that I now found myself living in a seven-bedroomed house with a two acre paddock and extensive gardens, a large balance in Lloyds Private Bank and absolutely nothing to fulfil me.

Now I had a hole in one and Rosemary was ecstatic even if I wasn't.

"Maggie got a hole in one on the twelfth! You should have seen it. Fantastic shot. Never looked like going anywhere else." Rosemary was leaning across the polished wood bar and speaking excitedly to Marco the Club's Majorcan bar steward. The group of ladies in the corner looked up. They smiled at each other and one of them shook her head. "Maggie? A hole in one? Now that's something to shout about. Why Maggie's lucky to play to 36 handicap most days and that was when the fairways are baked hard and she manages to hit her tee shots far enough to clear the heather!"

"I am so pleased for Mrs Miles. She is very pleased also I think. Where is she?"

I remember I'd changed out of my golf trousers and sweater and was wearing my 'Tuesday outfit'. This consisted of a dark brown flared skirt in a satiny material with a rather fashionable 'crinkle-cut' hem, a snow-white cashmere V-necked sweater. I had put on my chunky gold necklace with the large pearl in what Frank had called a mussel shell but was in fact the shell of some exotic shellfish found on the beaches of Phuket. Frank had bought it for me when we holidayed there.

"Well done Mrs Myles. Things are looking good – and so are you!"

Marco was such a flirt but we ladies loved him. I patted my hair and said something half-joking back to him. I've always considered my hair as one of my better features. For years I had had it cut and styled by a salon in Ascot although it required rather more blonde highlights now. I tried to keep it short and modern. I didn't want to join the blue-rinse brigade. I had a few acquaintances who were little older than me yet seemed to have given up and spend their time in slippers, knitting and watching Countdown. I didn't want to be like them. Frank had always liked me looking smart. But then, Frank was no longer around, was he?

I got a polite round of applause as I entered. An eagle was a rare bird among us ladies that lunched at West Downs Golf Club (founded 1909). I wasn't likely to get another hole in one – I was happy to savour the moment.

"Well done Mrs Miles, you have holed one on the twelfth." Marco's English was fluent after 20 years working bar in the Home Counties but still lacked anything approaching sensible conversation.

"Yes indeed. Thank you Marco, please have a drink on my card."

"Very kind, very good. Thank you."

Rosemary was adding up our scores and looked up as I approached with our drinks.

"With your five points on the twelfth, I made you thirty eight so your handicap will come down." She pushed up her

Armani glasses a little more. The bar was now filling up with other players from our West Downs Ladies.

I wonder now what a casual observer would have made of the scene.

They might have supposed the group were meeting for a big night out. Jewels were everywhere. West Downs (founded 1909) might be traditional but that didn't stop the lady members from enjoying their bling.

The ladies of West Downs (founded 1909) might not be able to match Annika Sorrenstam when it came to shot-making but we could certainly outdo Paula Creamer when it came to dressing up.

As a group, we were aging. In fact the average age of the ladies section was north of 55. But these ladies didn't look like has-beens – at least not if plastic surgery and heavy make-up had anything to do with it. We were ladies who had married well; whose husbands worked in the City (God knows what he gets up to there but at least he's not under my feet at home all day!)

Of course, many of our husbands had now stopped being something in the City and instead were enjoying the fruits of their labours by playing golf every day that God gave them (anything to get him out from under my feet!)

Not that our Club was blingy. Oh no, far from it. West Downs was one of those golf clubs that understood 'tradition'. The flash clubhouse, the gym, even the fairway watering was not what West Downs was about. West Downs was about etiquette; knowing how to behave as an Englishman (or a Scot of course). It was a club that didn't have a 'social committee' but did organise weekly bridge evenings.

It was a club that some men aspired to join, to belong to, even to captain one day. People like my Frank.

"I've put you down for the coach trip next Wednesday Maggie. We're leaving at 9 o'clock so you mustn't be late. It's a fantastic shopping centre, loads of designer outlets and we're having lunch at a dinky little restaurant that Hilary's found by the port." Fiona was the Ladies Secretary. She was good at organising things. She liked organising things anyway. Things didn't always turn out as she hoped but she had an indefatigable energy that enabled her to pick herself up and smile, even after a total disaster. Like the time Wendy, Veronica and Margaret were left in the DKNY shop at Gun Wharf and no-one realised they weren't on the coach until Fiona announced that Wendy had won the raffle – and by that time we were approaching Basingstoke.

"Yes, I'll be there," I said. After all I didn't have anything else to do next Wednesday. In fact since Frank died I didn't have much to do with my time at all.

2

October 2007

Pyotr stretches out his legs and raises his arms above his head. He moves his head from side to side to try and get rid of the stiffness in his neck. Jarek, beside him, is still asleep, his sonorous breathing coming in regular smooth gasps like some enormous steam engine. The front of his shirt has a damp mark where he's dribbled during the night.

The dawn is beginning to lighten the flat countryside outside. Pyotr rubs the condensation off the coach window with his fist and looks out at the featureless landscape rushing by. He checks his watch and calculates. Two hours before the ferry so they must be getting near to Calais. The coach is speeding along the autoroute at around 100 kph. He sees a brown and white sign depicting a church and the words 'Charleville'. It means little to him. Maybe they are still in Belgium or maybe they have already crossed into France.

How easy it is to cross borders in the European Community. Land that had taken the World War 1 troops years to try and cross is now traversed at 100kph without even slowing down for the border.

How much easier than the first time he crossed a border. The one into the Ukraine. He remembers the queuing with his parents, the waiting to have their papers checked, the interrogation. And everywhere the Russian troops, the Kalashnikovs. No, it is certainly easier to move around Europe now the Wall has come down and the Soviet Union has split apart.

Now people like him and Jarek could get the bus to Britain! There's nothing to stop them, nothing in the way. Poland had always been in the way it seemed. In the way of the Germans, then the Russians. Even the Swedes years before. It was about time the Poles had a chance to get out from under. Good old Lech Walesa. Now the way is open and Pyotr is determined to make the most of it.

Jarek gives a loud snort followed by the hacking cough of a forty-a-day smoker. He wakes, and like Pyotr moments before, stretches out his legs.

"Where are we? Are we still in Germany?" Without waiting for an answer he heaves himself out of his seat and staggers to the back of the coach. "Need to piss," he mumbles.

Pyotr fishes out his iPod, a birthday present from his wife Saska. He puts the headphones on and presses the play button. He finds Cold Play's lyrics hard to understand and concentrates to try and make out the words of 'Lost'. His English isn't bad – he studied it after leaving school where he'd had to learn Russian and German.

The song echoes through his headphones. The lyrics have meaning for him. Rather like his life – no matter how much he studied, no matter how hard he worked, he hadn't managed to make it. He'd found every door locked. And he wants to make it. Oh yes, he owes it to Saska. He wants to succeed, to live in a fine house not a high-rise apartment made from crumbling Russian concrete. Maybe one day he'd have a house and a pool in L.A. like the ones in the movies and TV shows that had dominated the post-Soviet TV screens in Warsaw.

America isn't an option, yet. Britain is. Less than a day's travel, less than a week's wages and the promise of work.

Soon he'll see those famous white cliffs, with or without their bluebirds.

3

I climb into the coach, walk down the aisle and sit down next to Rosemary. It's raining again and I already regret having spent so long on my hair this morning. But one has to. It might be just a shopping trip to men but it's an occasion to indulge in retail therapy for ladies who lunch.

Rosemary starts talking even before I've sat down. She explains that Fiona has given her a list of all the clothes shops together with a hand-drawn map. She shows me where she's marked the restaurant where we are all to meet for lunch. I know the sort of place. Minimalist, tiled floors, serving Thai king prawn salads (so slimming!). We would all choose salads and then wash it down with one-too-many glasses of Pinot Grigio.

Not that I mind. A day out with the girls is something to look forward to. Anyway, I need a pair of new shoes.

Sitting across the aisle is Elizabeth. That surprises me. She's normally too busy with her charities to come on 'frivolous' outings, not her style at all.

"How are you managing, Maggie? Are you getting

along OK without Frank? It must be so difficult for you. I know just how you feel, having to do everything yourself now."

God, is that how she treats her charity cases? OK I know she means well but does she have to bring Frank up? "Oh I'm managing, it's not bad." I flash her a smile. "People have been very kind. Lots of dinner invitations, very kind."

People have been kind. They've invited me to dinner parties but the conversation always skirts around my newly widowed status. It was as though no one knows how to deal with it. Frank had been popular at the Club but the nature of his death, drunken driving, I guess is something none of them feel comfortable to mention.

"Oh that's good, Maggie, I'm so glad you're getting plenty of invitations."

I know the invitations will soon dry up. Single women don't make for convivial dinner parties – spinsters or widows. That's why Elizabeth gets so few. Of course there are a few single men in the Club, widowed like me. I suppose that sooner or later, once a suitable interval has elapsed, I'll find myself invited along with one of them.

"Your family must be a great source of support." Elizabeth has an annoying way of asking questions that she's already answered herself.

"Yes, of course."

I turn to Rosemary to get away from Elizabeth's well-meant questions. She's texting on her new phone. No help there!

At last the coach sets off. The coach driver puts the coach in gear and turns out of the golf club car park. We're heading for Portsmouth. It's a change of scene, I tell myself as I lean across Rosemary and wipe the steamed-up window. It's raining.

Yes, the family have been good to me. They helped me arrange the funeral; Simone came and stayed for a few days. Hugh of course has made a big show of playing head of the family. But then, I suppose he is now – head of the family. He was so good at the funeral, took care of everything, spoke with the vicar, phoned the guests and he did speak so well about Frank.

I was silly to think he could spend more time with me afterwards. He's got a very important job, and a family. I smile at the thought. "The city never sleeps" he's always telling me. "24/7 it's happening and I need to have my finger on the pulse at all times. Need to be able to give a head ups on the global markets, provide them with solid data for their blue-sky forecasting." What nonsense he speaks now – just when did my little boy grow up and start to speak in jargon?

Still he **is** something in the City and at least I can leave all the financial affairs to him to sort out.

4

Pyotr and Jarek hug each other at Victoria Coach Station. "Good luck with the potatoes," jokes Pyotr, "I'm sure Peterborough is a great place – just don't spend all your money in the nightclubs!"

He watches as Jarek and most of the others walk towards the coach for their journey on to Peterborough. They hope to find employment crop picking in the East Anglian fields. It's back-breaking work, long hours and only £7 or £8 per hour. But that translates well into zlotys and with cheap hostel accommodation, a year in the fields could provide a tidy sum to take back to Poland.

But Pyotr hasn't come to dig potatoes. He doesn't do that in Poland. He has studied agriculture at college. He worked for the State Forestry Commission. What he wants is a good responsible job that pays good money. Yes he's Polish, but he speaks and writes English and knows lots about plants and cultivation. And now he is "European" he is entitled to work anywhere in the Union.

He looks again at the address that Lech has given him.

Woking is only half an hour by train from here. And Woking was a place to find well-paid horticultural jobs, Lech assured him.

"There are lots of famous gardens," he had said.

Pyotr knows about the Royal Horticultural Society Gardens at Wisley, about Kew. He has also Googled and found there is a specialist agricultural college nearby. It sounds promising.

He walks across the road and into the railway station. He changes every Polish note he has for English money at the bureau de change on the concourse. He doesn't get much. It is going to have to last until he gets his first pay packet. He is determined to be successful. He will bring Saska over, they will have a fine house in England, he will stop smoking and learn to put milk in his tea.

He goes to the ticket office and buys a single ticket to Woking.

5

That Sunday the committee meets in the clubhouse. Members of the committee get together most Sundays to discuss matters but today is different. Today will be decision day. For three years the committee members have deliberated. They have met, looked at plans, reworked the figures, argued about the likely response from members and then retired to the bar for a couple of gins before lunching and playing foursomes. Today they must decide.

Jim has been captain for more than six months and is used to chairing meetings. He isn't one for long meetings, arguments over points of order. He's had a successful importing business and knows how to make quick decisions. But this isn't a quick decision. It is something that will have a long-term effect on the Club and there are people on the committee who need to commit rather than continue to raise minor issues.

The arguments over global warming were in the past. The truth is, water is going to become scarcer because there are so many new houses in the area. Without an adequate water supply, the golf course will die. Jim isn't going to go down in the Club's history as the captain who failed to respond to the crisis. Already they've had restrictions imposed on their use of the bore hole.

Jim begins by trying to instil a sense of urgency.

"We need a reservoir if we are going to continue to have the quality of greens we've always enjoyed, month in month out. And we need to carry out the tree clearance to bring the character of the course back to where it was in 1909". There is a low murmur of approval as the committee, as one, respond to the Club's founding date. "The problem is, can we afford to do both now?"

"We need to preserve the Club as an example to all these 'Johnny-come-lately clubs that have sprung up." Arthur has been head of finance sub-committee for about as long as anyone can remember. He still plays in Plus-Fours (much more traditional than Plus-Twos) and although now playing with the biggest-headed titanium driver ever made, he constantly harps back to the time when golf was played 'as God and Old Tom Morris intended'.

He ignores Jim's look of annoyance at the interruption and carries on, clearly warming to his subject. "Because of the status of this Club, and my own relationship with Dylan's Bank," he pauses and lets his words sink in. He wants to remind the two younger members of committee of the fact that he has been a director of the boutique bank with offices in Moorgate and Sunningdale. "Because of our unique position," he repeats, "we do not need to levy members in order to finance both these schemes. We can borrow against our own security, paying it off across, say, twenty five years. Which means most of us will not still be playing and won't need to worry!"

"But what about the interest payments? Add those to the capital that needs to be repaid and we're going to be talking pretty big numbers. Even over twenty or twenty five years that's going to mean pretty sizeable monthly payments." Arthur glares at the younger man who has dared to interrupt him. The trouble with the new breed in the City is that they all think they know it all. They all want to work 24/7 and show off because they've got a first in economics. And this one, this forty year old who dares to interrupt him – where had he got his degree – Oxford, Cambridge? No, a bloody provincial university – Manchester or something. What audacity! To question him, a man who has guided successive captains through the financial dealings of the Club for years. He, a man who knows you learn more from knowing what school a man went to than you could ever learn from a spreadsheet.

"I had of course allowed for that, if you'd only let me finish. We won't need to levy existing members as we can expect an increase in joining fees with a top-rate course. The annual subscriptions will, naturally, have to rise a bit, but probably no more than 10%

"I doubt that would be enough," says the young banker. "With interest at, say 7%, we'd need to be paying......" he taps some numbers on the keypad of his Blackberry.

"Will you please let me finish? You have probably forgotten that there will be an increase in income once the women become full members next year and pay the same as us. So with that and the £5000 joining fees we'll easily afford it. Especially as I have been promised a particularly low interest rate due to my past history with the Bank." Once again, Arthur stops and looks around the committee room letting his words take effect.

The younger man isn't going to be pacified however. "What about security – what are they demanding for the loan? Are we going to have to mortgage the Club? Isn't that a risk?"

Jim tries to bring the meeting to order. He looks at Arthur. "Actually that's an important consideration, Arthur."

Arthur's lipped curls into a condescending smile. "Might I point out that under 'current assets' we have an item 'investments' standing at nearly a million pounds. That is the amount which we have achieved through careful and knowledgeable.." another pause, "purchase of shares as well as judicious use of high interest deposit accounts. We are not short of the means to pay the interest on our debts. We just don't want to cash in those assets while they are earning us so much. After all they have almost doubled in value in the past three years!"

Later in the bar, Jim questions Major Silvester the Club Secretary who had been in the meeting. "You're sure we don't have to put this to a vote at the AGM?"

"Absolutely. The committee has the power under the articles of the Club to make proper provision for maintenance of the course and that's exactly what this is."

6

Pyotr looks around the room. It's cheaply furnished, a couch where he would sleep, a small TV on a low coffee table, in the corner a formica-topped table, folded, is propped against the wall. There are grimy slatted blinds over the window.

He crosses and parts them a little to look out. The room is on the first floor above a betting shop. Across the road are similar shops in a terraced row. They have two storeys of flats above them. Between every second shop are the doors that give access to the stairs leading to the flats.

One of the shops opposite is boarded up. Next to it is a shop selling model kits and next to that a fast food outlet, the smell from which accosted his nostrils when he got out of Lech's Polish-registered VW Golf. There are two other rooms and a bathroom in the flat which is shared by four Poles. Pyotr will stay, sleeping on the couch, for a few weeks until he finds somewhere of his own.

It had taken them 20 minutes by car from Woking station to Addlestone where Lech has his flat. Twenty minutes for Pyotr to realise how crowded Britain was. The roads were filled with traffic, very new cars, many of them big 4x4s. Pyotr supposed that these vehicles dealt with the potholes better than ordinary cars and certainly better than Lech's Golf.

They had stopped on the way at a small grocery shop that sold Polish food and which had notices in its window in Polish.

"This shop is owned by two brothers from Krakow, they've been over here for four years – before we joined the EU. Quite a few Poles came over before we joined – couldn't officially work here but there's plenty of casual work if you want it. Surrey is a rich area and the Brits don't seem to like getting their hands dirty!"

"You'll see a lot of guys coming into the betting shop under our flat. They don't seem to have a job but they've got money to bet with. The state pays quite a lot as benefits each week."

"Don't they have to get a job?"

"Doesn't look like it to me."

*

The next morning he wakes up to the smell of bacon cooking. It's still dark outside. In the little kitchen two of his flatmates are frying bacon and buttering white sliced bread.

"Hi Pyotr. You slept alright on the couch then"

"Yeah, pretty good." He rolls off the couch and stretches. The couch wasn't long enough for him to lie straight and he rubs his neck to get the blood flowing again. The mug of coffee revives him and he crosses the room and looks out. The street lights are reflected in the puddles and the cars have their headlights on.

"What time is it?"

"Just before six. We're off in a minute."

"How far is the depot?" Pyotr has learned that Mikhail and Marek had, like Lech, jobs driving vans delivering groceries to people.

"About three kilometres. We get a bus down the road unless Lech drives us. It's not a bad job, you get tips sometimes from customers too."

"Lech always gets tips," laughs Marek. "Especially from the pretty ones!"

"I just like to practise my English," Lech enters the room. He straightens up, pushes his hair off his forehead and in English says "I hope you like your food. I learn English so I can talk you up."

Pyotr smiles. There is something wrong with 'talk you up' he knows but he can't think what.

"I want to get a job in horticulture, not a delivery job," he says and then instantly regrets it. He hadn't meant to sound disparaging; he knows a lot of Poles work for Ocado the delivery company. They advertised in Poland and even paid for people to come over. It's just that he wants to be successful for Saska's sake. He needs to earn a lot more money. Today he would make some phone calls to Kew and Wisley and Merrist Wood. A job there and he could start looking for somewhere to live – somewhere with a proper bed where he could stretch out his full 180 centimetres. He rubs his neck again.

7

I'm going to have to phone him. It's no good. It's still growing, the damn grass and he didn't come yesterday. All this rain just makes it grow more than ever.

I look across at the paddock. The grass is even worse there. It needs the tractor mower going over it. Frank would have seen to it. He liked riding that tractor mower. Drove it as fast as it would go, round and round the field. Frank always drove fast, too fast.

Alberto and Frank had got on pretty well in a boss/worker sort of way. Frank told him exactly what needed doing, Alberto retorted that it was impossible to do it all in the time, only for Frank to tell him that if he didn't talk so much and got on with the job it would all get done.

Since Frank died I haven't been able to get Alberto to do much at all. He arrives late, spends time talking to God-knows-who on his mobile phone and complains as usual that the garden is too big for one man to handle.

Last week he arrived an hour late, finished early but still demanded his £50 plus another £18 for fertiliser. I'm sure he was trying it on. Didn't like it when I asked for receipts for the fertiliser.

He complained that he was being insulted. Frank never asked for receipts. I paid him. I don't want to lose him.

I half expect him not to come again. I'm right. I ring his mobile and leave a message. He doesn't ring back. Oh well, I think, I'll have to get Hugh to do it at the week-end.

I hear the postman's van and am just in time to see him put a pile of letters in the box by the gate. I get the mailbox key, throw on my old anorak and wellies and go down the drive to fetch the post.

It's all very well having electric gates, and Frank was very keen, but it's always me that has to go out in the wet to empty the mailbox.

Among the letters is one from our management company in Portugal. I read it through twice. Apparently there's to be a meeting of residents about a new tax the Portuguese have brought in for foreign owners. Frank always sorts these things out. He likes meetings, especially where he can hold forth. I'm always doing this. Forgetting he's not here to do things anymore. Perhaps I can ask Hugh when he comes down. But he's always so busy and he may have to spend time cutting the paddock anyway.

Since Frank died I think I'm in limbo. I know I'm widowed, he's not coming back, yet somehow I don't know what that means for me. I can't see what my life is going to be like – I mean what does the future hold for someone like me? Frank always made all the important decisions, even if we'd talked them through together. I mean he knew about those things, finance, forms, tax. I've always been happy to leave it all to him.

I've only just got around to sorting out Frank's clothes, removing them from the wardrobe in our bedroom. They are now bundled up, in the garage, waiting for me to take them to the hospice shop.

For weeks, I haven't opened any letters addressed to Frank. The pile had grown higher. Last week I gave them all to Hugh.

I look again at the Portuguese letter. It would be easier to pass that on too. Let Hugh deal with it. But today I feel somehow different. I think about my hole in one. Why should that make me feel any different about tackling the letters? I don't know. But maybe it's the realisation that I can still do things without Frank. OK, so maybe it was a fluke, just a lucky shot. But still I have done it. Maybe I should start believing in myself a little more. Hugh does have more than enough things to sort out what with the probate and everything. Surely I should at least take another look at the letter?

Still I prevaricate. I make another cup of tea. Come on Maggie, get a grip. I sit down and reread the letter. It all seems very clear. The decision is easy. I'm not about to jump on a plane to Faro, not going to go to a meeting in Portugal just to moan about the Portuguese government's attempt to extract more tax. If they have decided to tax expatriates who own villas through offshore companies as we do, then what can I do about it? Why only last week I read in the Daily Mail that the Portuguese government was so short of money they couldn't afford fuel for their navy! If I have to pay a property tax, so be it. The others can have their meeting and moan, I'm staying in Britain.

I get some note paper and write back to the management company. I tell them that if they are unsuccessful in stopping the new law I'll pay the tax.

I feel energised. It's such a small thing. A quick letter, an instant decision. But again I feel like I'm starting to come back to life, to think for myself. I don't have to rely on others all the time. Filled with a new burst of enthusiasm and confidence I pick up the other letters. I go into Frank's study. On his desk is the computer screen and keyboard. Beside it lie half a dozen letters that have arrived in the past week.

OK Maggie, you can do this. You've emailed people before, it's not that difficult – it's not rocket science as Hugh would say. You just have to remember how to switch the damn thing on.

I press the button, the screen flickers and gradually the Microsoft logo appears. Then the message 'Enter your password.' Password? What the hell was Frank's password? Maybe he's written it down somewhere. I open the desk drawer. I'm looking for his golf club diary. Maybe his password's in that. I find that Frank's attempts to frustrate would-be hackers were pretty feeble. 'F's PCSARACENS' must mean his favourite rugby team is his password. I'm beginning to enjoy myself.

The clock strikes and I automatically look at my wrist watch. I find it hard to believe I've been sat at this computer for two hours. I've sent emails to the Residents' Association in Portugal, accessed our joint bank account through further detective work on the golf club diary and found a rather healthy balance from which I pay two outstanding bills I find among the unopened letters. Yes, it's been a good morning.

I manage to print out the bank statement. I take it with me into the kitchen and put the kettle on. While it's boiling I study the printout. I'm pleased to see that most of the household bills are settled by direct debits that Frank must have set up. Nevertheless the size of the balance surprises me. Hugh told me last week that most of Frank's assets were in stocks and shares. He says he's going to talk to the stockbroker about them, I shouldn't worry. Thank goodness I have a clever son, he understands these things.

I perch myself on the breakfast stool, and sip my coffee. The rest of the post seems to be junk mail. There's a couple of magazines. Frank subscribed to many magazines and there were always stacks of them on his desk. He swore that he read them all but I often found issues weeks old still in their polythene wrappers. I make a mental note to try and cancel the subscriptions.

I look at the two I've just opened, the Economist and Investor's Chronicle. So boring. Nice cover on the Economist though. A depiction of an Arab Sheik and a Texan oilman. Special Relationship? Isn't that what we're supposed to have with America? Apparently it was what 'Dubya' now had with Saudi Arabia. Oh dear, how things change.

I flick the pages and stop when I come to the article. Is this how politicians really behave? Is it all just about oil and money?

I'm startled by the harsh ringing of the phone. "Maggie, we were worried. You didn't come. Is everything alright? Would you like me to come over?" Elizabeth sounds concerned but also rather annoyed. I feel a pang of guilt as I realise I'm supposed to have gone to a coffee morning at Elizabeth's. With the excitement of mastering the computer, I'd totally forgotten.

"I'm sorry."

"I know you must find it hard to face people but it would have been good for you. Give you something to do.

What are you doing now? Would you like me to come over, I've got a catalogue you could see."

"Er, I was just reading an article in the Economist about Bush and the Saudis."

There's a silence down the phone.

"I'm coming over. You need to talk to someone. I'm worried about you."

"No really. I'm fine. And I've got a lot to do. I've got to go to Waitrose, do the shopping later anyway."

Elizabeth sounds hurt. "I'm sorry, I didn't mean to sound ungrateful. It's very kind of you and I'm sorry I forgot about the coffee morning. I don't know what I was thinking. I was doing things on the computer and I forgot the time."

"The computer?" In my mind I see Elizabeth shake her head.

"Well I hope you won't forget you're playing in the match against Maidenhead tomorrow. 10.30 for 11."

"I won't"

8

By the time we reach the twelfth hole Rosemary and I are two up.

It's my turn to tee off. As I place my ball on the tee I hear Rosemary telling our opponents about my hole in one. The two ladies look at each other. Their concentration is suffering from Rosemary's constant prattling and they're in no mood to see me repeat my feat.

With a sense of inevitability, I address the ball and swing the club. The ball never rises above hip height, skims over the water, bounces off the surface two or three times in Barnes Wallace style before coming to rest a few feet from the flag.

Embarrassed, I look at Rosemary and then apologise to our opponents.

We leave the twelfth green three up thanks to Rosemary's putt. It seems to me that whatever I do things still seem to come out right. It's a good feeling.

There's an etiquette at West Downs Golf Club (Founded 1909) that, following an inter-club match, and after changing into smart clothes, you assemble with your opponents in the mixed lounge for a drink before going through to the dining room for afternoon tea.

The problem is that few other clubs go to the same lengths as we West Downs Ladies do when it comes to dressing up. Indeed some ladies from other clubs do little more than change their shoes and brush their hair.

By contrast, we unzip our suit covers and matching shoe bags and proceed to transform ourselves from golfers into something akin to ageing debutantes. Make-up must be applied, rings and necklaces taken out of jewellery wraps, skirts and tights put on and hair lacquered. There are a number of dressing tables in the ladies locker room, but never enough.

Consequently the visitors usually arrive in the lounge several minutes ahead of their hosts and often resort to buying their own drinks. When, eventually, the West Downs Ladies sweep into the bar, en masse, the difference in appearance between the two groups is very marked. It leaves the visitors shuffling nervously from foot to foot wishing they had packed something rather more glamorous than a pair of clean trousers and a cardigan.

But that's how we are. And I guess it'll never change. We are just different!

I see Marco smile, or is it a smirk, as we enter. He's used to this. The swans and the ugly ducklings. It was always like this. The swans and the ugly ducklings. There are hardly any men in today so really our effort is just to impress each other.

I see our opponents already seated, a glass of orange juice in front of one, a glass of wine for the other. The younger one, Fiona, is probably in her mid-thirties, unmarried and works in London. A good golfer, she's taken the day off to play.

I rather admire her. She runs an interior design business in the City, doing up plush offices for overpaid bankers and fund managers. It must be nice to have the confidence to do that, to succeed in a man's world. It isn't something that many of us would relish even if we were capable of it, which we're not. She doesn't seem the least impressed by the fashion parade from us West Downs Ladies.

I find her conversation strangely stimulating.

"You must find it difficult having to negotiate with bankers and lawyers and all the other clients. I mean men can be so domineering can't they?"

"Not really. Not these days. And anyway a lot of those lawyers and bankers and people we design for are women. The City's not just a male preserve these days."

"The world is so different now. Women are respected for their abilities, their intellect."

I feel she's being slightly condescending, probably thinking what do these rich bitches know about work? Always pampered by their husbands. I search for something to say to sound more modern, to shatter her stereotyping. "Not everywhere," I say. "I was reading an article yesterday in The Economist about women in Saudi Arabia – they're not even allowed to drive! It's the same in many Arab countries."

"That's true and just look at the result! Half the population unproductive, repressed women and uncompetitive economies"

"My goodness Maggie, what are you two on about? This is a golf club not Question Time."

9

The wine Jim has chosen for the Annual Dinner is South African, and very good. Of course every previous captain had chosen a good French burgundy white followed by as good a Bordeaux chateau-bottled claret as he could afford. But Jim appreciated wine and was increasingly impressed by the efforts made in other countries to improve the quality of their offerings. Jim went to South Africa for a few weeks in the winter and had trawled the areas around Paarl and Franschoek visiting the vineyards. Far better value than the French, he believed. And so he had arranged for the Club to serve a particularly crisp Chenin Blanc with the starter followed by a Cabernet Sauvignon/Shiraz from the Robertson vineyard with the Beef Wellington.

Judging by the noise that is rising from a loud hum to a crescendo of competing voices as the evening progresses, the meal and the accompanying wine is proving to be a great success. So now it's time for his speech Jim is more than confident that his decision to press ahead with the reservoir and the tree clearance without levying members will be approved. There isn't a vote – Major Silvester has scotched that idea – but there are no dissenting voices either during his speech or afterwards in the bar.

Beside him, on top table, sits Arthur. His thin lips are formed into a permanent smile, he nods sagely as Jim speaks and quietly complements himself on his negotiations with Dylans. The interest rate he's achieved is a full point lower than HSBC, Lloyds TSB or any of the other banks would offer, and while the bank has (rightly in his view) insisted on some 'force majeure' clauses, Arthur knows that he has saved the members thousands of pounds.

Even Jim's announcement that annual subscriptions would have to rise nearly 10% is met with equanimity, After all, everyone knows that it has been a bad year what with so many of the older members dying or no longer playing and the shortage of new applicants. Most of the members present are more interested to hear about the Centenary arrangements. Nigel Grant-Jones is already working on the official history of the Club and will publish it time for the celebrations in two years' time. Members will be able to invite their friends to their Club 'over a hundred years old you know'. It's a satisfying thought.

Later that evening as the taxis and wives arrive to carry their inebriated husbands home, Jim puts his arm around Arthur's shoulders. "Thank you Arthur, the Club owes you a huge debt of gratitude. What we're doing will ensure West Downs becomes one of the most respected clubs in the country."

"It already is," says Arthur quietly, while inside his heart swells with pride.

10

The Royal Horticultural Society's gardens at Wisley cover hundreds of acres alongside the A3 just north of Guildford. Hundreds of thousands of visitors come each year to wander around the gardens and admire the thousands of different varieties of plants that are grown there.

It is rightly world-famous and Pyotr has studied the organisation's website for weeks.

When Pyotr arrives in the borrowed Volkswagen Golf he finds the car parks nearly empty. It's too early for the coach parties. The weather is damp and cold. Visitors will be sparse today. He walks past the café where two young girls in dark green RHS sweat shirts are wiping tables. They don't look up. To the left he sees the visitors' entrance and walks across to speak to the lady sitting in the kiosk dispensing tickets. He explains his reason for being there, showing her the piece of paper with the name of the man who has agreed to talk with him.

She calls on her intercom and another young girl wearing the same dark green sweatshirt and cargo trousers arrives and leads him to the old, creeper-covered house that serves as the main offices.

Pyotr expected jobs to be easy to find in the UK, especially with his qualifications and references from the Polish Forestry authorities. But each of his phone calls has been met with a negative, if sympathetic response. Only Wisley has agreed to a meeting.

But half an hour later he is shaking hands with Mr Williamson and, packing away his papers. The RHS isn't hiring 'at the moment'. They have a large project building a computerised greenhouse that is employing construction workers but there is no requirement, or budget, he explains for horticultural staff. He gives Pyotr a card which offers free access to the gardens for a year and promises to keep in touch, but there is no job.

Pyotr spends an hour or so walking around the gardens after the interview before returning to Lech's car. He has decisions to make and the stroll round the gardens helps him to think. He will give it another week, but by then his money will be used up and he will return to Poland.

11

My knees stiffen up if I sit for too long and now I need to rub them to help the circulation. I've been sitting for far too long. But, at least it's another milestone. Well that's a bit grand – perhaps another step in the right direction might be more appropriate.

It might have taken a long time but I'll get quicker each week. And at least it means I don't have to get in the car and fight my way along the aisles of Waitrose.

I glance at my watch, an anniversary present from Frank, and realise it's later than I thought. I had got up early today, like every day now, I suppose. Don't seem to be able to sleep so well without Frank. I'd better get used to it though. I'm not likely to find another one to share a bed with at my age – even if I wanted to, which I don't. I guess I'll just rattle around this big house until it all gets too much, or I get Alzheimers and the children put me in a home. I wonder what would happen then? Would Hugh move in? Knowing him he'd feel it was his right. But what about Simone and Estelle? Estelle's husband wouldn't like

Hugh taking everything. The two of them don't really hit it off at the best of times. There'll be a real falling out. Oh dear!

But come on old girl. You're not ready for a care home yet. You've got years and years before you. I don't feel old. Anyway there are the grandchildren and then of course there's the golf club. Plenty of friends there. I might need some more lessons, try and improve my handicap. After all I've got a hole in one now! Yes the golf club is the one constant in my life, that won't change.

As if on cue, the phone rings.

"Just checking you'd remembered our tee-off time at 11.15."

"I hadn't forgotten, Daphne, I'll be there." I check my watch again. Half past ten. Hadn't realised it was that late. Daphne is already at the Club, probably been hitting balls on the range getting ready for their 'big match'. She's a bit too keen.

I turn off the computer and go upstairs to get ready.

The first thing I see as I drive into the car park is a group of our ladies and Joe, one of the greenkeepers huddled around a large 4x4.

The object of their interest is Marika, a large Dutch lady who hits one of the longest drives of any of us and who is one of the most fashion-conscious. Even by West Downs' standards her wardrobe is extensive. Her husband's large salary seems to fund an inexhaustible supply of outfits, normally in pale pastel colours that Marika thinks complement her generous figure but probably have the opposite effect. It's not unusual for her to arrive at the Club in one outfit, change into her golf ensemble, and then change back afterwards into a third outfit. Oh dear, I'm so bitchy.

Marika is a lady who either is your best friend or biggest critic. One day you can do nothing wrong, the next you are being run down by her to every member of the Club. She's a dangerous woman to cross.

And cross she is right now, I can see as I walk over. Marika is standing, red faced and her hair awry. There's dirt on her cheek and on the end of her nose. Her pale apricot coat has large patches of damp mud on it and there are dirty patches on both her knees.

Joe is crawling under the large Mercedes. There's a loud whining noise which suddenly stops. Joe's body snakes backwards from the vehicle and he emerges dragging an electric trolley.

"The stupid, stupid thing! It just set off on its own, I couldn't stop it." Marika looks at the offending trolley and then down at her coat. "It's absolutely ruined – I've got nothing to wear."

I try to hide my smile. "She's just got this expensive new electric trolley," explains Caroline Templeton. "Apparently she was assembling it and when she connected her battery it set off across the car park and ended up under Betty's car! She tried to stop it but fell over in the mud, still holding onto the handle as it went under the car. Joe saw her lying there with the trolley motor still whirring."

"Oh dear, oh dear," the tears run down my cheeks and I start to laugh. Daphne arrives trying to find out what is happening. She sees Marika and starts to laugh too. It's all too much for Marika. "Don't laugh at me," she cries, "It's not funny. I am totally ruined. I will have to go home."

Twenty minutes later as we prepare to tee off, I'm still chuckling. By now Marika will be safely sipping a large vodka in the bar. She did not go home but has taken off her coat and washed the mud from her face but there's a graze on her nose where it hit the gravel.

I'm glad to see you're laughing again, Maggie. We've missed that."

"Well, Daphne, I'm just glad I didn't miss Marika's fall from grace!" I start to laugh again .

12

The intercom sounds and I look out to see the Ocado van waiting at the end of the driveway. I press the buzzer that opens the gate. I notice how long the lawn has grown – still Alberto hasn't returned my calls. I check my hair in the hall mirror on my way to open the door. Why do I do that? Force of habit. After all it's only a delivery man.

Opening the door I am greeted by the widest smile I can remember. The man has sparkling blue eyes that smile at me as well. He holds up his Ocado badge and announces in heavily accented English. "Mrs Miles? I have brought you your shopping. Please may I enter your lovely house and unpack it for you?"

I'm amused by the over-politeness of the Pole. I assume he's Polish, there are so many now in England. I show him to the kitchen noticing that he removes his shoes before following me. He puts the purple basket on the worktop and proceeds to empty it, asking where he should put various things.

"I don't know why I never used this on-line shopping

before," I think. This is marvellous service. As I stand watching him I feel guilty for not helping.

"Are you from Poland?"

"Yes, Gdansk, it is in the North where Lech Walesa started the Solidarish movement in shipyard."

"Oh yes, we saw a lot of him on television at the time. He has the same name as you, Lech!" I am pleased that I remember the name on the Ocado card. The surname had defeated me with its absence of vowels.

"How long have you been in England?"

"For almost one year. I hope to make a lot of money so I can buy a house in Gdansk."

As we chat I learn about his flat in Addlestone and how he had been recruited in Poland to work for Ocado. How he had found it difficult at first, driving on the left, speaking little English. "I got lost many times."

I find myself enjoying his company. He has a pleasant outgoing manner with just a hint of mischievousness which women find attractive.

I offer him a cup of tea. He hesitates, looks at his watch and then accepts. "My next call isn't until three."

"You have a lovely house here," he says looking out of the kitchen window at the large back garden leading down to the paddock. "Your husband must be a very rich man I think."

"My husband died. Just last month."

His face falls, the smile vanishes and I see suddenly a more serious Lech. "I'm sorry. Very sad, and you so young."

I smile at the compliment. "He had a car accident."

The words hang in the air. Neither of us seem to know how to continue the conversation. Lech stirs his cup again. Finally he speaks.

"Your garden is very big. Who is looking after it?"

"I have a gardener, an Italian called Alberto."

"I think this Alberto needs to come quickly and cut down your grass."

"Yes, you're right. He should have come last week, and then today but I haven't heard from him."

"Very bad, you need a man to work in this big garden."

"I expect he will call tomorrow." I try to sound confident, but I'm not. Alberto had definitely gone off in a sulk when I queried the cost of the fertiliser. Hugh didn't come down at the week-end and the garden is already beginning to look unkempt.

Lech looks at his watch and stands up. He extends his hand - a quaint gesture I think. He thanks me for the tea.

I watch as he goes down the winding drive and turns left towards Sunningdale. I press the buzzer and the gates close. What a polite young man. I'll definitely order again. Then a sudden thought strikes me. Oh, I never gave him a tip! I'm sure you should. Oh dear. Remembering to tip, that was another thing I have always relied on Frank for.

13

"Well quite honestly I don't know what we'd do without them. I mean Roy's mother, in a home, wonderful staff and not one of them English. Filipinos, West Indians and now the Poles.

"You're right Daphne," I say. "The Poles are real workers. I took my car into that place near the station, just along from Waitrose, you know the hand car wash. Ten pounds, the car was gleaming!"

"Yes but we managed before, without them. They're costing the country a fortune." Colonel Matthews is one of those military types who has been everywhere, seen it all and learned nothing. He has an unshakeable belief in his own judgement. Everything to him is black or white – preferably white.

I put a piece of chicken in my mouth and look across the table at the Colonel. He's only a few years older than me yet seems to belong to another generation. A generation of Empire builders, of missionaries spreading the gospel – or the parts of it that fitted their purpose, of land owners and proud families insulated by their own sense of importance. Next to him, his wife Veronica is busy chatting with Daphne's husband. She gesticulates a lot. The fork rises and falls like a conductor's baton. Each movement is accompanied by the tinkle of metal from the large gold bracelets she is wearing. I can imagine her playing the triangle in the London Philharmonic orchestra. Veronica likes jewellery, the bigger the better. She wears more jewellery on the course than most women wear to a dinner party, but that is nothing to the amount she's wearing tonight.

I've dressed up to, but not to this extent. It's another dinner to which I've been invited by well-wishing Club members. Another where I am only too aware of my new-found status, husbandless.

I drag myself back from the melancholy. The Colonel is expanding upon his theme that all immigrants are parasites living on the handouts of honest taxpayers like himself.

"But there wasn't a hand car-wash at all before the Poles came," I venture, looking at the Colonel to see his reaction.

"It's taking jobs from the Brits, that's what it is. God knows we have enough unemployment in this country without giving jobs to every Tom, Dick and Harry from Eastern Europe. You won't find the French or the Germans allowing immigrants in. Oh no, they look after their own kind first."

"I think, George, you'll find they both have larger immigrant populations than Britain." Laurence, Daphne's husband, takes the opportunity to get away from Veronica's tale of woe about their last trip to Tuscany. "And we need young people working to fund our pensions."

"Nonsense! The Germans turfed out all those Turks and you can bet that none of these Poles and Romanians pay their tax. It's all cash in hand, cutting out the British tradesman."

"George, have some more wine. Laurence, fill George's glass." Daphne moves to change the subject. Dinner parties were for polite conversation, a little gossip and fine food and wine. She doesn't want to get George started on politics. It was bad enough at the Club. George was always holding forth about UKIP, the UK Independence Party and how Britain should never have joined the Common Market. "Bled us dry," he used to say. "Paying a fortune to have some Belgian civil servant say I can't eat a bent banana."

Veronica seizes her chance to get back in the conversation. "The way the Italians organise things is just unbelievable. Do you know when we were in Tuscany last month we had to wait ten days for them to fix the phone in the villa. Ten days! And then they found that last people had pulled the plug out of the socket. It's just as well I had my mobile or I don't know what we would have done."

"Saved a fortune, that's what." The colonel's voice is several decibels louder than the other guests, military training I suppose. "Your mobile phone bill while we were in Umbria would have paid one of these Polish chappies for a year!"

Oh God, back to the Poles. Time to change the subject. I pick up my glass and cradle it. "What do you think about this new reservoir scheme and cutting back all the trees? Isn't it going to cost an awful lot of money?"

"Well," George puts down his knife and fork, wipes his mouth with the linen napkin pausing for dramatic effect. "As chairman of the Greens committee, I've seen the agronomist's report. With this damned global warming we're going to need our own water supply. We've got to be forward thinking if we want to get the course back to how it was years ago. And of course we have to cut down a lot of trees. They suck up the water so the fairways dry out and they stop the sun getting to the greens so we get fusarium. And now those bloody Belgians are saying we can't use certain chemicals on the green, so we have to give them more air."

Oh, back to Brussels and politics again. "But how are we going to afford it?"

"Well they've put up the fees by 10% for a start. And the ladies will be paying full subs next year too." chips in Laurence.

"Yes, and we have negotiated a very substantial long loan from Dylan's Bank at a very low interest rate. They know how prestigious West Downs is. The directors still have their annual golf day there." The Colonel's voice is growing louder by the glassful.

"Well that's alright then," I say, returning to my Armenian chicken. Men understand finance. I don't. That's why I left it to Frank. Or now, to Hugh. Let them deal with the banks and insurance companies and tax offices – it's a man's world after all.

George and Veronica drive me back home afterwards. I'm worried about George's competence to drive after so many glasses of red wine, the opening gin and tonic (or was it two?) and the brandy to follow. I'm only too aware of what drinking and driving did to Frank, and me. I make a mental note to drive myself next time. As the car's headlights pick out the gravel driveway and lawn, George booms "The old lawn's looking a bit shaggy Maggie." He chuckles at the rhyme. "What's that Eyetie been up to?"

"Who knows, never returns calls."

"Don't talk to me about Italians darling. They couldn't organise anything. Do you know it took them ten days ...."

"Thanks Veronica, thank you George. Very kind of you. Drive carefully now won't you?"

I watch the gravel spray up behind the rear wheels of the Jaguar. The Ocado driver had driven much more carefully.

14

I wake early again. It is Sunday and I have Hugh and Letitia and their two children coming. It's three weeks since I've seen them. A week or two after the funeral in fact.

I'm going to prepare a real Sunday lunch for them. I get out the sirloin of beef that Lech put in the fridge for me. I whip up the batter for the Yorkshire pudding. I still have lots of apples from the orchard, wrapped in paper in large cardboard boxes. It was something Frank and Alberto did just before he died. I'll make apple crumble, Hugh likes that. Smoked salmon to start with for the grown- ups, melon for the children.

I'm glad to be doing something positive. Life has purpose. A family to feed. I look out of the window at the garden and the paddock beyond. Grass isn't supposed to grow in the winter. But the seasons are all over the place now. It's been so warm for October and the grass has continued to grow. It's getting really long in the paddock.

I go out to the garage. The sit-on mower is there. Beside it is a large can of petrol. I pick it up and shake it. There's a reassuring slapping sound as the petrol rushes from side to side of the can. Good, plenty of petrol. Hugh can cut the grass in the paddock.

The beef is in the oven, the crumble made and the vegetables cut and peeled, I move to the dining room. I check my watch and then peer out of the window. No sign of Hugh and family yet, but they are always late. I go into the hall, press the switch to open the electric gates so Hugh can just drive through.

I go into Frank's study. I suppose it's my study now. Funny that, always been Frank's study. I switch on the computer, type 'Saracens' and check Frank's email account.

There are four messages. Frank has been dead for six weeks but to the cyberworld FVMiles26@aol.com still exists, still lives on in the ether, still receives mail.

There's an email from the golf club. Really! Surely they could have amended their records by now. That lazy Silvester, never does a thing. No, Frank will not be entering the captain's prize this year, or any other year come to that.

I click through to the web. I tap in Lloyds TSB and log on. I check the balances on the accounts. There's over £200,000 in a high interest deposit account. Our current account has a healthy balance too. I must change the accounts to reflect my change of circumstances. Hugh said it would all be done once he's sorted out the probate but that will take months.

In the meantime I can still operate the joint account but I won't be able to access the £200,000 because it is in Frank's name only. I'm joint executor of Frank's will along with Hugh so perhaps I can do something myself. I'll ask Hugh to see if things can be moved along more quickly. I know he'll ask me why I want to change it so quickly. I don't have any plans to move the money but somehow, I feel I should take more charge of my own affairs.

I don't hear the car arrive, I'm too engrossed in the computer. It's not until I hear a car door slam that I turn and glimpse the twins running towards the front door.

I hurry into the hall, check my hair quickly in front of the mirror by which time young William is pressing the doorbell for all he's worth.

We congregate in the kitchen. Hugh's eyes take in the saucepans ready with the peeled vegetables and the unbaked apple crumble. The smell of roast beef fills the kitchen.

"Oh, you've cooked. I thought we were eating at the golf club," he says.

"We thought it would be easier for you," adds Letitia.

"No, I wanted to do you a roast. And I've done apple crumble for you specially."

"With custard?"

"I thought we'd have cream."

"I prefer custard."

"Well I'll do that then." I go to the cupboard and search for the Birds tin.

"Why don't you and Lettie have a chat while I go and sort out Dad's things? I need to get details of bank accounts etc. for the probate. I've written to the bank but they move so slowly, I thought I'd try and see if I can get into the accounts on line. Trouble is Dad will have a password which I don't know so it may be a problem – we may have to look at the old statements. Have they sent you any?"

"Saracens."

"Sorry?"

"Saracens. That was Frank's password."

Hugh looks at me in astonishment. "Did he tell you?"

"No, I found it in his Club diary. I've got the balances. I was just looking at them when you arrived."

"Now mother, you need to be careful. You shouldn't go messing with Dad's computer. It's very easy to press a wrong key and transfer money by mistake."

"Hugh. Give your mother some credit. I'm not that stupid."

"Well I'll go and have a look."

"Will you have time to cut the grass in the paddock this afternoon? It's awfully long."

Hugh shot a glance at Letitia. "Well we had hoped to get away after lunch, certainly by four. We're entertaining an Icelandic banker and his wife this evening. Can't you get Antonio to do it?"

"Alberto you mean. No he hasn't been here for two weeks. Anyway, it was always Dad who did the paddock on the tractor mower."

"I'll do it granny! I'll drive the tractor."

"No William, You're not quite big enough yet."

They leave at four. The paddock is cut. Hugh was clearly not happy and Letitia had sulked, hardly talking to me at all. Even the twins seemed ill at ease. "I'm sorry we can't stay any longer but you know what it's like in the City. You're away from your desk for a day and the whole market's changed. And this dinner tonight could be very important. But don't worry, I'll get Dad's affairs in order and the probate will all be finished in a few weeks.

"Thank you Hugh." I stretch up to kiss him. So tall! My little boy, now so big and important. The twins are hopping up and down on the doorstep anxious to leave. I stoop and kiss both of them. They turn and run to the car. Letitia gives me a kiss on each cheek.

"So nice to see you again Maggie. You're looking much better."

"Thank you, I feel better now."

They're gone.

I go back into the house. I don't feel better. In fact I feel rather miserable. It has been nice to have company, to see Hugh and the twins. But somehow I feel they only came out of a sense of duty. They were wrapped up in their own lives, it has nothing to do with mine. Hugh was really quite nasty about me using Frank's computer.

I wander from room to room. It **is** a big house. Too big for little old me. What do I need all these rooms for? And the garden? Who will I get to do that if Alberto doesn't come back?

I empty the dishwasher and clear the teacups from the lounge. Already it's dark enough to need the lights on, the heavy overcast sky is threatening more rain.

I look at the photographs on the mantelpiece. There's me with Frank in San Lourenco looking all tanned and happy. Frank was wearing a bright green Boss polo shirt with the Sun City logo he'd picked up in South Africa. It was his favourite. He still wears it for important matches, No. Not anymore. Not anymore.

What am I going to do with all his clothes? They're all in the garage. I should have asked Hugh if he wanted any. Probably fit him. But no, Letitia wouldn't let him wear someone else's 'cast offs'. Oh dear no. Probably best just to give them to a charity shop. What about Elizabeth's hospice. Yes that would be good, I'll do just that in the morning.

Decision made, I feel better. I look at the clock. Still not five o'clock. Too early for a drink. Hugh hadn't wanted wine at lunch because he had to drive so we'd just had a sherry beforehand. Now I feel the need for one. Too early? No, blow it! There's no one to tell me the sun isn't over the yardarm. There wasn't any sun today and what's a yardarm anyway?

I speak the words out loud. They seem to echo off the walls. Then silence. Emptiness.

I go to the drinks cabinet, pour a good measure of Bombay gin and go to the kitchen for some tonic and ice.

Returning to the lounge, I lift my glass towards the ceiling. "Cheers Maggie!" The words sound forced. "Cheers all of you" I reply, toasting the family assembled in silver frames along the mantelpiece.

I'm lucky to have my children and grandchildren. The grandchildren love to play down here, especially the twins. So much more space than they have in Barnes. Don't know how they can put up with all that noise and grime.

The chimes of the grandfather clock in the hall strike five. As the last chime fades away the house seems more silent than ever.

I walk around the lounge, glass in hand looking at the paintings, now illuminated by their own individual picture lights. Frank had a good eye for paintings, and a good nose for a bargain. The Victorian portraits of young girls in pastoral scenes suit the room and its furnishings but are far more than ornamentation. I know that they are very valuable. Frank complained to our broker about the insurance premiums. That was one of the reasons for fitting the electric gates and upgrading the alarm system.

It's almost dark outside now. I walk into Frank's study and pull; the curtains. I look at the golf trophies lined up on the bookcase. They're cheap metal cups on wooden bases, the sort you bought in those little shoe repair shops, where they engrave your name. The cups he's won for Club competitions are silver and bear the names of scores of players who have triumphed over the years. They are safely locked in the golf club trophy cabinet.

The cups here are from corporate days or even holiday golf. There's a large cut glass decanter and I pick it up to read the inscription. "Winner – Financial Times Challenge 1976". That would have been while Frank was still at Reuters. So long ago. Before we lived here. Before Frank made so much money.

I gaze at the paintings on the study walls. Scenes of early Victorian industry. Dockside scenes with tall-masted ships being unloaded. Horses drawing haycarts with men walking back from the fields, while on a nearby road a large steam engine is pulling more wagons.

My reverie is shattered by a metallic voice announcing "You have email!"

Hugh's left the computer on. I lean over and hit the return key. The screen flickers to life displaying the inbox. There's a new message.

It's to me from Ocado offering a free bottle of wine if I order again in the next week. I sit down and start typing. "I might as well go shopping now," I say to the men in the hayfield.

15

It's Tuesday and the weather has improved. The rain didn't materialise and I awoke to find the sun shining in a perfectly blue sky. There was a heavy dew on the lawn and the air was crisp and clear.

The improvement in the weather makes me feel better too. It seems that as the clouds lift so do my spirits. A nice day for golf. I am looking forward to getting out of the house – seeing my friends. A bite to eat afterwards, a drink.

The Club car park is unusually full. "The bloody Major has fixed a society to go out before us!" Daphne tells me as we change our shoes. "One day a week is all the ladies get and he has to put a society out. They're playing fourballs and half of them look like they don't know a driver from a drumstick."

Daphne's way with words is always original, if bizarre.

"I don't know how you can smile Maggie, we'll be late for lunch and I've got so much to do this afternoon too. I'm going over to Reading to look at curtains for the dining room. Do you want to come with me, help me choose?"

"No I can't, my groceries are due this afternoon"

"Sorry?"

"I've got this online shopping thing. They deliver it to your house – even unpack it and put it in the fridge."

The round is slow and Daphne becomes increasingly frustrated. I don't mind. I'm in no hurry. I'm enjoying the company, and the cool sunny day. And I'm enjoying my golf. My shots seem to be going a bit further and a bit straighter. I'm three putting less. At the end of the round Daphne congratulates me. "Forty one points Maggie! They'll cut your handicap now."

The society men were in the Club dining room, talking and laughing loudly.

We change and go to the mixed lounge to order sandwiches.

"And how did Mrs Miles play today? You catch another eagle?"

"'Fraid not Marco, but I scored well."

"Good. Good for you. You're looking particularly nice today!"

"Oh you're such a charmer Marco, Don't listen to him Maggie."

"Why not?" I rather like the compliment. It's nice to be out again, have people notice me. I consciously pull my shoulders back and lift my head as I walk across to the coffee table. Yes, it's nice to be noticed.

*

There's a buzz on the entry system. I pick up the handset. Before I can say anything I hear Lech's voice. "Hello Mrs Miles, it is Lech. I have your groceries."

I press the buzzer to open the gates and walk back down the hall until I reach the mirror. I pick up my handbag and fish out my lipstick. I pat my hair again. The face that reflects back from the mirror is flushed. Perhaps it's the effect of the winter sunshine when I played. Or maybe it was the wine afterwards. The bleep of the van's reversing sensors of the van make me hurry to open the door.

Lech is there sorting groceries into a big purple basket. He turns to me. He grins and I smile back. "Hello again! You are keeping well I hope?" His English is improving.

"I'm fine thank you."

He struggles up the steps with the basket. "I see Alberto has not come to cut the grass." I'm impressed that he remembered the gardener's name, Hugh hadn't.

"No, not yet."

He puts down his basket on the step and removes his shoes. He follows me down the hall carrying the groceries. I put on the kettle to make tea. I don't ask him. He starts to unpack the groceries then glances out the kitchen window at the paddock. "Ah big grass over there, it is cut. Who do that?"

"My son. He came on Sunday. He cut it."

"Why not cut up other grass in front?"

"He didn't have time. He's very busy. He has an important job in the City."

"Which city?"

"London. He's a kind of banker."

"Ah, I like kind bankers, maybe he would lend me money?" He chuckles.

"No he's not a kind banker. He is a, type, of banker. He does research and ...... things." I realise that I don't actually know what Hugh does in that big building in Canary Wharf.

I wave my hand across my body as if it would explain Hugh's job better.

"So where is this Alberto? Why is he not coming?"

"I think I upset him. I think he doesn't like being told what to do by a woman." I push the plate of chocolate digestives towards him. I turn to the window, following his gaze. A wind is getting up and clouds are forming. It's already dusk. Leaves are blowing from the trees and fluttering down in the gloom.

Lech pushes his chair back, the wood squeaking against the terracotta floor. "I have to go now. But tomorrow I have no work. I bring my friend Pyotr; we work in your garden. OK? You can pay us, not Alberto."

I am startled by his forcefulness, his assertiveness. I haven't asked him to help with the garden. And who is this friend he's bringing? I like Lech but I hardly know him. It's only the second time I've met him. And what would Alberto say? My natural English reserve is screaming no, no, no. I stall for time.

"Your friend. Is he a gardener?"

"Much better, he has studied all flowers and trees in Poland. He has papers," he searched for the word. "diplomats. He is wanting job but no job yet, so he needs money. We come tomorrow"

It's settled. I can say nothing. I show him to the door. He puts his shoes on and waves as he climbs into his van.

I pour myself a drink. It's early, I know, but why not? I'm drinking more these days, I realise. I try to collect my thoughts about what has just happened. It can't harm to have some help in the garden and it looks as if Alberto has gone for good anyway.

Tomorrow will tell if it has been a good decision.

Although I don't know it my life is about to take a dramatic turn.

16

Lech and Pyotr arrive at 9 o'clock the next morning in Lech's Volkswagen. I hear the buzzer go. I'm up early, unable to sleep and have finished my breakfast.

I press the gate release and open the front door. Lech pulls up outside and the two men climb out. They are both wearing warm jackets. The low cloud has returned and although the wind's dropped, it's threatening to rain. Looking at their big boots, I decide to show them around to the side of the house and bring them in through the kitchen. Pyotr is not as tall as Lech and seems shyer. Inside the kitchen he politely extends his hand and says in excellent English, "Good morning Mrs Miles. I am very pleased to meet you. We will work hard to tidy up your beautiful garden."

As he speaks his dark brown eyes hold mine and I find myself thinking 'What a handsome man!" His complexion is tanned and he has a firm chin, blonde hair that is cropped fashionably short, and a broad mouth with lips that turn upward at the edges in a permanent smile. I realise I'm staring and turn away. My cheeks feel flushed. Stop it Maggie! Behave yourself!

I lead them to the garden shed and show them the tools and the mower. The tractor mower was only used for the paddock; Frank kept a petrol mower for the front and back lawns.

The two men sort out the equipment and I see that Pyotr is clearly giving instructions to Lech. He's pointing out things in the garden to him. He walks around with Lech, stopping by certain bushes and talking animatedly to his friend. I walk back to the kitchen but continue to watch them from the window.

First they rake the leaves on the lawn, forming a big heap. Then Pyotr starts the mower and adjusts it so it's running just right. He says something to Lech in Polish and Lech nods in agreement. The grass is awfully long – it may need two cuts I think.

Lech manoeuvres the machine into position at the edge of the lawn. He sets off on the first cut. I watch as he turns and begins a second row. Soon there are parallel dark and light stripes across the lawn.

I'm so busy watching Lech that I don't notice Pyotr until he taps on the kitchen door. I turn, embarrassed that he has found me watching Lech. "The leaves Mrs Miles, do you want me to compost them or do you have bags for them?"

Again I'm impressed at his command of English – so much better than Marco's at the golf club. I watch as he returns to the garden and begins to collect the leaves and place them in the wheelbarrow. Such a handsome young man.

For two hours they labour, anxiously looking at the sky from time to time. But the rain holds off. The lawns have both been cut once and the edges trimmed. The leaves have been placed in a large heap at the far end of the garden near the paddock, along with the grass cuttings ready for composting. Lech is about to start on the second cut of the back lawn.

I call out to him. "Come and have some coffee."

The two Poles remove their heavy shoes before entering. Lech points to the sink and asks if he can wash his hands. Pyotr follows.

"Well you've certainly done a lot. Would you like some cake? It's a chocolate one from Waitrose. An awfully nice man brought it yesterday!" We share the joke together as they take a piece of cake each.

"So tell me Peter, do you work for Ocado too?"

"No I have arrived in England only ten days since. I am hoping to work at the Royal Horticultural Society Gardens at Wisley." He enunciates Royal Horticultural Society slowly and carefully.

"Have you been for an interview?"

"Yes but they do not have any work for me now. Maybe after Christmas. I have also spoken to Kew. He pronounces it more like Kev. "They are not hiring now. So I must find somewhere else."

"Lech told me you studied horticulture in Poland."

"Yes. I have studied plants and trees and how to grow them. I am very interested in how to grow things better but without using chemicals. I like the natural way."

Lech had been looking nervously at the sky and now spoke to Pyotr in Polish.

"We think it may rain and we should finish the grass before it does. So please excuse. We will go now. Thank you for the cake."

The rain holds off and they finish the second cut of the lawns back and front. One of them mows. The other empties the grass box into the wheelbarrow and takes it to the compost heap. It's nearly 1.00 by the time they've finished.

"We could cut the hedge over there if you like. It should be cut now in Autumn, before the ice comes."

"Before the frost comes." I correct Pyotr.

"Before the **frost** comes," he repeats.

"Well yes it does need doing. Alberto normally does it over the winter. "

"Alberto is not a good gardener. This hedge should be cut now before the.....frost ... comes. Also that Euonymus bush, it is getting very big and the plants around it are suffering. It hides all the light."

I can tell he knows about plants. Very impressive.

Lech speaks to Pyotr in Polish who responds, nodding his head.

Turning back to Maggie he translates. "Lech says that he promised to do your grass for the same price as Alberto, fifty pounds. He says that if we work this afternoon we will have to charge you more."

"Yes, yes of course. You have already done much more than Alberto and I would like you to do the hedge. But it is a big job. It will take you a long time."

"OK, thank you. First we must go to shops for lunch."

"No, no. You must have lunch with me. I'll get some ready."

I make some sandwiches. I find a couple of cans of vegetable soup in the cupboard, look at the two men outside and decide I need both.

As the soup's heating Pyotr comes into the kitchen, carefully removing his boots first. Lech stays outside smoking a cigarette.

Once again I find myself looking at his strong face. Those eyes, brown and warm, complementing his smile. I drag my gaze away. "What will you do if you don't find a job?"

"I hope to find a good job where I can use what I learned. I need to earn more money than Lech gets driving his truck. In Poland, in the forestry department, I organised which trees we cut, which we preserved. I organised the renting and buying of the vehicles and tools. I had responsibility for fifty men."

"So why come to England?"

"The pay for such a job here is three times what I got in Poland. In Poland I earn less than my wife Saska. She has learned economics and accounting and works for a big accountancy company in Warsaw. They pay her well."

I look at the young man standing in front of me. He isn't some labourer who might replace the indolent Alberto. I can see he is ambitious and proud. He obviously wants to succeed in earning a high wage so as not to depend on his wife's earnings. I think of the sacrifice he's prepared to make to come to England to earn more money. Leaving his wife, his country, his children?

"Do you have children Pyotr?"

"Not yet. First we must make enough money to buy a nice house to bring out our children. I must get this good job in England."

"But you must miss your wife, Saska isn't it?"

"Of course, but if I get a good job here she can come to England too."

I find I'm enjoying talking to Pyotr. He talks about his job in Poland and how he studied at night for his business diploma to add to his other qualifications. He tells me how he's studied the plans of famous gardens all over the world and how he likes to design gardens himself. "But no one in Poland is paying to have gardens designed. Most people live in apartments. No gardens. Not like England."

We both look up as Lech comes into the kitchen. His hair is wet. He curses in Polish and says something to Pyotr.

"It's started to rain. If it continues we will not be able to cut your hedge."

We finish our sandwiches and soup. The rain has got heavier. We sit and talk. It's good to have people in the house again – especially such good-looking ones! All too soon they get up to go. Pyotr gives me his cell phone number and asks for mine. He says he will find another day when he can come over and do the hedge and the euonymus. Perhaps Lech will lend him the car.

I pay them £50 each – after all they had done far more than Alberto manages. They are delighted and Lech's face bursts into a big grin.

"Good luck with your job hunting," I wave them goodbye.

"Thanks. I will try some other places," Pyotr calls from the car.

As they turn out of the drive I press the button to close the security gates. Then the idea strikes me.

17

I have no time to act on my idea. The next few days, uncharacteristically, are very busy.

Thursday is the day that Mrs McGraw comes. She's my cleaner although I never refer to her as that to friends. She's 'my lady that does'. She's worked for me and Frank for almost the whole time we've lived at the house. At first, with the children still at home there was a lot for her to do. Cleaning all the rooms, helping me in the kitchen and generally tidying up after the five of us.

Gradually the work diminished as one of the children after another left the nest. Now there's just me, the old broody mother hen left. But I still pay Mrs McGraw to come each Thursday.

Of course Mrs McGraw (even after all these years we still call each other by our surnames) is a lot older now. Not so nimble and her eyesight isn't what it was. Dusting and cleaning is a bit more of a hit and miss operation. But I've never thought of telling her that she isn't needed. And Mrs McGraw needs the money. Her husband works for the

Council, a desk job, the same job for twenty years. It doesn't pay well but there is a pension at the end of it. Mrs McGraw lives in a small terraced house on the other side of the A30, the main road that bisects Sunningdale. It is a mile or so away.

When she first came to work for me she would arrive on a push bike, slightly red faced but full of energy. These days she comes in Mr McGraw's car, a small hatchback that they keep in pristine condition. She has a remote control to open the gates and keys to the house. When Frank and I were away she would come up and check on the house, empty the mailbox and sweep the leaves off the porch step.

This morning when she had taken off her coat and then put the kettle on for a cup of tea, (Mrs McGraw never started work before having a cup of tea). She had looked out the window at the striped lawn and cut paddock. "I see that Italian has finally decided to do some work. About time. The garden was looking all-uncared for. He's a lazy so-and-so."

Mrs McGraw has never liked Alberto. She has met him only occasionally but there had been an instant mutual distrust between them.

"Actually I've not seen Alberto. He's not even returned my calls. Hugh mowed the paddock on Saturday and I got some new chaps to cut the lawns and clear the leaves yesterday."

"And a fine job they've made of it to. Very straight lines on that lawn. Mr McGraw always says you can tell a good gardener by the straightness of his lines on the lawn. Where did you find them?"

"From Waitrose," I joke. Mrs McGraw doesn't joke. She takes everything very seriously.

"From Waitrose?"

"Well it was the chap who does the deliveries for Waitrose, Ocado, who offered to do it with his friend Peter. They're Polish."

"Polish? Oh no Mrs Miles, you mustn't use them. They are taking all the jobs from the British workmen and they don't pay any tax because they are illegal immigrants. And they're claiming benefits for their children who are still in Poland. Oh you mustn't give work to the Polish."

I'm not sure whether to be annoyed or amused by Mrs McGraw's illogical prejudice against the Poles. I settle for being annoyed. "They are very polite, very hard-working and very intelligent."

"Oh no, they don't know how to do things properly. They bodge things. Mr McGraw says they don't stick to any of the rules on health and safety and that's why they can charge less than the English they are putting out of work."

I'm about to remonstrate when the buzzer goes. I pick up the handset. "Open the gate it's Alberto."

My heart sinks. In my mind I have written off Alberto. I never thought I'd see him again. Now here he is. What will I say? Suddenly I miss Frank. He was used to things like this. I'm not. I haven't had time to adjust to being the homeowner – the person who deals with the tradesmen.

I watch as his pick-up negotiates the drive. I watch as he gets out, walks around the house and goes into the back garden. I rush into the kitchen where I can see him. Mrs McGraw follows me.

"You're in trouble now Mrs M. You should never have employed those illegal Poles. You should have stuck with that good-for-nothing Italian."

He's walking towards me now. His face is a stern, unsmiling mask.

"You have had someone using my mower!" There's no 'good morning', no pleasantries, just a stark accusation.

I think about lying, saying that Hugh had done it all, but he would not believe me. The lines are too straight, the compost heap too neat. Oh, I wish Frank were here to deal with this stroppy Italian. I've upset him already over the fertiliser receipt. Now he's clearly furious.

But I don't have Frank to do things and anyway who is Alberto to criticise me? Who hasn't answered my calls? Who left the grass uncut for weeks. **His** mower indeed!

"Yes Alberto, and they've made a very good job of it too. Why didn't you come last week? Why didn't you return my phone calls?"

Alberto stops a few yards from her. He shakes his head as if trying to get something out of his mind, an insect out of his hair. His sulky, accusatory expression changes to one of uncertainty. This is a new Maggie, I realise. He didn't expect this. He's not used to be talked to like this by a woman. No woman in Sicily would dare to challenge him like this.

Taken aback by my riposte he looks suddenly unsure of himself. He shuffles his weight from foot to foot. He looks at me standing on the kitchen step and behind me Mrs McGraw craning her neck to see his reaction.

"I am busy. Very much to do for many people at this time. I don't have time to call you." He turns to look at the beautifully-mown lawn. I can see he's calculating. This is a good contract; we pay him well. Without Frank to chide him he thinks he can do it in his own time, when he pleases. He was annoyed when I caught him out over the bill for the fertiliser. Although I've paid him for it he knows I suspect him. That angers him.

As if to show me who's boss, he'd deliberately not come last week, ignored my phone calls. Let her wait – she would soon see that she needed to be nice to Alberto!

But it hadn't worked. Without really trying I have already found a replacement for him. And someone good by the looks of things. I wait. He's obviously still calculating his next move, how to retain my business.

His expression changes. Now it's aggressive. I realise I've put my hands on my hips and am glaring at him defiantly. "Well?"

Men are so easy to read! Torn between wanting to placate me and wanting to prove his superiority Alberto hesitates. The Sicilian male hormones win. "Very well. I go. You find someone else to do your garden!"

He turns and strides off, his rotund body wobbling from side to side but his head upturned, chin pointed forward. He slams the side gate behind him. It doesn't latch and springs back open so we can still see him marching back towards his van, kicking at the gravel.

He gets into his van and reverses it too fast, the stone chippings flying from the rear wheels and clatter against the underside of the van. He speeds down the drive only to come to a screeching halt in front of the electric gates.

Mrs McGraw, looks at me and I see a smile spreading across her face. "I'd better push the buzzer and let him out or he's likely to smash the gates down!" We laugh to ease the tension.

"I'll make us a cup of tea Mrs M."

"Good idea!" I should be depressed. I've just lost my gardener. But strangely I'm not. In fact I feel quite elated. It's another change in my life. I'm beginning to take control, to make my own decisions. Yes, life is changing.

*

That afternoon I go shopping. I buy myself a new pair of trousers and a bright scoop-necked jumper. I have my fortnightly hair appointment.

"Just a little spruce? Trim it a little, Mrs Miles?" says Jenny, my hairdresser.

"No, I think I'd like you to reshape it, something a little different. I feel like a change."

*

Friday morning I'm up quite early and after a quick breakfast I examine my new shorter hairstyle in the hall mirror, patting down a stray wisp here and there.

I check it again in the car mirror on the way to the golf club. It was only 8.30 and there are few cars in the car park. I haven't brought my clubs. I don't need them today.

The greenkeeper's compound is on the south side of the clubhouse accessed down a narrow bush-lined path. I am looking for Tom, the head greenkeeper and find him talking with two of his staff who have just returned from cutting the greens.

He looks up as I approach, treading carefully across the shingle path in my court shoes. My woollen suit in dark blue keeps the early morning cold out and makes me feel more business-like.

Tom raises his hat politely and wishes me a good morning. He knows me quite well having had a lot of dealings with Frank when he was chairman of the greens committee. However, I can tell he's intrigued to see me coming over to the staff compound so early in the morning, dressed as if I'm going to a business meeting.

I tell him about Pyotr and ask whether he needs extra staff for the tree clearance work, particularly trained ones like Pyotr.

He listen and then shakes his head. "They don't want us to do it. We're not involved. The whole project has been contracted out to some golf-course development company. We just have to keep out of their way!"

Tom is obviously not pleased with the decision. He asks more questions about Pyotr.

"Seems like a useful chap. Maybe he should try and get a job with the contractors. They start next week. The Major's keen to get it all done over the winter."

He gives the name of the contractor and I write it down. I toy with the idea of asking the Major for their contact details but I've never really got on with him; none of the women do.

On the way back to my car I meet Terri who works in the office with the Major. "Morning Mrs Miles, you playing this morning? There's a society due off at 9.30 so you'd need to get off before them." Terri can always be relied upon to know what's happening.

"No, I'm not playing but perhaps you can help? It's about the tree contractors……"

When I arrive home the answerphone is blinking. There's a message to call Simone, Daphne had called about a game on Sunday and there's a message from Pyotr to say he can borrow Lech's car on Saturday and come over if I want him to.

*

Saturday is beautiful, warm and sunny, one of those rare days in October when England shows off in all its Autumn glory. Pyotr arrives soon after nine and starts immediately on the long hedge. He sorts out the hedge trimmer, runs a long extension lead from the kitchen through the window and even puts on a hard hat and goggles that he's brought with him.

I decide it would be nice to be in the garden too and, secateurs in hand, begin to dead-head the roses. After a bit Pyotr comes over and explains about the right way to prune the roses to ensure flowers in Spring. I watch closely as he demonstrates and then copy him. I turn to him to check I'm doing it right. His brown eyes twinkle and he nods. "Very good, very good."

We work happily for a couple of hours until I go inside to make coffee. I bring the two mugs and a biscuit tin out onto the patio and we sit down together, surveying our progress.

Two hours is enough gardening for me. I feel hot and dirty after my efforts and go upstairs to wash and change. I glance out the bedroom window and see Pyotr on the step ladder by the hedge. His polo shirt is damp with perspiration and there are dirt marks where the dust from the hedge has fallen. As he works I find myself looking at his strong muscles, his weather-beaten arms. He looks very fit.

By lunch, the whole hedge has been neatly trimmed and a large heap of cuttings has been prepared for burning. We talk over the tuna sandwiches and I ask him about his job hunting.

"I have a possibility of a job at the big garden centre on the A30 but the pay is not so good. But maybe I take it as I have to pay rent."

I tell him about the golf and the tree clearance project. I give him the details of the company and the owner whose name and details I've got from Terri. I also fetch the plans and the original agronomist's report. Again Terri had supplied these. He looks at me inquisitively as if trying to sum me up. I can see he's impressed that I've gone to all this trouble for him.

I refill his coffee as he bends over the plans and report. "It is a good report but I am not sure the activity plan from the contractors is so good. You see here," he points to a spot on the map near the 11th hole, "these trees are marked to be cut down but if you do that it will channel the wind down here, and here. That will not be good for the rhododendrons here."

He points out one or two other problems that he foresees. I'm not sure I understand all of them but I nod enthusiastically, enjoying being close to him.

"With this information, I could talk to the boss of the contractors and maybe he would hire me. Thank you. I will phone him on Monday, Thank you.

*

Michael Hamilton, the owner of GMS Contractors was delighted to receive his call. This was the biggest contract he had undertaken and in truth he wasn't sure how he was going to manage it. His idea to recruit Eastern European labourers, kit them out in smart GMS sweatshirts and hardhats was fine. It would bring him a handsome profit over the six months. But since Sean, his Irish contracts manager had quit, he had been faced with managing the project himself. And Michael's talents were selling not organising.

He had made his money selling – everything from insurance to loft insulation. Meeting Sean, who ran a landscape garden business had sparked off an idea. Cheap labour from the continent, 'rich bitches' in Sunningdale and an experienced project manager added up to a business opportunity he couldn't ignore. But when Sean got fed up with working all hours managing dissident workers whose language he couldn't begin to understand, while Michael drove around in his flash car sipping tea and more often Sauvignon Blanc with prospective clients, he quit.

Michael now had thousands of pounds of equipment on lease, a clientele more inclined to complain than compliment him, and absolutely no idea of how to manage an Eastern European diaspora of low skilled workers.

Normally he wouldn't have dreamt of bidding for the West Downs contract or anything of this size. Furthermore he wouldn't have expected to get it even if he had bid. But then he had met Arthur at a Rotary Dinner. In his usual fashion he had talked up the company and his expertise. Arthur was impressed. He was also available now, he said, and Arthur was keen to get the project carried out well before the Club's centenary.

When Michael received Pyotr's call it was as if all his prayers had been answered. Here was someone who had already studied the plans, had the qualifications to manage a project like this and was going to cost him much less than Sean. The fact that he was Polish was not a drawback. In fact it was a bonus as most of the workers were Polish and problems of translation would be a thing of the past.

Pyotr just wondered at the twists of fortune that had landed him this job. If it hadn't been for Maggie, and in turn if it hadn't been for Lech....... Now all he needed to do was find somewhere to stay close to West Downs.

That proved easier than he imagined. He moved in with Maggie as a lodger on Tuesday.

18

The past few weeks have simply flown by, although not without critical comment from just about everyone. When my friends found out I had taken in a good-looking Polish lodger I was chided as having a 'toy boy' and not all the jokes were flippant.

Hugh was particularly angry. "For God's sake Mother. It's not as if you need the money and you know nothing about him. It's not right for you to be living alone with him."

Estelle and Simone were less critical, understanding perhaps more of the loneliness I was feeling after Frank's death. But they both made excuses to come down and see me and meet Pyotr. Simone even stayed a couple of nights prompting me to joke that she was trying to pinch my 'toy boy'!

I've been shopping on line each week and Lech more often than not stops for a coffee with Pyotr and me.

One evening I spoke to Saska, who phoned Pyotr after he had gone out with Lech and friends. She told me how grateful she was for my helping Pyotr.

But it was the evenings I've enjoyed the most. Then Pyotr and I sit and chat. I tell him about the children, about life with Frank, while he gives me an insight into how life was in Poland before the Russians left and the rapid changes since then. He's such good company and I can't help liking his enthusiasm when he talks about his plans to make a lot of money for Saska's sake, his interest in garden design and organic farming.

One Saturday we drove over to Wisley Gardens to see the enormous greenhouse they are building to house extra plants. He talked with the project manager there about how all the temperatures and humidity levels were computer-controlled and how they conserved water etc.

I was also pleasantly surprised to find that Pyotr was a whiz at computers. He asked one night if he could use the computer to look up things on Google. Since then he's showed me shortcuts and how to get everything from weather reports to recipes. He loaded in a program he had got from Michael Hamilton which enabled him to prepare scale drawings and plans for different garden layouts. He's really clever.

We talk about his job at the golf club, and he gives me regular updates on the progress of the project. The initial clearance work is going well, they are ahead of schedule in fact. But there are some more difficult works scheduled for after Christmas.

He seems happy to be earning good money and he's able to control his Polish workers well. I helped him open a bank account, a lot easier now he has both a regular job and a fixed address.

Hugh and Lettie come down one Sunday. Hugh has completed all the probate process and wants to explain things to me. Under the terms of Frank's will nearly everything passes directly to me with no inheritance tax problems at this stage. So I'm now the sole owner of the Sunningdale house as well as the sole shareholder in the offshore company that owns our Portuguese villa. I've got a share portfolio worth several hundred thousand pounds and nearly quarter of a million pounds in various bank accounts. The only disappointment is the expensive life assurance that Frank paid for during our wedded life. It is invalid because Frank had been over the drink limit at the time of the crash.

Hugh says I've still got more than enough to enjoy life in comfort and travel wherever and whenever I want.

*

The Christmas Party at West Downs is a black tie affair which enables all the ladies to dress up and show off their jewellery.

I was undecided whether to attend. Daphne and several of the others insisted I join their group so at seven o'clock I find myself standing in front of the full-length mirror in the bedroom adjusting the straps of my long black evening dress. Black always looks elegant and given the absence of Frank, might be more appropriate. Not that I'm in mourning. Far from it. I seem to have found a new lease of life in the past few months. It's just that the Christmas party has brought it all home to me that for the first time in forty years there would be no Frank to share it with.

I hear the buzzer on the electric gates. The taxi has arrived.

"Your taxi's here Maggie." Pyotr calls up the stairs. Quite when he had stopped calling me Mrs Mills I don't recall.

"You look super! Really elegant." Pyotr is standing at the bottom of the stairs and I feel I'm blushing like a young girl on her first date.

" Dziękuję, Pyotr." I curtsy and smile , thanking him in Polish. I've insisted he teaches me a few phrases.

*

"Oh, I do like that dress, Maggie." Veronica greets me as she enters the ladies changing room where I've left my coat and am making final adjustments to my hair before joining the throng of partygoers in the lounge.

Veronica slips off her short mink jacket; she's not one to wear fake fur no matter how many animals are killed or how many protesters may yell their abuse at her. Taking off her jacket reveals another black dress but shorter and lower than mine, revealing not only Veronica's still-shapely legs but a considerable amount of cleavage that I'm convinced is plastically-enhanced.

A large red stone pendant jostles for room between her tanned breasts.

She sees me looking at it. "It's a ruby – used to belong to George's aunt. She was out in India you know."

I didn't know and don't really want to know. Veronica can be such a tart. But I force myself to look down her cleavage as she leans forward and lifts up the pendant necklace so I can admire the size of the ruby.

"How are you getting along with your new toy boy?"

Veronica looks at me and I search for signs in her face that she's teasing, but find none.

"Very well, thank you. He's been teaching me a lot."

"I bet he has. I wouldn't mind learning a few new moves from him myself."

"Oh Veronica! Trust you. No he's taught me a lot about the computer and we're learning a lot about garden design. We're hoping to redesign the back garden and introduce a water feature. Pyotr thinks that…"

*

I find myself seated between George, the Colonel, and Sean, a young committee member.

"The tree clearance project seems to be going very well don't you think Sean?" The Colonel leans forward and speaks across me.

"They seem to be working hard whenever I'm playing," replies Sean.

"Damn good workers, the Poles. I suppose you know they're Poles don't you? Whole lot of them. You can hear them jabbering away in Polski." The Colonel takes another generous slurp of his Chardonnay.

"I thought you didn't approve of the Poles coming here and working, George?" I am determined not to be ignored.

"Well I don't like the fact that so many are over here all enjoying our benefit system, but at least this lot seem to be getting on with the job. Better than some of the blokes you see working for the council. I guess we're saving a packet using them anyway if I know Arthur Balfour."

"Actually," says Sean, "I don't think we are. In fact it's costing us rather more than we budgeted. The firm GDS isn't cheap, or Polish. It's run by an ex-insurance man that Arthur met at Rotary. But they were the only company who could do it in the time."

"Well whose fault's that? We left the decision too late as usual. The problem with this Club is everyone likes to sit on committee and pontificate instead of making decisions. No way to run a business. Wasn't like that in the Army – we'd never have got anywhere. Decisions, action, that's what you need. Anyway I'm glad we've got Arthur – he seems to get things done and have his finger on the pulse."

I start on my prawn cocktail. The Colonel and Sean are obviously not into small talk with a woman.

*

Pyotr has waited up. He had the front door open as I alighted from the taxi. His case, packed ready for his return to Poland in the morning, is in the hallway.

I follow him to the kitchen, taking off my coat as I go. I sling it over the end of the bannister. I don't notice as it slips gently off and lays crumpled on the carpet. I need to sit down. I grab a kitchen chair and drag it across the tiled floor. It makes a loud noise but I sink into it gratefully. It's harder than I expect.

"Thank you for waiting up for me. It's not nice coming into an empty house. I shall miss you when you're away."

A bottle of vodka is on the kitchen table. Beside it are two glasses. The brightly-wrapped present sits to one side. "I hoped we might have a pre-Christmas drink, to celebrate our friendship." He smiles as he unscrews the bottle, already half-empty and pours the white spirit into the two glasses.

He looks at me. I smile back and feel my face flush. I've drunk too much tonight, I can tell. I feel not quite in control, but never mind, it's nearly Christmas. I'm not bad looking for my age, I think. And this dress may not be as low cut as Veronica's but it still shows off my shoulders and my skin is still soft. I laugh.

"What's funny?"

"Oh it's nothing, just something Veronica said."

I'm thinking about Veronica and her remarks about Pyotr. He is certainly very handsome – and not **that** young. Yes Veronica would definitely be showing off her large ruby to him, leaning forward as she had in the locker room. I wonder what Pyotr would think of Veronica's ample cleavage? I pull up one of the straps on my dress that has slipped down my arm, hoisting up the neck of my dress. I reach for the vodka, the strap slips off again. I let it stay.

"Cheers!"

"Cheers!" He downs the vodka in a single gulp. I try to do the same. The fiery spirit makes me cough and the coughing makes my eyes water. I rub at them and notice mascara on my fingers. Oh God. My eye liner's running. I must look a fright.

He comes round the table and pats me on the back. I sniff, then laugh. He pours two more glasses. "Perhaps a little bit slower this time," he says, his bright eyes dancing with amusement and for a moment making him seem more like the flirtatious Lech.

He pushes the present across to me.

Inside is a large, hard-covered book on Poland. I leaf through the beautiful photographs of Polish cities and countryside, in the different seasons. "Thank you Pyotr, it's lovely." I sip the second glass of vodka.

"I have a present to give you too. It's upstairs." I feel his strong arm supporting me as we climb the stairs.

19

This time he takes the plane, not the bus, to Poland. Maggie drives him to Heathrow Airport. He now has money enough for a ticket as the job with the golf club is going well. It will be thick snow when he lands in Warsaw.

The plane breaks through the low clouds and circles over the newly-named Warsaw Chopin airport. Everything is white with just the black streaks that mark the runways. As he comes through the immigration he sees Saska waiting there. She is wearing the fur hat that he gave her last Christmas. He sees her before she sees him. He puts down his case and takes her in his arms. Then he holds her shoulders and pushes her away so he can look at her better. "I've missed you, I had forgotten how beautiful you are."

"It's nice to have you back here in Poland".

"Yes, but now I have a good job in England you will soon be able to come over and live with me there."

She smiles – his excitement is infectious and it's good to have him back. He is so much more positive than a few months earlier when he boarded the coach for England.

"Yes, Pyotr." Now is not the time to tell him. She'll wait until Christmas Day after mass.

It feels strange to him to be back in the old apartment. It's so small and full of Saska's things. He's never liked living in the city – but they moved there when Saska got her job with Price Waterhouse. The Forestry Department was also headquartered in Warsaw but he missed the forests of Silesia. The apartment is very central, not far from Lazienki Park. He looks out through the windows over a city already growing dim in the fading light, the solid slab of the 'Birthday Cake', a farewell present from the Russians, dominates the skyline.

That evening they eat a simple meal at home and talk. Or at least Pyotr talks. He tells her everything about his time in England even though she says he has told her most of it before in letters or on the telephone. He describes the lovely house where he's living with Maggie, tells her how the men who work for him laugh at some of the golfers they see. He tells her about his boss, Michael. He is a strange man, he seems not to like the work; he likes to stay in his office which Pyotr thinks is at his home and rarely comes to the Club to look at what the men are doing. He asks Saska what she has been doing without him. She says she has to work very hard but the job is going very well.

"Maybe they will promote you," he jokes.

She doesn't laugh. She's tired he thinks and tomorrow they leave early for Saska's parents' home in Poznan.

*

The next morning they take a taxi from the small apartment near Lazienki Park to the Central Station. It has snowed

86

heavily and the taxi makes slow progress. The thick cumulus clouds hang over the concrete city like a dirty tablecloth, making the Russian architecture look even greyer and starker than usual. They pass the new shops bedecked with Christmas decorations. Already people are out shopping, wrapped up in thick coats with wool or fur hats on their heads.

They descend to the underground platforms and wait for their train. The Warsaw – Berlin Express will take just under two and a half hours to reach Poznan Glowny station where Saska's father will meet them.

They watch an express arriving from Minsk, the roofs of its carriages encrusted with snow. Smoke rises from the roof of the restaurant car billowing up until it meets the concrete roof of the station where it spreads out into a cloud just like the snow clouds outside.

Their train is a German express headed for Berlin that stops at Poznan. In a little over two hours they are there and her father is standing at the barrier. He takes one of the suitcases and they follow him to the car park.

"You have a new car!"

"Yes, it's not new but only two years old and Volkswagens are really good." Her father tells them his work is going well and he is being paid more. Still, Pyotr thinks, he must have saved for some time to buy the car.

The snow crunches under the wheels as they turn into their little road and see the cottage. The paths are swept clear and the December sun is reflecting off the banks of shovelled snow either side. He sees the satellite dish on the roof. Her father follows Pyotr's gaze. "You can watch your English football now. We have Sky!"

20

The turkey went in at 8.00. I've chosen the biggest one the butcher had. It will take five hours at least. I had a moment of panic as I tried to get it into the Neff oven. It fitted, but only just, sitting on the base of the oven rather than the lower shelf. I worried about the breast drying out so put even more rashers of streaky bacon over it than usual.

Estelle and Simone come down together and start to make coffee.

"What do you want for breakfast? Just toast?"

"Yes, toast is fine. We ate so much last night. Have you any juices?"

Justin and Tim come down a little later and the girls put more toast on. The men sit down at the kitchen table nursing mugs of coffee, chatting quietly. The girls insist on doing 'sprout duty'.

I had heard Estelle's two children get up very early, running into their parents' room with their stockings. They had been told to be quiet and let granny sleep. Now they appear, still in pyjamas, at the kitchen door eager to show everyone what Santa has brought them. Christmas is for children and I love to see their faces so excited.

Hugh and Lettie have decided to drive down on Christmas morning with the twins. They arrive around noon. Hugh has probably got a hangover. He drinks several cups of black coffee and is short with the twins.

Because there is a blue sky and a watery sun, I suggest a quick walk round the garden so I can explain all my new ideas including the water feature. Justin, Simone and Estelle join me, wrapped in thick anoraks despite the unseasonably-warm weather. Tim, Hugh and Lettie remain inside with the children. Tim has set up the new Wii computer game and is trying to keep all four children under control. Lettie is sitting reading a magazine while Hugh busies himself choosing the wine for lunch from the cellar that Frank built.

*

By five o'clock on Boxing Day, everyone has gone. I look around at the debris. I reload the dishwasher, cling-film the cheese and wonder what to do with the remainder of the turkey.

I wander around the bedrooms collecting up the torn wrapping paper. I wonder if I should strip the beds but decide tomorrow will be soon enough.

I push open the door to Pyotr's room where Justin and Estelle stayed. The new laptop computer I gave him for Christmas is on the side chest. His hard hat and two pairs of shoes are inside the wardrobe. His GMS coat hangs on a solitary hook.

I close the wardrobe door and walk downstairs. The house is quiet, just the ticking of the grandfather clock. All that preparation. All that effort. And in 48 hours it's all over, for another year.

The phone rings. The strong clear voice sounds as if it were next door. "Maggie. I wish you and your family a happy Christmas. I hope you are enjoying it as much as we are."

The Polish accent is there but the English is perfect. In the background I can hear music and laughter.

"Pyotr, are you with Saska's family? Is it snowing?"

"Of course it's snowing. It always snows at Christmas in Poland. You are having a good time?"

"Yes, lovely thank you," I lie

"Here is Saska. She wants to say Happy Christmas."

21

She doesn't tell him until they are on the train back to Warsaw. He should be happy about her promotion. She has done so well. It means a lot more money. It means she will move from Warsaw to Lodz where she will work on three of Price Waterhouse's biggest clients. But it means she will not be coming to England. The job pays much more than she could earn in England. She is now earning more money than Pyotr.

She tells him that maybe next year she can get a transfer to England, to Price Waterhouse in London. But he doesn't believe her. It is better that he thinks about returning to Poland and getting a job in Lodz. Then they can be together again. His dream of making lots of money and bringing her to England is over.

He waves goodbye at the airport. The job for Michael Hamilton will be finished by Spring. Then he will return.

*

He takes a bus from Heathrow to Staines and then a train to Sunningdale. From there he walks with his small case all the way to Maggie's. He hadn't wanted to call her out. Pressing the button on the gate he hears her voice answer and then the buzz as the gate swings open.

She gives him a big hug, excited to have him back, pleased to have company again. But Pyotr's thoughts are still with Saska and Poland. He feels a long way from home.

She has cooked a meal and they eat together in the dining room – a big table for just two. Maggie opens a bottle of wine and they toast the New Year. Later, Pyotr goes to his room and fetches the laptop that Maggie had given him for Christmas. He shows her the programs he has already loaded, anxious to show his appreciation.

He then goes into the internet and looks at his bank account to check how much money he has. How much will he be able to take back to Saska and Poland?. Michael Hamilton had paid him by cheque when he finished just before Christmas. Pyotr paid it into the bank on the way to the airport.

At first he didn't understand the words 'Refer to drawer.' The account shows the money going in and then a week later coming out. He asks Maggie to look. She goes white.

"It means that there wasn't any money in his account to pay the cheque! We'll ring the bank in the morning. And Michael Hamilton."

But the next morning is a bank holiday and Michael Hamilton's mobile is off so Maggie leaves a message for him to phone.

It isn't until the following day that they learn the truth. GMS has closed. There is no money to pay the men and no sign of Michael Hamilton.

Pyotr is distraught. He turns to Maggie "I don't know what to do. I have no money left. Maybe I should just get the bus back to Poland."

Pyotr wasn't the only one who suffered a sleepless night. Arthur Balfour received the news from one of his friends at Rotary. They were at a cocktail party. His friend took him to one side.

"I just heard about that Hamilton chappie. How's that going to affect things at West Downs? He was the guy who was doing all your tree clearance wasn't he? You'll have problems finding someone else to finish it."

Arthur paled. Finding someone else to complete the contract was the least of his problems. How to explain that he had paid Michael Hamilton hundreds of thousands of pounds just before Christmas, retaining just 10% of the total value of the contract? Not only would the contract not be finished but the Club now had little money left to pay for it.

22

January 2nd is the day the Polish workers are due to report back.

Pyotr is up early. I hear him making coffee in the kitchen. I know he's worried. We spoke of little else yesterday. I have phoned around anyone at the Club who might have news but no one was able to shed any light on the situation. They were all as surprised as me, and none of us at that time was aware of the full story, of the payment that Arthur Balfour had made just prior to Christmas. Not that Arthur had acted improperly; cheques of that size required two signatories and Major Silvester had been happy to countersign. Improperly no. Inadvisably certainly.

I keep telling Pyotr it was probably just a mistake and all would be sorted.

He is quiet as I drive him to the Club. His main worry seems to be that the men had not been paid, but since most did not have UK bank accounts they were paid weekly in cash and had received it just before Christmas.

They are all there, ready for work as usual except for one who remained in Poland.

"His girlfriend doesn't trust him to come back! She's heard about the English girls. And she's a good Catholic." The men laugh.

Pyotr doesn't know what he should do. The men are there, expecting to work. The diggers and other equipment are there. The job needs doing. I watch him from the warmth of the car.

He sits down on the wheel of one of the tractors and calls the men around him. He's explaining what has happened.

The men are quiet. I expect them to throw down their hard hats, to kick the nearest piece of machinery. But they don't. They just stand there looking at him.

I step out of the car and walk over. I want to know what's happening.

One of them is asking Pyotr something. He translates for me. "So what are we going to do? Who will pay us now? The golf club is very rich. We don't need GMS – you can run the project and the golf club can pay us."

Pyotr shakes his head. If only it were that simple, I think. Pyotr hadn't wanted me to come with him but I had insisted. I feel responsible. After all it was me who introduced him to Michael Hamilton. It was all my crazy idea.

The men continue to talk, questioning Pyotr. I can't understand the Polish but I am picking up the atmosphere. There is no resentment toward Pyotr. They just seem to be looking to him for guidance.

One of the men walks over to Pyotr. He turns to the assembled men. Putting his arm on Pyotr's shoulder he speaks loudly and firmly to them. At the end his voice gets louder still and ends with a question. As a man they respond.

They pick up their tools and walk to the tractors and diggers and fire them up.

The work will go on!

At nine o'clock Major Silvester arrives. I am still sitting in my car, wondering whether to wait until the Club opens and have a coffee. Before he can get out of the car, two more cars arrive. From one, a man in a smart suit and briefcase appears. The three men with him remain in the car. The second car also contains four men, casually dressed. All remain in the car. I rub the windscreen to see better. I lower my window a bit so I can hear what they're saying.

They're looking for the secretary and the Major introduces himself.

The suited man passes him a business card. As an insolvency partner, he explains, it is his job to ensure that the assets of an insolvent firm are secured so they can be used to help pay off creditors. GMS had failed to make the lease payments on its vehicles and equipment. There were few other creditors – it was a labour-intensive business – but HM Revenue and Customs had not received PAYE or VAT for several months and Her Majesty's revenue collectors are not reticent when it comes to forcing companies into liquidation if they believe they will, as preferred creditors, recover the taxes due.

The leasing company was also keen to recover its assets which it did not want impounded by the liquidator.

I sink down in my seat in case Major Silvester should see me. I want to hear everything. The Major tries to bluster his way out. "This is nothing to do with West Downs, sir. We are a club that goes back nearly one hundred years and

I can assure you that we have never failed to pay our bills. Why the very…."

"I understand entirely sir. No one is blaming the Club. All we need to do is to establish what equipment, vehicles tools and other assets GMS may have here on site which I will need to have appropriated by my men here." He nodded towards the men in the two cars. The men climbed out. "These men are with you?" Major Silvester looks disapprovingly at them. I know what he's thinking. The Major detests jeans. To have so many men standing in the members' car park unsuitably attired is guaranteed to offend his sensibilities.

"Technically, no. They are employed by the finance company but we often work together in these cases."

I hear the noise of a truck and they turn to see Pyotr driving into the car park from the side of the clubhouse in a green pick-up. The foreman who had stood up and addressed the men is seated beside him. In the back of the pick-up I can see a collection of power saws and ropes.

The liquidator looks amazed.

"Who is that? Is that a GMS vehicle? Are they still working? Don't they know the company's gone bust?" He motions to one of the men in jeans who rushes across in front of the truck, raising his hand imperiously for it to stop.

Two more cars now drive into the car park. In the two Jaguars are Arthur Balfour and Jim.

"Let's go into my office," says Major Silvester, obviously embarrassed. Perhaps he's seen me. He leads the way into the clubhouse followed by the liquidator, Arthur and Jim. Pyotr gets out of the truck and follows them in. I settle down to wait.

It's a long wait. I see members arriving with their clubs, a few hardy souls prepared to brave the weather. I realise I'm getting cold in the car and decide to go into the clubhouse and try and get a cup of coffee.

As I pass the office I can hear raised voices from inside. I want to stop and listen but someone might see me eavesdropping. I walk along to the bar and get a coffee from Marco.

It's nearly an hour before I hear the men coming out of the office. I rush back outside to my car and grab Pyotr's arm. "What's happened. What did they say? Tell me everything."

Apparently the Major at first objected to him joining the meeting. But Jim and the liquidator had prevailed. After all, Pyotr was the project manager and there was nobody senior from GMS around. He was also apparently a preferential creditor for the bounced salary cheque.

"What did you say?"

"I didn't say anything at first. I just listen. They all argued about whose fault it was. They seemed to be trying to blame each other."

Gradually I piece the story together. Hamilton had taken over a million pounds from the Club, had missed payments on the vehicles and equipment and then transferred almost all of the cash in the bank to an account in Cayman Islands. The liquidator said he had people trying to find out the owner of that account although the suspicion was that it was Hamilton. His house in Ascot turns out to be rented and he is behind with the payment there as well. When Jim had heard that Arthur and the Major had written out a cheque shortly before Christmas to cover virtually the whole contract despite the scheduled completion of March he burst out with a string of expletives.

Pyotr wants to check on his men but I tell him not to be long. Again I find myself sitting in the car as the windscreen fogs up. Eventually, after what seems like an hour, Pyotr returns.

He climbs into the car. "We're going to the pub for lunch," I tell him.

Pyotr says nothing.

We walk into the pub which I know serves good food and select a table. I order a bottle of burgundy.

"Now what's our plan Pyotr? What are we going to do?"

23

The rain started before we leave the pub. It streaks down the sides of the Mercedes and in the headlights the raindrops seem to bend and hurtle towards the windscreen across which the wipers hurry back and forth like batons wielded by a frantic Proms conductor.

By the time we reach the house the rain has already turned to sleet. I park the car by the front door and splash across the gravel and into the house.

We take off our coats and shake them leaving puddles on the mat and carpet. Pyotr unlaces his boots as I slip off my shoes. We pad into the kitchen.

I drop the blinds, cutting off the sleet-filled night sky and fill the kettle.

Pyotr goes upstairs, returning with his laptop. We sit, side by side at the table as the laptop fires up. Our hands are cupped around our mugs of tea.

My head is spinning and it isn't from the burgundy. For the first time in a very long time I feel important. Someone really values my opinion. Someone really trusts my judgement. For years, business and finance have been strictly something that concerned men. Like the Men's Bar at the golf club, you didn't go there.

Maybe the world really is changing. Now women are being made full members, equal rights. The men's bar is being redesignated simply as the spikes bar. And here am I, Maggie, 60 year-old widow, putting together an audacious business plan to take over the work of GDS Contractors.

Pyotr seems more circumspect. His initial excitement as the men had hailed him as their saviour, telling him they didn't need GDS and would carry on working for him, has subsided. The meeting with the liquidator and the Club's officials has pointed out the impracticalities.

For a start, all the equipment needed to carry out the clearance had been leased and is being repossessed. Anyone taking over the contract would need to lease more equipment, lots of equipment. That meant having capital, trading records, credit rating. Pyotr has none of these.

Then there's the question of whether the Club has the money to pay for the project. That's to be the subject of an extraordinary general meeting which can't be convened for weeks.

We work in the kitchen until late that evening. Pyotr constructs spreadsheets, listing the work to be done, the equipment needed, the time frame. He calculates labour costs, builds in finance costs and contingencies.

I'm surprised at how easily I understand as he explains his workings. Maybe it's the way he explains it – simply, directly without the technical jargon of which Hugh is so fond.

But the conclusions are clear. The project cannot be taken over by Pyotr without a substantial down payment from the Club. The prospect of the Club agreeing to pay money in advance again, is remote. Given that Arthur has already paid nearly the whole contract amount before Christmas, most of which is now sitting in some Cayman Islands bank, unlikely to ever be returned, there's no way the Club will, or can make prepayments.

The leasing company is unlikely to offer to extend credit to a start-up firm, connected, however innocently, to a defaulting customer.

"But someone has to fund the work and soon," I say. "We're only a couple of years away from our Centenary."

"With weather like this," says Pyotr as he lifts the blinds to look outside, "no one will be working on the course, or playing on it."

24

The New Year is a time of celebration, quickly followed by melancholy as the Christmas card deliveries are replaced with bills. Why is it that so many annual bills have to be paid at the beginning of January, just when everyone is counting the cost of providing an ever-more expensive and extensive amount of presents?

In Barnes, Hugh was in a black mood. He yelled at the twins who had left toys on the floor outside his study for him to trip over. He cussed Lettie for leaving him at home while she went to the first day of the Dickens and Jones Sale.

The snow that had fallen overnight had already melted and been turned into dirty slush by a thousand feet and countless car wheels. Everywhere was blanketed in a grey slush. The lights were on in the house and an Anglepoise lamp illuminated a pile of bills on Hugh's desk.

Apart from the utility bills there were the prep school fees for the twins. Living in London there was no way he would countenance sending them to the local state school where the mother tongue of two thirds of the pupils wasn't

English. Not that the twins new classmates were all 'old-school' English. There was a smattering of other nationalities among the new intake, Europeans, Americans and several Chinese. But they were all children from rich families whose mothers (or au-pairs) drove them to school in 4 x 4s. They were the 'right sort of people' in Hugh's mind. But private schooling didn't come cheap – even the uniform cost as much as a month's wages for the average man. But Hugh wasn't your average man. He was a fund manager, and a damned good one. This meant he earned an annual bonus that was ten times the average man's annual salary.

Of course, the bonus wasn't guaranteed. Oh, no. It had to be earned. Earned by long days at his city desk in Docklands, early morning commutes, interrupted holidays and a 24/7 Blackberry. All of this made Hugh feel important, almost indispensable, investing millions, hundreds of millions, of Mr Average's pension contributions in corporate bonds and US equities. As long as he kept his fund's performance above the average he was rewarded with big bonuses. At the end of April the results were calculated and a few weeks later Hugh's bank balance dramatically improved.

This meant that school fees, mortgage payments and even Lettie's insatiable appetite for Jimmy Choos and Prada handbags could be paid for with a scrawl of his signature on his Private Bank cheque.

Not that Hugh blew all his bonus on Ferraris and Crystal champagne, let alone lap dancing clubs as some of his contemporaries did. No, Hugh liked to practice what he preached, investment. Most of his bonus was used to increase his share portfolio. But mindful of the warning that accompanies every equity investment, he was careful to keep a large amount of his wealth safe and accessible in a high interest offshore deposit account in the Isle of Man.

He worked methodically through the New Year paperwork, just occasionally yelling at the twins to keep the noise down. January 1st was a bank holiday so it was a rare opportunity to sort out his affairs, and Maggie's.

He was surprised at the changes in his mother. Once she would have left everything financial to his father. She wasn't interested in finance, invoices, investments. But since Frank had died she seemed hell bent on becoming an amateur financier.

It had all started when he found she had accessed Frank's computer and checked on bank accounts. That was his role, Hugh thought. He had been entrusted to sort out her financial affairs. He was named executor on the will; obviously Frank knew that poor Maggie would never get her head round such matters. A little knowledge is a dangerous thing he had told her. Leave me to sort out what to do with your investments, that's what Daddy would have wanted.

Then she had taken a shine to that Polish gardener, even had him lodging with her. Frank certainly wouldn't have approved of that.

At first Hugh thought she would quickly tire of the finances and leave it all to him. But on the contrary. As the weeks passed she seemed to be getting more and more interested. She would phone him in the evening just when he had returned from work tired and longing to put his feet up and relax in front of the telly. "Why was he suggesting she move her money out from Lloyds and into some Norwegian bank?"

"No Mother it's not Norwegian, it's Icelandic. They pay so much more interest than Lloyds do."

"Why had he insisted on investing Frank's pension fund in equities rather than taking a nice annuity for herself to live on? "

"Because you don't need the income now and I can earn more on your money than Zurich Insurance will pay you. It's what I'm good at for goodness sake – it's my job!"

He blamed the influence of her Polish lodger. He seemed to be filling her mind with all sorts of ideas, even teaching her all sorts of programs on the computer – Frank's computer.

His reverie was interrupted by the phone. It was Maggie.

"Hello dear, how are things?"

They exchanged pleasantries. Then she came to the point of her call.

"You know we've transferred most of the Frank's savings from Lloyds to Kaupthingamejig?"

"Kaupthing, yes."

"Well, how easily and quickly can I get hold of that money if I need to?"

Major Silvester switches off the engine and sits back in the seat for a moment. He gazes at the painted concrete wall of the underground car park bearing the numbers of the various apartments.

It's three years since he and Nicola moved into the gated apartment block in Sunninghill. Three years since they moved down from the Warwickshire. The move then hadn't been planned. They had been pleasantly surprised by their Warwickshire surroundings. Not nearly as bleak as they had feared. The job, his first as a golf club secretary, hadn't proved too onerous. His military training had enabled him to delegate anything he couldn't or didn't want to do.

Of course the members were nothing like as glamorous or important as those at West Downs but still very acceptable to him. Indeed the facilities of the Club were far better than he remembered from his days playing courses around Aberdeen.

The staff weren't a problem either, at least not before the 'incident'. In fact he didn't really get involved in the nitty gritty of Club finances, or suppliers and the course equipment. He preferred to spend his time cultivating the more influential of the men members. Perhaps if he had, he might have realised what was going on. But details had never been Silvester's strong point and in the regiment he had always been able to rely on his sergeants to manage everything. He liked to think of himself as more of a strategist.

His staff had always been deferential to him, polite, welcoming. Why would he have suspected foul play? He said as much when confronted with the evidence by the captain accompanied by the senior partner from the Club's auditors.

"How much?" he had demanded. "That's preposterous. I'd have noticed if £100,000 had gone missing."

But he hadn't noticed, had he? He hadn't cottoned on to the scam that the chef was running with the meat supplier, nor the missing vehicles from the green staff's compound. It had been a close decision for the Club. Prosecute the chef and the head greenkeeper and have the news of their secretary's incompetence plastered all over the local media for rival clubs to gloat over or dismiss them both and the indolent secretary and say nothing. With negligible prospects of recovering any of the missing money, the Club had decided on the second alternative even going as far as writing a somewhat ambiguous reference for Silvester.

It's quiet in the car park – just the metallic clicks from the cooling engine echoing off the concrete walls. The lights were dim giving the whole scene a foreboding atmosphere. He sits, unmoving, just thinking. Thinking what Nicola would say to him. She had liked Warwickshire and had quickly found her way to the good restaurants and the better shopping malls around Birmingham. She seemed to enjoy the company of her new girlfriends much more than the officers' wives in the regiment. But then, thought Silvester, the new friends had been so much younger than the officers' wives. And Nicola was more their age.

She had been very young when they married. He, by contrast, was old for his first marriage, but then he had never been good with women. Of course she wasn't quite from the same class as his Scottish family – not by a long shot but at 45 his mother had been only too pleased when a cousin introduced them. In fact it had done wonders for his image in the Mess. Nicola was a 'looker' according to his fellow officers so what did it matter that she hadn't been to university or even the right school?

When the 'incident' happened in Warwickshire and he had told her that they would have to move and find a new job, she had thrown a fit. She had always got on well with the chef and the greenstaff and told him so. She even said if he'd done his job right instead of being 'such a lazy bastard' they'd never have been tempted to con the Club.

Now it was happening again.

A golf club had been conned – totally conned by a crook who had hopped off to the bloody Cayman Islands. And it was he, Major Silvester, who had countersigned the cheque.

Next day in Sunningdale the snow had not yet melted. Indeed it was still snowing and although the main roads were clear the West Downs Golf Club car park was covered in a thick blanket of virgin snow. The path from the two bungalows where the Club steward and head greenkeeper lived had footprints on it but the members' car park was as smooth as the icing on a Christmas cake.

Major Silvester was the first to arrive, his Volvo crunching across the snow and up to the notice announcing this place was reserved for the Club Secretary. Not that the wording was visible today.

A couple of minutes later a Jaguar saloon slid into the space next to the Major's car. Jim, the captain, got out gingerly. His feet sank into the thick powdery snow and the bottoms of his pale grey trousers turned a wet charcoal colour. He reached across for his briefcase, turned up the collar of his North Face anorak and headed for the clubhouse.

The Major was fussing around trying to get the coffee machine working. He turned to Jim as he entered the office. "Arthur's not coming. There's a message from his wife on the answerphone. Says she thinks he has a bad cold."

"Cold feet more like. It's his fault we're in this mess." Jim drew up the chair, accepted the cup of coffee and opened his briefcase.

January was a time when West Downs received half its annual income – the membership fees. The notices had gone out, along with the Christmas card and the Captain's Christmas letter.

The letter described the committee's decision to press ahead with the major tree clearance and the new reservoir. It had stressed the importance of having the projects completed before 2009, the centenary year of this famous Club. It had explained the necessity of borrowing two million pounds rather than levying members and pointed out that, even with the 10% increase in fees, West Downs was only a little more expensive than other great clubs.

Traditionally about half the members sent in their cheques straight after Christmas while the rest dribbled in during January and February. So half of the expected money had been received and the cheques had been sitting in a file on Major Silvester's desk when the bailiffs had arrived.

"We need to get a grip on the situation Hamish. I've spoken briefly to George and Malcolm and explained what's happened and they're pretty upset, as I am. I can't believe that Arthur was so naïve as to pay all that money upfront. He was so cavalier with the Club's money. I also told Sean and his reaction was much more critical – after all there's no love lost between them as you know. I need to get a handle on exactly how bad our position is before next week's finance committee meeting."

The Major shuffled papers on his desk. Or rather he moved two large piles of files from the right to the left. Truth be told, the Major never cared for figures. He saw himself as an organisation man. He liked organisations as long as that meant there were people to do all the detail work while he discussed the matters of the day with the officers of the Club. Rather like the army in fact where he had never been happier than reporting on the activities of the various platoons to his C.O.

His three year tenure at West Downs had been relatively trouble-free. There were Club rules and regulations and he was good at writing notices and pinning them on the

Club notice board reminding members of dress codes, the importance of fixing matches on time and announcing upcoming events.

He left the day-to-day running of the bar to Marco and the catering to Dorothy who had been with the Club for years. Recently he had made one of his rare decisions which had not met with her approval, but so what?

He had never got on with the head greenkeeper but solved this by passing every problem over to the chairman of the green's committee to adjudicate.

If he was unpopular with the staff he was not aware of it. After all his job was to preserve the traditions of the Club and take it through to its centenary, and he spent most of his time planning for that.

As a result, he did not have his finger on the pulse when it came to the Club's finances. West Downs employed a book-keeper to write up the accounts and a local accountant (a friend of Arthur's who played off a very good handicap of 6) to audit them.

At the finance committee meetings the Major would present the figures on bar sales, green fees and overheads but these were invariably several months old. West Downs was a rich club and its borrowings, now rather heavy because of the tree clearance and reservoir project, were more than covered by the value of its investment portfolio.

Jim waited for the Major to speak.

"Well we've obviously been running an overdraft up to Christmas, but that's fairly normal. We get lots of our income from the membership fees of course. About now in fact." He tapped the file with the cheques.

"Do you think we should pay those in now, Major?"

"Why ever not?"

"Well I'm wondering what the reactions of the members is going to be to the news."

"Well we have to get the work completed and we'll need the membership fee money to pay the new firm."

"The new firm?"

"Well yes. I thought we'd be putting the contract out to tender. I thought I'd draft up a report on what has been completed so far and what still needs doing to get things ready for the work on the reservoir to start.

"You think it's wise to go ahead with the reservoir?"

"We've spent a lot of money getting all the plans through the local council so we'll have to."

"Not if we don't have the money."

"But we have to. The Centenary. It's only two years away. We must get the reservoir started as soon as the trees are cleared.

"But what about the money? We can't just ignore the financial mess we're in."

"Well," the Major moved one of the piles of folders to the other side of his desk. "That's really up to Arthur, he's the finance man."

Jim tried another approach. "What's our bank balance at the moment and how much do we have in members' cheques so far?"

The Major shrugged. "Arthur probably has those figures. I haven't counted the cheques yet, Marjorie normally does that and she's not in today."

The two men carried on talking for more than an hour. By the end Jim realised that he wasn't going to get any meaningful answers or decisions out of the Secretary.

It was becoming clear that putting the remainder of the tree clearance out to tender would mean a delay of several months before work commenced which meant major disruption in the main golfing season. The work needed to be completed before April when the main competitions started and the first societies began arriving. The Club needed the income from these societies more than ever now.

It was also clear that they would need to have to find more than half a million pounds to pay the new contractor, even if they could find one willing to finish off a half-completed job. Another million was earmarked for the new reservoir.

He knew that Pyotr, the Polish site manager, had been willing to carry on the work but then the leasing company were repossessing all the machinery which made it impossible. The Pole wouldn't have the money or the creditworthiness to pay for new machinery. Not for the first time did Jim ask himself why he had ever volunteered for the job of captain.

He couldn't see any way out of the problem.

But a mile or so away was a lady who was hatching a plan that just might provide him with the exit route.

25

PYOTR

I find it hard to sleep tonight. Maggie and I have been talking for hours and my head is full of figures, of ideas, of plans and of doubts.

Maggie's so enthusiastic. It's hard to criticise but I do worry that it's just a big game for her. She seems to have a simple answer to every objection I raise. I find myself believing that it really could work. But then what does she really know about business and finance? And I've never run a business before – not in Poland and certainly not in this foreign country.

She thinks we should join together and set up a company. We should be partners. She says she can persuade the leasing company to rent the equipment to us for a few months – but how does she know? They looked pretty unhelpful to me.

She says she can get the golf club to pay us weekly so that the workers could get paid in cash. I know we could do the job and get it finished in time but I'm not so sure about her ability to get the leasing company and the Club to do the other bits. After all, she's a woman and she would be operating in a very man's world.

It all sounds so simple. But I can't sleep. What if the leasing company won't rent us the equipment? What if the golf club decides not to go on with the tree clearance? What if they appointed someone else? What if they wouldn't pay until it was all finished? I could hardly blame them after the last time.

I wake from a fitful night when I had dreamed about trying to chop down trees in a Polish forest but all the saws we had were blunt and the trees wouldn't be cut. The harder I tried to saw them the more the saw blade just bounced off the bark of the tree.

I decide to call Saska and ask her advice. After all, I was only in England to make a better life for her and I haven't told her yet about not being paid and the collapse of the company.

She answers my call herself. I have a direct line number for her at her new office in Lodz. I had pretended to be happy for her with her promotion but inwardly I worried that I was falling even further behind her in earnings. It wasn't right that she should be the one to earn the money – that was my job – or would be if I still had one.

"Oh Pyotr, I'm so glad you called. I am so loving the job here. They've given me responsibility for two of their biggest clients – it's a real step up. There's an Englishman overseeing the accounts but most of the work is going to be down to me. I've already spent a morning in the factory of one of them and it seems ….."

"That's great," I say interrupting her, "but I have some news for you too."

"Oh good, Pyotr. Tell me how is the tree clearance going – I read there was a lot of snow in England – is that delaying things?"

I tell her what has happened. I don't tell her Maggie's plan. She is silent. Then she tries to reassure me.

"Oh Pyotr, I'm so sorry. But I'm sure you will find another job."

I tell her about Maggie's plan. I expect her to be critical, to throw cold water on it as the English say. After all she's used to dealing with major companies with millions of zlotys of assets, not a little start-up firm like we are planning.

"But Pyotr, that's wonderful. This Maggie seems such a resourceful woman. And it is a great opportunity for you. If you do this contract well then you will surely get lots of other golf club contracts and make lots of money."

"But it's such a risk. And what if it doesn't work?"

"Well you'll never know until you try. It's not going to be easy I know, convincing the other companies to back you but you can try – you can always try. Now, you'll need to set up a limited liability company. Does Maggie know how to do that? If not I can ask my boss here, the Englishman. He'll get you set up, no problem."

After the phone call I feel surprisingly elated. It seems that it's not such a 'madcap' scheme after all. I start making some coffee and then hear Maggie coming downstairs. Her face lights up when she sees me smiling.

"Now you've slept on it Pytor, are you still keen?"

"I am. I am. I've just talked to Saska and she can help us register a company and everything. "

Maggie smiles back. She has that lovely smile that makes you think everything is wonderful. I feel confident. I want to get started right away.

"Maggie. Can I borrow your car? I want to go to the golf club right now."

26

The clubhouse was open and there were a good number of cars in the car park. The regular Tuesday crowd had arrived, without clubs, but still wanting to get away from wives at home and meet their friends. There was a snooker table and plenty of people to play bridge as well as Australian cricket on the Club's Sky TV.

Marco was busy dishing out drinks and the news of the previous day's happenings. Snooker and bridge were forgotten as everyone pontificated on the news and what it meant for the Club.

The Major had locked the door to his office where he had retreated as soon as members started to arrive. Only Terri, his secretary was left to field members' questions and she knew no more than they did.

"All I know is that the Major has asked me to get the bank balance up to date. He's already had a long meeting with the Polish man, Pyotr I think it is. The Major's in a bit of state, he's very agitated about something. I've never seen him like this before."

*

The Major was reading the Captain's letter. He unlocked the door and called Terri into his office. "I need you to type this out and send it to every member – today!"

The notice of the extraordinary general meeting was attached to the Captain's letter. The date for the meeting was just over two weeks away, fourteen days' notice being required by the constitution.

*

It's already dark by the time I return to the house. I stopped off to see the foreman of the men after leaving Addlestone. I press the remote control that Maggie keeps in the front of the car. The gate opens and the car crunches up the gravel drive that's still covered in snow.

Maggie has heard the car engine and has the front door open by the time I reach the steps.

"Pyotr, Pyotr. Guess what's happened! Such fantastic news."

My heart skips a beat.

"Guess what? I got a phone call from Simone. She's pregnant! The I.V.F. has worked. I'll have another grandchild in the summer!"

"That's wonderful Maggie. I'm so pleased for you." Inwardly I feel deflated. For a moment I thought that Maggie had good news about the business – perhaps had heard from the leasing company or the golf club. But it seems she has thoughts only about a new grandchild. Will this alter things? Will she still want to be involved in the business? Women are fickle.

For the next hour or two as she works away preparing the meal she keeps chattering excitedly. Over and over she marvels that the I.V.F. has worked, wonders if she'll have a granddaughter or another grandson. What will they call it? How will they manage in that house? Will they be moving to a bigger one? She never once asks how I've got on.

"No coriander seeds! I knew there was something else I needed from Ocado. I'll have to get Lech to bring me some more next week."

Why does she always assume it will be Lech who delivers the groceries? One week a different man, a Scotsman, had come instead. Maggie had been most put out.

I watch as she works away with the different ingredients. "You're going to an awful lot of trouble for me."

"Don't be silly, it's for Jim. We need to make a good impression. Oh didn't I tell you? He rang for you and I explained we had some proposals to put to him. He was most intrigued." She smiles coquettishly. "So I asked him to join us for dinner!"

"You forgot to tell me?"

"Well, what with Simone's news it went right out of my head. Anyway, tell me. How did you get on with the Major?"

27

The next two weeks fly by. I have never been happier. I spend a couple of nights with Simone at her place. She shouldn't drive in her condition on these icy roads. We talk about how the spare room will be decorated, whether Simone should give up her job, what names are in fashion.

Then there is the bring-and-buy sale at the golf club in aid of the Lady Captain's charity. I'm running the bookstall with Daphne.

"Isn't it terrible about Arthur's friend running off with five million pounds of our money?" I smile to myself. I never fail to wonder at how misinformation spreads around the Club. An innocent remark about someone's dress sense becomes a major contretemps in no time at all as the original remark is embellished with every telling. Chinese whispers? They have nothing on West Downs whispers.

"It was only one million Daphne and some of that covered work that's already been done. And anyway there's a good chance the liquidator will be able to get some of the money back."

"My, my. You are well informed. Anyone would think you understood all these shenanigans." "Anyway I hear you're to be a granny again. That's marvellous news. Is it going to be a boy or a girl?"

Before I can answer we are interrupted by Elizabeth wearing an expression of impending disaster.

"Have you heard what's happened? The kitchen say they haven't any cakes at all! Apparently the company that they get all the bread and cakes from hasn't delivered! What are we going to do?"

"Let them eat bread," I say. But the wit is wasted on Elizabeth.

"Well the sandwiches have all had to be made from frozen bread which was left over in the freezer. It's not good enough – you wouldn't get this trouble at Wentworth or Sunningdale. Oh no, the Secretary there would have been on to the supplier immediately. Immediately!" she adds for emphasis.

"But our Secretary has rather more serious things on his mind right now," I think.

And indeed he had. The extraordinary general meeting was less than a week away and for once, Major Silvester would have to come up with some hard facts. The bakery, who had stopped delivering in protest against the Club's slow payment, was another problem.

28

Annual General Meetings at golf clubs are strange affairs. Around half the membership dress up and attend clutching copies of the previous year's minutes, the Club accounts and the agenda. There is much discussion prior to the meeting about the improvements that need to be made, the competitions that need to be better monitored, the price of certain drinks in the bar and so on.

But at the actual meeting everyone listens politely while the captain talks about what a wonderful year he's had and how his successor will be a safe pair of hands. The nominations for committee and vice captain are voted through unopposed and the new captain then stands up and says how proud he is to be entrusted to the office of captain and that he would be pleased to buy everyone present a drink in the bar – even if the prices are a little steep. This is met with applause and laughter and members' concerns about the running of the Club are forgotten for another year.

But an Extraordinary General Meeting is entirely different. On the rare occasions when it is called, it is normally to decide on action on a serious problem. There are no free drinks, no light-hearted heckling and no jockeying to see who can propose or second the most motions.

The meeting takes place in the dining room, the largest room in the Club. Every chair in the building has been requisitioned and has been placed, theatre style, in the room. There are still many people forced to stand at the back of the room.

At a table at the far end sit the committee, the Club Secretary and an empty chair. Arthur sits between Jim and Major Silvester shuffling his feet and gazing at the clock on the rear wall above the members' heads. He avoids all eye contact.

The Major clears his throat, stands up and explains why the EGM had been called, confirms that all necessary notices have been given and that everything is being carried out according to the constitution.

Daphne sits next to me on the second row. "It's a pity Arthur and the Major didn't think about giving us notice that they were giving a million pounds to a crook!"

As quickly as he can, the Major passes over the microphone to Jim, sits down and begins writing in his notebook. I can't imagine what he suddenly finds necessary to write down.

"As you know, your committee decided last Autumn to engage in a major tree-clearing exercise and to go ahead with installing a reservoir. The object of the exercise is to return the course to its traditional 1909 state and to ensure, in these days of global warming, we have adequate water for our fairway watering system. We wanted to have all this in place by the time of our Centenary."

There's a murmur of approval.

"As you know," he repeats, "we decided that the work should start immediately and we were lucky enough to find a contractor willing to commence straight away."

"Unlucky you mean," shouts one of the younger members from the back.

"Well, yes, as it has turned out that contractor has gone into liquidation so is unable to complete the contract." Jim pauses and sips from his water glass. Now for the bad bit.

"Unfortunately the Club had paid the contractor for the work so we are now left with the problem of finishing the work and paying for it all over again. And of course we need the work done now to ensure the course is playable by April." He coughs, helps himself to more water. The meeting is silent, expectant.

"I'm sure members will have been impressed by the speed and efficiency of the work carried out by the Polish workforce employed by G.D.S." He pauses again. There is a murmur of approval. "I am glad to say that, due to the generosity of one of our members, we are in a position to continue the work using the same team under a new company."

"Are they going to run off with money too?" The young man at the back turns to his friends who laugh.

"Seeing as the co-owner of that business is Maggie Miles I feel that is extremely unlikely," says Jim. "Indeed I should like Maggie to join us on stage to explain."

Daphne looks at me, open-mouthed. "What Maggie? You? What's going on?"

I get up and move to the table alongside. The noise level in the room rises and I can feel their eyes on me.

"It's quite simple really," Jim moves the microphone closer to me. "It's quite simple really. Can you hear me ok?"

"It's obvious we can't leave the job half done. It's not the Poles' fault that the boss ran off with our money. Pyotr's wage cheque bounced too – he hasn't been paid for December. But Pyotr can finish all the work if the Club wants but he needed the equipment and vehicles that GDS had hired. So I've put money into the new company so we can pay the leasing company who'll rent us the equipment. Of course it would have been easier if the Club had given him an advance but after the last time and what happened" she looks pointedly at Arthur, "we couldn't expect that. So I know Pyotr and his chaps will do an excellent job and I just want you all to back the decision to use him, er us."

I know my face is flushed, I can't wait to sit down. I hand back the microphone. There, I've done it. Two frantic weeks of meeting and planning and now it's over to Jim to sell it to the membership. Some things have been easier than I'd hoped. Jim's been really supportive, even enthusiastic. The costings that Pyotr prepared were agreed by the committee. The leasing company whose vehicles are still parked at the course and part-covered in snow, are happy to recoup some of their losses. The only real problem has been Hugh.

He was furious at my request to pull £240,000 out of the Icelandic Bank and put it into Lloyds TSB. He was incensed that I had promised to bankroll Pyotr. But I didn't care. I was not going to give into him. The money is now back in Lloyds and, if the motion is carried, tomorrow I'll transfer it to the new company.

I suppose I expected everyone at the Club to thank me, but obviously they're not going to. The questions from the floor are about the committee's incompetence in their dealings with GDS. Somebody questions whether it's right to just get the Poles to finish the work rather than get a 'proper' firm, a respectable, trustworthy firm. It takes all of Jim's persuasion to convince them that there's little alternative to the Poles. To cap it all I see two of the older members jumping to their feet together in their haste to get Jim's attention. One of them demands to know who would be responsible for managing the contractors and ensuring they don't exceed their estimate or time as obviously this was not a job for a woman!

But eventually the motion is put, seconded and carried, although there are several dissenters.

But a second motion is defeated. The committee proposed, in view of the financial situation, to delay the reservoir building until after the centenary. But the older members in particular are vociferous and one of them purporting to speak for them insists that the project continue as it would be too embarrassing for an ancient club like West Downs to admit it no longer had the money to pay for it. Since Arthur has such good connections with Dylan's Bank they are sure the bank will extend the loan. Arthur, who has kept the lowest of profiles during the entire meeting sees this as an opportunity to partially redeem himself, and nods enthusiastically.

By a narrow majority the committee's motion is defeated and the next day the committee will endorse Jim and Arthur's signing of two contracts – one with Petmag Contractors and the other with a large Irish construction company who would start drilling and surveying within a couple of months.

After the meeting I leave immediately to drive back to the house. Pyotr has waited in the car for news. Now he wants to hear everything from me. I feel tired and depressed. I'm close to tears. There is no spring in my step and I don't return his smile. I turn the key in the ignition, select drive and swing the car out of the car park and out of the Club.

"Well, Maggie? What happened? Did they accept our offer?"

"Yes, it's all going ahead as we planned. Jim will sign your contract tomorrow."

"**Our** contract Maggie, it's not my company. You're the one who has put the money in."

"Well you wouldn't have thought I'd done anything if you listened to some of the old farts there. Oh no, just rude comments about my ability, being a woman, to manage a contract. It's not as if the men have actually got an unblemished record in that field – who was it that gave the contract to GDS in the first place?"

"They didn't thank you?"

"On the contrary I could see them muttering about profiteering from the Club's predicament. And then they went ahead and decided to go on with the reservoir project. Apparently Arthur will magic a loan from Dylan's Bank to pay those contactors."

"I think, Maggie, that you should ignore those old men and their views on women. They are not like the rest of the Club members. Just ignore them."

"It's not just them. It's the women too. The ones I thought were my friends. Instead of being pleased for the Club, pleased for me, they are being really horrible. Daphne didn't say a word when I got back down from the platform while Elizabeth said it was not right for a member, a woman member, to get involved with 'trade'."

"I don't understand what you mean – 'trade'. What's wrong with 'trade'?"

"Everything apparently. N.Q.W. Not Quite West Downs!"

I notice Pyotr gripping the door handle and realise I'm driving rather too fast. He says nothing but he must be thinking I'm strange, not celebrating the fact that we've got the contract. I know he's desperate to make it work, to make money and make Saska proud of him.

He reaches into his pocket for his mobile phone. Saska answers the call almost immediately. The excitement in his voice is obvious although I understand not a word., The same excitement is apparent when he phones Tadeusz, the foreman and then Lech.

I'm being silly. I should have known what their reaction would be at the meeting. It's been hard enough to get them to accept women in the Spikes Bar, much more so to accept that a woman could save the Club from its biggest ever cock-up. And anyway, I'm not just doing it for the Club. I'm doing it for Pyotr and he's obviously grateful. So cheer up – you've got a business to run now!

"There's a bottle of champagne in the fridge. We'll open it as soon as we get back and toast our success," I laugh. Pyotr's phone calls have cheered me up. Pyotr looks at me and smiles. He shakes his head 'Women, I'll never understand them!"

The headlights pick out the driveway to the house. The electric gates are open, the lights on in the house. Hugh's Range Rover is parked by the front door.

Half an hour later when Hugh leaves, I no longer feel like opening the champagne. Although Hugh and I have argued sometimes in the past, tonight it's a full-blooded row. And Hugh has been so rude to Pyotr, accusing him of exploiting a vulnerable woman with no head for business. He's insisted that I talk to a lawyer friend of his before putting any money into the company. My protestations that my reputation at West Downs is at stake is met with further accusations.

"How do you think I feel? How am I going to explain to my friends at the Club that I've let my mother get involved with some itinerant Pole and she is throwing away my father's hard-earned cash and my inheritance?"

Pyotr has remained silent through most of the exchange but now interrupts saying merely "I'm not itinerant. I will not leave your mother in trouble. We will be successful and she will become rich."

"She's already rich," spits Hugh.

He leaves, promising to speak to Simone and see if she can talk some sense into me.

29

Brendan Matthews, the business manager at the Ascot branch of Lloyds TSB had been expecting my call. News of the EGM votes had reached him the evening before. He quickly agreed to meet me and Pyotr and £200,000 was transferred from my current account (to which I had recently transferred the money from that Icelandic bank,) into the new Petmag account with me and Pyotr as joint signatories. I have at least heeded Hugh's advice about that, even if I spurned his offer of a lawyer.

I look at Brendan's face to see if there is any of the disapproval I had encountered at my meeting with Hugh but I can detect none. Indeed he seems very positive about the whole affair. Probably thinking of his commission.

We arrange payment to the leasing company and ring the representative to inform him. He checks with his accounts department and then agrees to release the equipment immediately. In truth this is a figure of speech since the keys had been left with the Major and the equipment is still in the Club car park.

By the time we arrive at West Downs the vehicles are already being used by the Poles. Pyotr smiles and waving me goodbye heads for 'his' pick-up truck.

I feel suddenly alone. After the last hectic 24 hours, suddenly there is nothing left for me to do. I look around the car park. There are lots of members' cars around. I recognise Daphne's Golf GTi with its personalised number plate. Elizabeth's little Mercedes is there and the Lady Captain's space has a Lexus 4x4.

I realise this is the day when the ladies meet and take down the Christmas decorations. Not only are women at the Club considered 'jolly good at flower arranging' but we are pretty useful at managing the Christmas decorations.

Walking into the clubhouse I turn left into the dining room. It's empty. I retrace my steps and enter the main bar where I find Daphne and Elizabeth, together with Marco the steward. Daphne is holding a step-ladder while Marco, perched precariously on the top step, is unfastening the Christmas decorations.

"Do you need a hand?" I ask putting my handbag down on the table.

"I'm sure you've got more important things to do." I'm taken by surprise at Elizabeth's manner, her normal 'mother-hen' concern replaced by barely concealed sarcasm. Daphne shoots me an apologetic smile but then turns her attention back to the ladder.

I try again. "Really, I'm not doing anything this morning, I'd like to help. I always do."

I pick up a decoration that Marco had dropped and put it carefully in one of the large cardboard boxes.

"We could start on the Men's Bar," Daphne says and I follow her into the adjacent room, now named the Spikes Bar but still referred to by most members as the Men's Bar despite the fact that ladies were now permitted to use it as well.

Elizabeth says nothing and remains helping Marco.

What's up with her?" I ask as soon as we are out of earshot. "What have I done to upset her?"

"Shown us all up, that's what. Especially the men. They don't like the fact that you've stepped in to sort out this mess."

"But they should be pleased. After all it's my money. And I didn't see any of them rushing for their cheque books."

"Yes, I know. But that's what I mean. You've shown them up. All these alpha males have been trumped by a woman."

"Maybe, but that doesn't explain Elizabeth's attitude."

"Oh she's just worried for you. She thinks you're having an affair and it's turned your head. You've put your money into something with a young Pole just because you've fallen for him."

"Oh, that's preposterous! He's half my age and I've got a son older than him."

"That doesn't stop the tittle tattle in the ladies room. I think we're all rather jealous!"

"What you too? You don't believe that rubbish do you?"

Daphne smiles knowingly, "It's none of my business."

*

I would normally have stayed at the Club for lunch but Elizabeth's attitude still annoys me and I drive home. The news is on the car radio but I barely listen to it. I catch a bit about the stock market being down by a large amount again. There's an interview with someone in America talking about 'toxic assets' and the default of a major merchant bank. I feel depressed enough already and switch channels to Classic FM.

Back home I make myself a sandwich before going into Frank's study. Funny how I still think of it as Frank's study. There's a pile of unopened letters on the desk and I start to open them with Frank's silver paper knife, the one I gave him for Christmas how many years ago? There's lots of catching up to do. I really haven't come to terms with having to deal with all the bills myself. That was always something that Frank did.

I open the letter from the golf club and extract the bill. I feel rather guilty that I didn't pay it before Christmas but there just didn't seem to have been any time. The amount had gone up – even I notice that although Frank had always paid it. I no longer get a 'spouse's' discount and there is a general increase of 10% - Arthur's way of part-funding the reservoir and tree clearance projects.

I get out my Lloyds TSB chequebook and sign across nearly £2000 to West Downs Golf Club. "Still," I think, "they'll be paying my company ten times that amount every week!" I think of Pyotr working away right now in the cold.

The phone startles me. I pick up the extension on the desk.

"Hi Mum, how are you?"

"I'm fine darling, just fine."

"I'm sorry I haven't been in touch this week but Justin's been having to work late. Things are a bit dicey at work. It's left me with the kids."

"Don't worry, Estelle dear, I've been so busy myself that I haven't had time to phone **you.** There's been such a to-do at the golf club and now Pyotr and I …."

"Yes, I heard from Hugh. He's worried that you're making a big mistake."

"Oh no," I think "Doesn't anyone believe me. Why does everyone think I'm acting like some gullible old woman who is having the wool pulled over her eyes by some Polish lothario?"

I change tack.

"What's the problem with Justin's job?"

"Well they've just had two of their biggest contracts put on hold. Apparently the firms have just cut their budgets because of the financial situation or something. It was on the News about some big American bank. Did you hear it?"

"I caught something about toxic loans or some such thing but I didn't really pay much attention."

"Yes, well Justin had a contract to fit that bank's London office and the whole thing's just been cancelled. And another job he was in line for, with a fund manager like Hugh's, they've just announced they're laying off a third of their staff so they won't be spending money on a new office! It's not looking good in the City."

"Oh, I am sorry dear. Look if you need some help, you know, need some money, you know I'd be only too happy to …"

"Thanks Mum, that's kind. But you know Justin, he's not one to sponge."

"It's not sponging, darling, it's family. You keep me informed. If things get bad you must have some money to tide you over. This financial malarkey – it's no big thing I'm sure. It'll soon blow over and business for Justin will be good again. It's not like we're going into a recession or something."

"You think not?"

"No. Even old pessimist himself, Gordon Brown, said we were the best placed country in Europe to deal with any crisis. I heard it on the News."

"And you believe him?"

After the call I go back to opening the post and sorting the bills. There's one from Portugal. The stamps, pretty ones that remind me of the times Frank and I spent in the villa. Normally at this time of year we would go over there for a couple of months to avoid the worst of the British winter. But this year the villa will remain empty until Easter when Simone or Estelle may go down. Or perhaps Hugh and his family.

I slide the paper knife under the flap of the envelope and withdraw the papers inside. There's a letter from our lawyer in Loule and some official-looking forms in Portuguese. Reading it I learn that apparently the Portuguese government have imposed a tax on foreign villa owners. The lawyers are saying we must pay more than £20,000. I'll have to talk to Hugh about that.

I plough through the rest of the mail. The bills are mainly settled by direct debit but I look through them and file them in Frank's cabinet. I'm getting the hang of this now. Poor old Frank would never believe it. And soon, I will have lots more to file – with the new business. That's going to keep me busy.

I look through the bank statements. My Lloyds TSB current account shows a very healthy balance while my

Icelandic savings account has dropped from the £250,000 to a mere £10,000 as a result of my withdrawal to fund Petmag.

I don't like to fall out with Hugh. He got so upset about Petmag. I know he doesn't think I've got a business brain. I probably don't. Maybe I am taking a big risk with Pyotr. After all, what do I really know about him? And now we're business partners and he's got £200,000 of my money. Well, not him exactly. Why is everyone so against me? Not just Hugh but everyone at the Club? And Simone and Estelle have obviously been talking with Hugh and they seemed to be ganging up on me. Can they all be so wrong? Oh, I wish Frank was here – he'd know what to do.

Yet in a strange way I feel rather good about the situation. I've got a project, something to give me a reason to get up in the morning. Something to take my mind off Frank and the prospect of years of loneliness and getting older. In fact I'm beginning to feel more confident about my abilities to cope. Damn it! It's my money, I'll do what I like with it. It's much more interesting than leaving it in an Icelandic bank.

The sound of the car tyres on gravel breaks my reverie. Then the phone rings. The security lights come on outside and I realise it has turned quite dark already. I pick up the phone. It's Hugh.

Hugh never phones me from the office. He is always far too busy making million dollar deals.

"Hugh, how nice of you to phone. How are you?"

"I'm fine," he replies. Only later do I discover he is far from fine. It has been another disastrous day on the stock market. The FTSE has dropped 400 points. Hugh has gone 'long' on most shares anticipating the post-Christmas slump would prove short lived. Instead the market has continued to fall. The value of the funds he manages has dropped even faster. It is too late to move into bonds or safer investments. The return on them, by the end of March, would not nearly cover his losses. Without increasing the value of his Fund's portfolio he would get no bonus at Easter. He is therefore hanging on to his equities and hoping and praying that the market will recover, and soon.

The problem is, he could no longer count on a big bonus and his personal bills are mounting. He needs a sizeable amount within the next month or two and his only source is me.

He broaches the subject carefully. "Just a loan for a few months until I get my bonus. I don't want to pull my money out of the Isle of Man account as there's a big penalty for withdrawing it now, as you know." He can't resist reminding me of one of his objections to my withdrawing the money from Frank's Isle of Man account.

"Well I'll see what I can do. I can't talk now because Pyotr's just come in and I want to know how it went – our first day of the company! Look why don't you come down on Sunday with the family?"

"Yes, OK Mum. We'll do that. Sunday."

I put down the receiver. Not like Hugh at all. Very subdued. And he just agreed to come on Sunday – no referral to her ladyship, Lettie, at all. That's a first. I wonder if he's not telling me something.

"Hello Maggie, I'm back." Pyotr has removed his boots and coat and is walking barefoot along the hall. He's carrying a big paper bag and grinning. Carefully he places the bag on Frank's desk. "It's for you. To celebrate our first day in business together."

I take the pot of snowdrops into the kitchen and place it on the window ledge. I open the fridge and take out the vodka bottle.

I look at his big hands, calloused and cut from a hard day's labour. The sinews on his arms trace dark lines on his fair skin. My vodka is diluted with tonic, a solitary ice cube floats in his.

"Na Zdrowie Maggie"

"Cheers Pyotr."

We laugh. The vodka slips down easily as Pyotr begins to tell me about his day.

30

I hear Maggie coming upstairs to bed. She calls out 'Good Night'. I hear her door close and turn back to the laptop. I know that I'm tired and should go to sleep. The winter makes for short days but I like to be on site before the men, to plan the day's activities.

The work is going well, better than I could have hoped. The men are pulling together, the weather, though cold, is dry, no more snow, so moving the felled trees is proving easier. The work will be finished on time or even earlier than scheduled. Either way in a couple of months the contract will be over.

But what then? Yes, I will have earned a good wage, hopefully there will be some profit as well to share with Maggie but what then? Will we look for more contracts? Where will we get those? Maggie seems to think that we will get more work from other golf clubs but she's an optimist. I read the papers, the economy is in trouble. Will golf clubs really be in a position to undertake major works on their courses?

I think of Saska. She's doing so well. She got a big rise when she was promoted. She seems to be really engrossed in the new job, in the new city. She won't want to give it up and come over here. And why should she? I'm earning a lot more than I did in Poland but for how long? I don't have any security to offer her. And what would she do here? All the Polish wives I hear of are working as shop assistants or waitressing. That's not for Saska.

If I had managed to get a well-paid permanent job at Wisley, or Kew perhaps, then maybe things would have been different. But although Petmag seems to offer opportunities we're not going to make a fortune out of West Downs, and we've no certainty of any other work. I can't help thinking that Maggie will tire of the excitement. It's made her happier to have something to focus on rather than her husband's death, but it won't last. She's got the new grandchild due soon. That'll take her attention. She hasn't got money worries – she doesn't need to make lots of money. She's never had to struggle like Saska and me. And then there's her son. What a pompous Englishman. Looks at me as if I'm a servant. Thinks he knows everything about business and money. I wonder. He deals with millions of pounds of other people's money but he doesn't do real work, doesn't make anything, doesn't create wealth. He just gambles with other people's money. And now I hear he's had to borrow money from Maggie so I wonder just how much money he really is making.

And if she gets bored with the business where does that leave me? Now if I had the capital to start my own business, I could move back to Poland and set it up in Lodz where Saska is now working. But how long will it take me to earn enough to do that?

I walk across to the window and draw back one of the curtains. It is dark outside but the moon is nearly full and the monochromatic layout of the garden can clearly be seen. Without the summer flowers and plants it looks almost surgically neat, anaesthetised, waiting for the Spring to warm it up and bring it awake. Waiting for Spring? What will Spring bring me? Can I afford to wait and hope that new opportunities will pop up like daffodils? And how long do those daffodils last anyway?

It's no use thinking like this. I've got to make the most of the current situation. Maggie's given me a great chance to make something of myself. The job's going well. Concentrate on that. Things have a way of sorting themselves out. Just as long as Saska understands that.

31

After the snow of early January had gone, the weather stayed dry and bright and work at the Club progressed well. Life seemed to have settled into a pattern. Every Friday Maggie would accompany Pyotr to the bank in Ascot where they withdrew the cash to pay the growing number of workers that Pyotr was employing.

Every evening they would sit together and drink a vodka or two or three. Maggie would make supper and then watch TV. Pyotr would take himself off to his room where he spent hours with his laptop 'surfing the net'.

Friday nights he would drive his pick-up (part of the leasing deal) over to Addlestone to see Lech. Sometimes he stayed over and Maggie was left alone for the week-end.

Hugh had come down with the family and she had written him a rather large cheque. Lettie and the twins were the same as always – Lettie rather distant, distracted; the twins boisterous. She had asked Hugh about the Portuguese tax. He confirmed she would have to pay it and she transferred some of the money from what was left in her

Icelandic bank account. She had wanted to discuss whether she should sell the villa but Hugh was in no mood to discuss things so she let it drop.

On the last day of January the Club was due to pay the first month's bill to Petmag. Normally she and Pyotr would have collected the cheque made out to Petmag and gone to the bank to pay it in and withdraw cash for the weekly wages. But Maggie had picked up a cold. It had started mid-week and got progressively worse. She felt terrible and wondered if she might have flu.

So she counter-signed a cheque for nearly £20,000 to be drawn in cash and gave it to Pyotr on Thursday night. The men were all due to be paid and work had progressed so well they had agreed bonuses for the men.

She heard Pyotr leave early in the morning. The front door slammed shut. She heard the pick up's engine fire up and the gravel crunch as he set off up the driveway.

By the late afternoon, she felt better and set about making herself a meal. Pyotr was due back and she would have a drink with him before he went off to meet his friends in Addlestone.

She put the vodka bottle and the two glasses on the table and waited.

But Pyotr did not return.

32

Lech phones me around six o'clock. He wants to know if Pyotr is with me? Apparently he hasn't been seen since lunchtime and the men haven't been paid.

Hugh has that 'told-you-so' tone when I phone him. He's depressed. The FTSE is still falling, his funds are falling faster. Things must be bad, I realise, otherwise he wouldn't be telling me this. He never discussed such things with me before. But Hugh has connections and after a few phone calls gets back to me to say he has spoken with Mr Matthews at the Ascot branch of Lloyds who confirmed that Pyotr had been in and withdrawn the cash. Surprisingly he says that he didn't deposit the big cheque due from the Club. There was no Dylan's bank cheque paid in.

"Phone the police," says Hugh. "He's obviously scarpered with your money. Twenty thousand pounds is just too much temptation for a Pole."

"Maybe he's had an accident?"

"Check with the police. Mum, phone the police."

They aren't helpful. "Are you saying he's stolen your money Madam?"

"No, of course not. I just want you to check if he's been in an accident."

Two hours pass. I ring the police again. I repeat the whole story to somebody new. They check. Yes there is a record of my previous call. No there have been no reported accidents involving a Hyundai pick-up truck.

It's a long evening. I can't think of anything else. I keep turning over in my mind different scenarios. Can he really have taken the money and run? I trusted him. I still trust him. Yet everyone is telling me I'm being foolish, risking my money for an infatuation. Could they be right? Is everyone wrong apart from me? Maybe I am just a silly old woman who got carried away with grandiose ideas.

I watch the News at Ten but it's all doom and gloom about the economy. Finally I ring Lech again. He tells me Pyotr isn't a thief. "I know Pyotr and Saska – he wouldn't do this to you."

I go up to bed. I open the door to Pyotr's room. Neat as ever. I look at his little table. The laptop is gone. I open the wardrobe. One pair of trousers and a couple of shirts hang there. There were clothes in the drawers but very few. The framed picture of Saska is still there.

But his precious laptop has gone. Why would he take it with him unless …?

In the morning, still tired through lack of sleep, I phone Estelle. I get only her answer machine. I try Simone.

"What did Hugh suggest?" Hugh was head of the family; the girls always deferred to him in an emergency.

"He's convinced Pyotr's run off with my money. He wants to call in the police."

"Maybe you should. I'll come over"

When she arrives I make some lunch. She's looking well and getting bigger. I feel happier at the prospect of another grandchild.

"Why don't we phone his wife in Poland?" she says. "Have you got her number?"

We go upstairs together and search through Pyotr's remaining possessions. We find a couple of letters from Saska but they have no address let alone a phone number. We can't read the Polish.

Then the phone rings and I rush downstairs to take it. It's Lech. He's heard nothing and has been talking to Pyotr's foreman. The men are angry at his disappearance and want to know how they are going to get paid. "After the last man went bust they are worried that Pyotr has left because he hasn't got the money to pay them."

"We have the money" I say, "At least we had. Pyotr took nearly £20,000 in cash yesterday and he didn't pay in the cheque that the Club gave him."

Lech whistles. "That much.? Do you still have more money left? Can you pay the men if we can't find Pyotr?"

"What do you mean?"

"Well the men are saying they will not do more work until they are paid. Tadeusz, the foreman phoned me. They need the money. You must go to the golf club Monday and explain. And pay them."

Simone tugs at my elbow. "Ask him if he's got Saska's phone number."

Lech doesn't think he has it. Saska has moved job and has a new number.

"Doesn't she have a mobile? "

"I'll check for Monday. You will go, won't you?"

"Must I? I don't know what to say and anyway I don't speak Polish. "

"I can come too if it helps?"

"Thank you."

I put the phone back and turn to Simone. I suddenly feel vulnerable. I need someone to talk to, to advise. I miss Frank. My whole involvement with Pyotr over the past weeks, the taking over of the contract, the moving of the money from the Icelandic bank – everything seemed to be going swimmingly. I couldn't fail. But suddenly I'm left, alone, to face 20 Polish workers who haven't been paid, who may throw down their tools and leave. Who might leave me to face the golf club and tell them once again the contract has gone caput.

Suddenly all the words of advice and criticism from Hugh, from Daphne and Elizabeth, even Simone, come back to me. I thought I knew what I was doing, could actually do business deals, set up companies. Now it has all come crashing down around me.

I look at Simone expecting to see her look of disapproval, or at least pity. But she's actually smiling.

"Come on, Mum. Cheer up. It's not the end of the world. Pyotr will turn up, the money will be there and everyone will carry on as before."

"But what if he doesn't come back? What if he really has run off with my money?"

"You don't believe that do you?

"No, I don't, but I don't know what else to think."

"Well you'd better think about drawing some more money out of the account so you can pay the men tomorrow. Do you know how much you owe them?"

*

Simone comes with me in the car. The police station is in the High Street in Ascot. The policeman tries to look busy as if that way he can get this stupid woman out of his hair quickly. No I don't know the registration number of the pick-up truck Pyotr was driving.

"But the lease company will have the details won't they?" It's Simone who is thinking now.

"I suppose so – I'll ring you as soon as I find it," I mumble.

He looks up from his notes. He smiles at Simone. "It's hard to trace him without that information. If he's left the country the pick-up is likely to be parked at the airport. We can check with immigration people at the airports but it takes time and C.I.D. is short-staffed right now. Are you sure he's not just gone to friends and forgotten to tell you? Most missing person cases are like that. They turn up a day or two later."

"You'd better tell him the rest Mum"

A trace of annoyance passes across his face. He looks pointedly at his watch. I start to explain about the money.

"So it looks like he's taken your money and scarpered!" His phrasing was almost identical to Hugh's. It wasn't a question, just a bald statement of fact as far as he was concerned. "In that case we can get the serious crime boys involved." He looks almost pleased at the prospect of a missing person report turning into a major manhunt. "Let me get one of my colleagues from C.I.D."

It's more than two hours later that we leave the station. We have been promised or threatened with a visit from C.I.D. to the house to examine Pyotr's room. I feel totally depressed. Not just about the money and the fact that even I am beginning to believe that Pyotr has run off. It was the knowing looks that the detectives gave each other when I explained I was recently widowed and Pyotr had been living with me.

We drive back in silence. It is Simone who notices the flashing red light on the hall phone.

"Maybe it's Pyotr," I cry pressing the key to play the messages.

"You have six new messages." The machine's robotic voice intoned.

"Hello Maggie. It's Daphne. How's your cold. Hope you're feeling better. Laurence and I wondered if you were up to coming round for supper tonight? Nothing special. Just Dolores and her husband. Give me a ring and let me know."

"Hello Maggie. Lech phoning. I found Saska's number and spoke to her. She will phone you, bye."

I look at Simone for reassurance. She looks sceptical.

"Hello, hello. Is that Maggie? It's Elizabeth. I know you've been ill but I wanted to know when you're playing the next round of the Hamilton. You're supposed to be playing Margretta on Monday and that is the last day. If you don't play then the committee may have to scratch you from the competition. I've already played my quarter final and I have to play the winner of your match. We need to get things sorted so can you please ring me, or maybe ring Margretta and if you can't ...." The message ended after the standard 30 seconds.

There is another bleep and then the sound of a receiver being replaced.

Then, "Hello. Message for Mrs Miles." There is a sound of throat clearing. The male voice continues. "Major Silvester here. I'm afraid I need to talk to you or Mr Wycenki about the works contract. Please call me before lunchtime."

"Charming fellow!" Simone grins.

"Hello, is that Maggie er Mrs Miles?" The female voice is heavily accented and the words come out slowly and deliberately. "I worry about Pyotr. Lech say he not come home to you. I will phone again, or," there is a pause, "you will phone here?"

The machine cuts off abruptly having reached the end of the tape. "You have no more messages."

My head is spinning and feels increasingly groggy. My throat is getting sore with all the talking. I reach for a tissue.

"I'll make us some lunch," says Simone. "You sit down. "You look exhausted."

I am. Really tired. I glance at myself in the mirror. My hair wasn't its normal groomed style – there are wisps and straggles everywhere. My face looks red and puffy and there are dark shadows under my eyes. So this was the executive woman running a construction company! I look more like an old grandma.

Simone comes in with soup and sandwiches. "Let's watch the news," she says. I look at the images of earthquake victims being dug out of a ruined building. The rest of the news is all financial and I concentrate on my soup. Alastair Darling is droning on about bad American banks that have caused our banking crisis. Then there's some analyst predicting a big recession, runs on our banks. It's all just too depressing and I switch it off.

I must have nodded off because it's already dusk when I'm awakened by the phone. It's Daphne checking again to see if I want to come to supper. I don't feel like going out but Simone persuades me. "Go upstairs, have a bath, do your hair and you'll feel much better," she says. "Anyway, I have to be getting back and you don't want to be on your own."

33

The taxi drops me at Daphne's. Laurence opens the door before I've even rung the bell. He takes my coat and gestures towards the lounge. I take a quick glance in the hall mirror and stop to pat my hair back into place. Despite the make-up I've applied the dark shadows are still visible under my eyes. My lack of sleep is showing.

I can hear the voices from the lounge and put on a brave face.

"Ah, Maggie, the businesswoman of the year!" Dolores's husband, Charles greets me by giving me a quick peck on each cheek while retaining his glass of chenin blanc in a vertical position.

I don't know Charles well, just as Dolores's husband.

"So you've turned your hand to tree-felling and earth-moving?" His tone is jocular, friendly and not the accusing tone I've come to expect from West Down members – particularly men.

"Yes, I've enrolled for lumberjack courses at the institute – such a change after pilates!"

They all laugh and I catch a look of relief in Daphne's eyes.

"So, seriously," says Laurence, "how is it all going with your Polish friends? I must say they seem to be getting on with it despite the awful weather.

I look at Laurence's face trying to read whether he knows about Pyotr. I don't think he does. I'm relieved. I'm still hoping there's an innocent explanation for his disappearance. Maybe I'll go home tonight and find him there.

"Laurence, give Maggie a drink for goodness sake, she looks like she needs one!"

"Wine, whisky, sherry?"

"Have you got a Vodka and some slimline tonic?"

"There's that Polish influence again, Maggie, " laughed Charles, "I fear he's leading you astray!"

The conversation turns inevitable to golf. The Club is always very quiet in February. Many members, certainly the retired ones, flee the winter weather and are to be found driving their golf carts in Florida or along the Garden Route. That leaves the Club nearly empty during the week. There are no societies booked and apart from a few hardy souls who brave the elements on Sunday and take lunch in the Club, the place is eerily quiet.

"It'll give that lazy secretary of ours time to sit and sort out his affairs," says Laurence. He never seems to know what's going on. If he did he might have prevented that chap from running off with the money."

So they know? I'm panicking now.

"Yes, though I blame that pompous twit, Arthur. He should have known better as a banker."

They don't know. They're talking about Michael Hamilton.

"Bankers! I hate the lot of them," Laurence speaks with a mouthful of humous-coated celery. "All those idiots buying packaged mortgage bonds that they knew nothing about. Toxic assets. I should say they're toxic. Problem is that it's us who'll suffer not them. They'll find a way to keep paying bonuses whatever happens."

"Yes and the politicians don't suffer. They've all got gold-plated pensions. It's poor sods like us have to fund our own pensions. Did you see the Footsie yesterday? It's falling like a stone."

Oh dear, no wonder poor Hugh is so worried, things seem to be really bad. I do hope he will still get his bonus.

Daphne looks bored and changes the subject. She has no head for business. Her role in life has always been to be the dutiful corporate wife which involves no decisions more taxing than deciding the appropriate clothes to wear or organising dinner parties. She is an accomplished hostess and I am looking forward to the meal. I realise I've eaten very little and am quite hungry.

We walk through to the dining room and I take in the array of cutlery. A full three courses at least and the crystal glasses sparkling in the light from a dozen candles forming the centrepiece of the table. I thought she said 'casual supper'.

Laurence and Charles follow us in with their whiskies in their hands. The conversation is football.

I hear Charles, "Not that I'm a soccer fan. Prefer rugby myself but even that's getting spoiled by money. But the money that Abramovitch has poured into Chelsea

155

– unbelievable. Then' there's poor little Reading down the road. Same division, none of the money. It's not a level playing field anymore."

"I agree. Foreigners are buying up all our top clubs. It's the Arabs who've got the money."

"And the Russians. I heard another Russian has bought some Scottish club."

"Must be a poor Russian!"

They laugh.

"I don't mind them buying football clubs, it's when they start buying our banks and newspapers I get worried. My son says the Russians could start buying our private banks if they are in trouble with this toxic asset thing."

"Laurence!" Daphne's voice, several octaves higher, halts their conversation. "Pour the wine, we girls are dying of thirst!"

As the evening progresses I realise I'm drinking too much. The room feels very warm, there's a real fire burning in the hearth. The alcohol is keeping my cold at bay. The conversation with Dolores and Daphne is inconsequential and largely about fashion and holidays. It's nice to think about such things instead of Petmag and Pyotr.

It doesn't help that Laurence is obviously under strict instructions to look after me and keeps topping up my wine glass. I realise Daphne is waiting for a reply from me – I have no idea what the question was. I mumble something about needing the loo and get up. I hold the back of Laurence's chair for support and head, unsteadily to the bathroom. There I splash cold water on my face but curse as I see my mascara is running. Then I chuckle at the sight. Maggie, pull yourself together, you're a mess, and you're tipsy.

I walk back to the dining room. Daphne hands me a cup of coffee. There's a tension in the room. They've been talking about me, I'm sure. Suddenly I want to be back home, tucked up in bed.

"We've got to be going now," says Dolores looking meaningfully at Daphne. "We'll give you a lift if you like, Maggie."

Back home, Charles helps me to the door, holding tightly to my arm. "I'm fine, I say" and as if to prove it insert the key in the lock first time. I grin, proud of my dexterity. "Goodbye and thanks for the lift."

The alarm is bleeping and I struggle to tap in the right numbers. At the third attempt the bleeping stops. Silence. The house is silent. I walk back to the front door and see the taillights of Charles car exiting the drive. Closing it, I turn and leaning my shoulder against the wall climb the stairs to the bedroom. I don't see the red light on the hall phone blinking.

My head is thumping and my throat is parched. I can feel my nightdress is wet and clammy. I feel for the bedside light. Its light illuminates the clothes from last night strewn carelessly over the back of the chair.

There's a dull ringing in my ears that's growing louder. There are voices. No just one voice. A female voice. The phone! The answerphone has cut in.

I stagger out of bed, vaguely aware of the damp nightdress clinging to my body.

"Hello, hello," I croak, coughing, There is a silence. 'Hello, hello?" I croak again.

"Is Maggie?"

It is the third time Saska has tried to speak to me. Her first call had left a message that had been cut short when the tape ran out. The second message, last night, is still unlistened to. Finally she is on the line. It's ten o'clock in Britain, Sunday lunchtime in Poland.

If I had any doubts before about Pyotr's disappearance, they are clearly unfounded. Saska's voice and her broken English convince me that she is as worried as I am. She's clearly distraught that something terrible has befallen him.

I try desperately to clear my hangover head. I know I must tell her everything that has happened, what I did yesterday. I tell her about the visit to the police, my conversation with Lech, the bank manager's news that Pyotr withdrew over £20,000 in cash but didn't bank the Club's cheque.

I have to repeat bits to her. Her English is not so good as Pyotr's. I tell her to hang on while I find a pen to write down her phone number. I catch the faint sound of sniffing and realise she's fighting back her tears. We both need desperately to know where Pyotr is.

34

Major Sylvester was a worried man. As he drove to the Club that Sunday morning to meet Jim and Arthur he knew that it would be a meeting he would not enjoy.

Figures had never been his strong point and fortunately he had little need for them during his long but undistinguished career in the army. He had relied on his public school accent to confound his sceptics and he had ensured that his NCOs kept a tight rein on everything, feeding him information when required.

Not that Major Sylvester was unintelligent. He had a liking for details and order. He had an excellent memory for facts but sadly not for names and faces. It was this memory that had enabled him to scrape the requisite 'A' Levels to get him into staff college.

What the Major was not good at was using all the information he had gleaned to make decisions. He had a fear of making the wrong decisions so he had always sought to make as few as possible. He tried to engineer situations so that others took responsibility. A tactical matter he would refer back to his sergeant with a comment such as "I'm sure you don't need me to tell you what to do Sergeant."

If the matters were more important, more strategic, he would bluster and say "I think this is probably a good one for a second opinion. If it were up to me of course I know what I would do but as this involves others I'll have to let them have their say."

Eventually the army noticed his indecisiveness and stopped promoting him. When he left he found a job with a local council where it was easy to appear diligent without actually making any decisions. But he didn't enjoy the lack of respect he received from his co-workers. They called him Mr Sylvester, not Major Sylvester. They were often as reluctant as he to make decisions, pen-pushers who saw the object of their job to report what happened, not make it happen.

Always a keen golfer, if not a very skilful one, the rules and regulations of the royal and ancient game intrigued him. So when he heard about the post of club secretary at the Warwickshire club, he applied. When, two years later he was forced to look for another post he was delighted to be accepted by West Downs and to move into a smart apartment in Sunninghill.

He made sure that he got on well with the 'right people' in the Club. This meant the captain and vice captain and the committee. He found dealing with the staff, difficult. Marco, the steward, was impossible to control; a fiery Spaniard who reminded him of Manuel in *Fawlty Towers*. Bill, the head greenkeeper was a no-nonsense Scot who viewed all public-school golfers as totally incapable of understanding anything about course management or agronomy. Since the Major had never so much as planted a daffodil bulb or ever mowed a lawn, he was quickly written off by Bill as a "bloody useless pain-in-the-arse."

In the army, catering was normally a male preserve, the mess sergeant ensuring food miraculously appeared on time. At West Downs it was Dorothy's preserve. And Dorothy didn't like being told what to do. The Major liked his food and, given his contract specified full meals, he was a frequent visitor to the dining room. She didn't mind so much that he would order coffee and a bacon roll as soon as he arrived in the morning, or the fact that he expected it to be brought to his desk. She didn't object to his mid-morning snack and generous helpings at lunch. What she objected to was how he tried to interfere with her suppliers.

Dorothy had been used to doing all the ordering herself., mainly from three local suppliers. The Major had other ideas. Applying army logic he insisted on her asking for quotes from a number of businesses including large catering wholesalers. The local butcher, who had for years supplied the Club, was not one used to tendering for annual contracts. The greengrocer who supplied, any of the fresh vegetables and the fruit for Dorothy's pies, was similarly non-plussed.

The contracts were awarded to two wholesale companies at a price that was expected to save the Club a considerable sum. The fact that the quantities had been wrongly calculated by the Major (his lack of numeracy for once being exposed) meant that three months into the contracts the terms had had to be revised and it was now doubtful if the Club was making any real savings.

Only the baker had remained local. Dorothy had stood firm and insisted that the members would be appalled if they didn't get their favourite rolls and cakes. Now, however, the baker had stopped supplying the Cub until his account was settled.

Unlike the two wholesalers who produced monthly invoices on a single page, with a detailed print-out of the items supplied, the baker wrote out daily bills which he presented the following day. This meant more work for the Major, who never bothered to check the wholesalers' print-outs, leaving it to Dorothy.

As a result, like a lot of the paperwork, the baker's bills remained in a pile on his desk waiting for him to find time to deal with them.

Things had come to a head after Christmas when the baker had come to the Club and insisted that the Major pay his account 'here and now'. The major was so taken aback that he lost his temper.

"I'm not going to be spoken to like that!"

"And I'm not going to give you any more credit," said the baker.

Dorothy was told she had to order her bread and cakes from one of the wholesalers. Dorothy had done as she was told but had refused to speak with the Major ever since.

So as he drove his car into the car park that morning, stopping in front of the newly-repainted 'Club Secretary' sign he was worried.

He had been very implicated in the decision to employ Michael Hamilton, although he insisted the real decision-maker had been Arthur. In fact Hamilton had been introduced to him by his wife. Nevertheless his job was to organise the running of the Club and losing half a million pounds wouldn't look good on his c.v.

Fortunately it seemed that the crisis had been averted after Jim, the Captain, had got the Poles to finish off the job. He tried to forget the role played by Maggie whom he considered just another lady golfer to be ignored. Nevertheless he had been forced to ring her on Saturday once it became clear that Pyotr had disappeared on Friday without paying the men. The woman hadn't even had the decency to return his call. Typical! That summed up women golfers in his mind.

Jim was already at the Club as was Arthur whose cold seemed to have disappeared.

The Major handed over the figures which his book-keeper had hastily prepared. "They are up to the end of November," he said, "and don't include the payment to Hamilton." He looked accusingly at Arthur.

"So what's our bank balance right now?" Jim liked simple facts, straight talking.

"Well, as of last Wednesday it was this." He passed a copy of the bank statement to Jim.

"That much overdrawn?" Jim pursed his lips and looked at Arthur. "You say Dylans are happy for us to run a deficit like this?"

"Yes, I saw to that." Arthur had regained some of his former confidence. "Although I would have thought with all the membership fees coming in that it should have been a lot better than that. You haven't paid Petmag anything yet have you Major?"

I paid them the first £50,000 on Friday but it's not shown on these figures. We've also got to pay around £100,000 as soon as they finish clearing behind the practice ground."

"But we'll have some more membership fees in by then?"

"Well I've still got some on my desk to pay in, but there's not many. People seem very late paying this year. And of course a lot of members are away." He tailed off looking down at his hands.

"I've had one or two members tell me they are waiting to see how we sort out the management mess before they pay," said Jim. "You really can't blame them. There's still no news from the police about Michael Hamilton and I don't rate our prospects of ever getting that money back."

Jim told the Major to send out a letter to those members who hadn't yet paid their membership fees urging them to do so without delay. "I don't like us owing this much. Maybe, Arthur, we should look at cashing some of our investments?"

"Not a good time, old boy, not a good time. Bottom's dropped out of the market since Christmas. Our investments have lost 30% since Christmas. Best to hang on."

For once none of them stayed for a drink afterwards. Marco carried on rearranging the bottles on the shelves. Not much to do today, he thought.

35

Hugh was also worried. More than he liked to admit to himself. It was no use talking to Lettie. She didn't understand money, only how to spend it. Any attempt to economise in the past had led to outbursts of protests from her. She drew unfavourable comparisons with 'our friends' who managed to afford it or told him she didn't put up with him working so long to be told that they didn't have enough money.

Hugh was worried about his bonus. His main fund was down 27%. Down! For years he had been used to only growth. The financial world had gone crazy since Christmas. He couldn't have foreseen how much and how quickly it had fallen. But that was his job to anticipate, to pre-guess the market. And he had failed. Worse, he had gambled his own money by taking large bets on the FTSE recovering. It hadn't and he hadn't taken out a stop loss insurance until it was too late. A twenty thousand pound investment that he hoped would make him two hundred thousand and make up for his lost bonus had gone disastrously wrong. He needed to come up with nearly a quarter of a million pounds by the end of the week.

The end of the week was when he was due to take the family for their half-term skiing holiday in Gstadt. He'd had to borrow money from his mother to pay for that along with the school fees.

Mother. The stupid woman had gone and taken £200,000 out of the Isle of Man Kaupthing account and thrown it away on that thieving Pole. That amount could have paid off his share dealing debt.

He's been too busy calculating his finances to think about Pyotr this morning, but now he started to have an idea.

He would go down and see Maggie and get her to agree to close the company and get her money out – or at least what remained of it. Except, - a sudden realisation came to him – he'd insisted on joint signatures on any withdrawals. It was meant to protect Maggie. But now, without Pyotr's signature she couldn't withdraw a penny!

The only other thing was to sell the Portuguese villa. But he knew that that would mean telling Simone and Estelle who liked to use the villa. He couldn't face them and their husbands and admit why he needed the money. There was only one answer. He must find that bastard Pyotr and get him to agree to close the company.

The detective who phoned Maggie on Monday morning was surprised to find the answerphone. In her experience, rich women in Sunningdale didn't stir from their homes before 10 unless they were on a school run. She rang at 8 a.m. No reply.

Maggie was already in her car on her way to meet Lech and the men at the Club.

I see Lech's old Golf in the car park. He's already talking with the men. There must be about thirty of them. I see a couple turn towards me as I get out of the car. Then Lech sees me and comes across.

"Hello boss! Nice to see you. The men said you wouldn't come!"

"I don't know what I can tell them that they don't already know. You haven't any news have you?"

I smile at the men gathered around us. My mind is blank – what can I say. I start by saying that I have asked the police to try and find out what's happened to Pyotr. Lech translates. The men look suspicious, unhappy. There is a murmuring of voices. I tell them that I will be going to the bank after this meeting to get them the money and will see them tomorrow. There is a polite applause from most of the men although one or two clearly don't believe me. I urge them to carry on with the work as I'm sure Pyotr will soon be back. In the meantime Tadeusz will be in charge.

He comes forward and shakes my hand. I gather from Lech's translation that the men will carry on today, but they want their money tomorrow without fail.

There's the sound of a car. It's the Major's. He looks surprised to see me addressing the men. I remember I haven't returned his call. He strides over.

"Where's that Pyotr chap? What's going on? Why didn't he pay the men on Friday? We gave him the Club's cheque."

I look at the Major in a new light. So far he's always acted so superior, so anti-women. Not just me, all women. Like he didn't think they should be members of the Club. Like the Club was a bastion of men, not of the weaker sex. Truth to be told I always felt a bit intimidated by him – he had that sort of effect. Loud, masculine, military.

Today though, the cards are stacked differently. Despite his accusatory tone I can see that he's unsure of himself. He needs me. He needs my help. He's seen me addressing the thirty-odd Poles. There's a grudging respect.

"Don't worry, Major. The men are just going to start. We had to rearrange things as Pyotr is, er, unfortunately not able to be here. The foreman here, Tadeusz", she moved her arm in his direction and he raised his cap to the Major, "will be in charge until Pyotr gets back. "

The Major looks impressed – whether by what I've said or the fact that I clearly have a knowledge of the men and Tadeusz's name. I decide to press my advantage.

"I'll go and have a word with Bill and his staff and make sure they know what's happening." I'm actually taking the Major's role, and I'm beginning to enjoy the feeling.

I gesture to Tadeusz to follow me and we set off towards the greenkeeper's building on the far side of the first fairway.

The Major remains standing in the middle of the car park. He seems perplexed. I realise that I never answered his question "Where is Pyotr?"

It's still only 9 30 and I'm already back home. I walk down the hallway and see the red light blinking on the phone. My heart skips – it's Pyotr, emergency over. But it's not. It's Detective Constable Shami Chandrasena. I call her back and arrange for her to come over this morning.

I realise I'm starving and start to make some breakfast. The coffee smells good and I'm about to butter the toast when the phone rings. It's Hugh. He's ringing in office hours again. Things must be bad. He tells me he's been thinking

168

about Pyotr and how it is essential we find him. He tells me to look at the leasing documents and get the registration number of the pick-up truck and ring him back. He sounds really concerned. I wonder if it's the pressure of work? I caught the headlines on the car radio – the stock market has fallen again.

After the detective leaves I phone Hugh back. He answers on the first ring of his cell phone.

"The police took away some photos and the number of the pick-up which I found as you said in the leasing documents. She searched his room but couldn't find his passport. He must have taken it. She said he would have needed it if he was going to skip the country. They hadn't heard anything from the airports although I get the distinct impression they haven't actually done anything since we reported it on Saturday."

"Give me the police's number. What was his name? I'll call and see if I can get things moving. We need to find that damn Pole and get your money back – and fast! That's if he still has it."

"He's a she and she's called DC Chandrasena."

36

As soon as I enter the branch one of the women comes up to me and ushers me into a manager's office. Brendan Matthews is there working on some files. He stops immediately, gets up and comes round the desk and shakes my hand.

"Coffee?"

I am at first intrigued, and then worried. Why am I getting this red carpet treatment. I was merely coming in to withdraw cash to pay the men – a large amount of cash admittedly, but enough to justify coffee? I sense someone entering behind me and turn to see a tall, immaculately-dressed Indian man.

"This is Mr Srinivassan from our London office," Brendan Matthews says.

"I'm very pleased to meet you Mrs Miles." His English is cultured public-school. Just a trace of the softness that one associates with Indians. His age I put at mid thirties and his handshake is firm. I notice the gold cufflink fastening his pristine cuff. "I thought I should come down to help out Mr Matthews here explain the situation. You see I'm afraid we have had to temporarily freeze your business account in view of Mr Lycenski's disappearance. I assume you have no further news?"

"No, none at all. But my account …?"

"The Petmag account."

"Yes, I've come in to draw out the men's wages. I've promised to pay them today. After Pyotr didn't come back on Friday."

"Ah yes, but you see technically you can't do that because the mandate you signed for the bank stated that any withdrawals had to be signed by two directors – and there's only you and Mr Lycenski."

"But that was just what I was advised to do by my son, he's a banker, of sorts. He did it to protect me. To stop Pyotr drawing out money without my knowledge. Not that he would of course, no, no he wouldn't."

"But I'm afraid it looks like he has, Mrs Miles. Over £20,000 on Friday. Are you saying he forged your signature on the cash cheque?"

No, no. I signed the cheque as usual. He just brought it into the bank."

"And then disappeared with the money!"

"But I've promised to pay the men, today. I have to withdraw the money."

Mr Srinivassan gave her an indulgent smile. He adjusted his right cuff with his left hand. "I understand that Mrs Miles but you see if we were to go against the mandate I'm afraid the bank could be held liable."

"But there must be some way to do it? Under the circumstances – and I've been a customer for years."

"It would always be possible for the company, your company, to elect new directors and possibly even remove Mr

Lycenski from the Board if he remained, er, lost. You would need to discuss that with your lawyer. But I would have thought that would take a certain amount of time. Weeks at least and until then I'm afraid your account will remain frozen."

For the first time, Brendan Matthews speaks.

"Look Mrs Miles. I know this all sounds very complicated," his tone was condescending, "but the bank has to obey its clients' instructions and I'm afraid they are very clear here, your son saw to that. But there is a way around the problem if you wanted it."

He looks at Mr Srinivassan for support. The Indian takes up the conversation again. "You could transfer money from your personal deposit account into your personal current account and draw cash from that. It would mean a loss of interest because your deposit account is not an instant access one, but you might consider that."

I don't know what to do. I desperately want to talk to Hugh, but he's the reason I'm in this mess. I'm sure Frank would have had an answer. No, I have to make the decision. If I don't pay the men they will quit, the golf club contract will not be honoured, I will likely have to resign from the Club, I'll maybe even get sued. And all because Pyotr has disappeared with our money, my money. Whatever his motives I am the one now left to face the music.

I accept the cup of coffee and sit down by Brendan Matthews's desk. Is it a case of good money after bad? Or is it a face-saving exercise in the now forlorn hope that Pyotr decides to come back?

Brendan insists on one of his male staff accompanying me back to the car. "That's a lot of cash to be carrying around," he says. "Make sure you go straight to the Club."

Saska phoned me again that evening. She sounds more in control than earlier. Like me she has heard nothing from Pyotr and tells me she is convinced he's had an accident. "Maybe I come to Britain to help you look for him," she says. I try to point out that the police are doing all they can, but she seems unimpressed. I tell her she can stay with me if she comes.

I try to collect my thoughts after the phone call. My head is still thick with the cold and I contemplate a vodka as a pick-me-up. No a Whisky Mac I think – more medicinal. It seems to have been a very long day. The trip to the bank, the realisation that I cannot access any of the money I've put into the company, the time at the golf club paying the men – so different from my normal visits to the Club. As I sit nursing my whisky I try to think objectively. Have I done the right thing backing Pyotr? Everyone told me not to but I went ahead anyway. Why? What on earth possessed me? Did I think I was really a businesswoman? Did I really think that I could single-handedly save the Club? I realise that I've been carried away with the excitement of it all. After weeks of purposeless existence after Frank died, this project gave me something to believe in. Something to occupy my time. Make me feel wanted again.

But now I am faced with a potential disaster. I can't control the Polish workers, I couldn't even if I spoke Polish. What do I know about tree-felling? And then there's the real elephant in the room. Pyotr. I keep telling myself and everyone else that he is an innocent victim, that something has happened to him. That it's not his fault. But what do I really know about him? He just turns up here having taken a coach across Europe, has no work and charms me into giving him a room and getting a job. Then I suggest he starts a company with me. No wonder the police look at me with a mixture of incredulity and compassion. The silly old bat, they must think.

Perhaps Pyotr didn't intend to swindle me out of the money. But maybe when the opportunity was given to him on a plate, he couldn't resist. £20,000 in cash was a lot of money. Perhaps he had just decided to 'cut and run' as Detective Chandrasena had said.

But what about Saska? Was she in on the act? No, I don't believe she knew. After all I would probably have been with Pyotr at the bank and even the Club afterwards had I not got this wretched cold. So it was probably a spur of the moment decision on Pyotr's part. I know he was desperate to prove to Saska that he could make money. He's probably on his way to Poland now to meet her. Maybe she has already heard from him? She didn't sound so distraught as the other night. Maybe she's just putting on an act?

It makes sense, I know. Hugh is right, he's no good. Daphne, Elizabeth the women at the Club, they're right – I've been a big fool.

Yet I still can't bring myself to believe it. I really feel that Pyotr and I have a special relationship. He trusts me and I trust him. I just have to hope the police come up with some information to prove me right.

I go into Frank's study and switch on the computer. I get out the piece of paper Tadeusz gave me. It shows the hours worked by each of the men and the hourly rate. It is a copy of the information he gave to Pyotr before he left for the bank. It had taken more than an hour to count out all the cash and put it into envelopes for each man.

I had asked Terri in the office to give me some paper and then I'd written down the men's names as best I could. Polish names seemed devoid of vowels and it wasn't easy. Then I wrote the amounts I was paying against each man's name. Later, Tadeusz would get them to sign against the amounts. I hadn't known if this was the right thing to do but felt I had to at least look as if I knew what I was doing. I don't know when, or if, Pyotr will ever come back.

The Major had sat in his office and totally ignored me. I didn't want to do it in the office anyway. I didn't want any of my friends coming across me. So I went across and found Bill and asked if I could work in the greenkeeper's building. He couldn't have been more helpful, even making Tadeusz and me a couple of cups of tea.

Now I am back home and need to type up details of what I've done. No one else can do it and if I'm to run Petmag, even for a bit, I need to do things properly. I start to type the list, slowly. I put the finished list in the file I found in Pyotr's room called 'wages'. I have brought down his files and now arrange them on Frank's desk. There are copies of the leasing contracts, estimates, and a copy of the invoice to the Club. I wonder, not for the first time, why he hadn't paid in the £50,000 cheque? What was he planning to do with it?

I'm still thinking about this when the phone rings. Elizabeth sounds annoyed. Her tone is accusing. I had completely forgotten about playing my quarter-final match with Margretta. To Elizabeth this was as inexcusable as it was incomprehensible. The golf club was her life and she was fastidious about detail.

"Margretta rang you first thing but there was no reply. Then someone said they saw you up at the Club this afternoon but I looked for you in the clubhouse and there was no sign of you. Margretta said she would have been happy to play this morning but you never contacted her."

"I'm sorry, Elizabeth, I've had a very busy day. But look, tomorrow is Ladies Day and I don't have a partner for the stableford so maybe Margretta and I could play our match instead?"

"I'm not sure the committee will allow it. I mean, the last day was today and we really must abide by the rules. It's very important you know."

"Yes, I'm sure it is but I'll have a word with Margretta now and see what we can do."

I put the phone down. Important! A stupid golf match. Here am I trying to save my company, find out what Pyotr's done, deal with police, sort out Hugh's problems. Important! Some people need to get a life!

Get a life. Yes that's what I have now. A new life since Frank died. A life now full of problems but still somehow satisfying. I've got purpose to my life now. But what if Pyotr is really gone? Just when I'm starting to have a new life another man is snatched away without warning.

37

Hugh left the house at 6.30 and took the tube to the city where he changed for Canary Wharf in London's Docklands. He was at his desk before 7.30. He checked the opening market prices in Shanghai, Tokyo, Hong Kong and Singapore. The European markets would not open for another hour or so.

Wall Street had rallied in late afternoon and Hugh hoped it would lead to a change of sentiment in other markets. There were rumours of increased mergers and acquisitions activity. With share prices having fallen generally certain companies became attractive takeover targets.

But cash was tight. Not only in the Hugh Miles household, but in business generally. The banks, heavily exposed to the sub-prime mortgage situation had stopped lending in a bid to bolster their capital reserves. Hugh reckoned that the major banks were too big to fail; it was unthinkable. But he knew some of the smaller, private banks could be in trouble.

He sat down at his desk clutching his Starbuck's styrene coffee mug. He switched on his computers and the four screens flickered into life. Other fund managers had already arrived but were engrossed in the figures on their screens. Since Big Bang in the stock market, things were unrecognisable compared to the leisurely pace before globalisation meant 24/7 working. The city never sleeps as Hugh would tell Maggie. These days Hugh found it hard to sleep, too.

The screens were showing rises across the markets and Hugh dared to hope that when London opened he'd see a rise in his main funds. He'd pulled out of financials and plumped for pharmaceuticals in a big way. Glaxo shares were trading higher he noted.

At eight o'clock the screens flashed the Reuters news. A Russian bank had acquired two old-established British private banks. With over 400 years of profitable trading behind them, Mortimers and Dylans had been forced to seek financial support. Their blue-chip clients would now be serviced by the Novaya Zemlya Kreditbank.

Hugh whistled through his teeth. His colleagues looked up. "Did you catch this about Mortimers and Dylans?" he called out.

"Yeah, I reckon Abramovich will be owning more than Chelsea before long!" Kevin was from Epping and his vowel sounds grated on Hugh's Charterhouse ears. But he was a red-hot fund manager who had a record even better than Hugh's.

"He's not involved in Novaya Zemlya, is he?"

"Wouldn't surprise me at all. That guy has got his fingers in everything. And I bet they paid a lot less for Dylans than he did for Drogba."

"The top-scorer for Chelsea." Justin explained to Hugh seeing his puzzled look. He knew Hugh didn't follow football.

The screens flickered with the opening prices in Europe. The room fell silent. Hugh watched as pharmaceutical shares opened higher. But his mind switched to Dylans. Dylans, that was the golf club bank where Arthur had been a director. He wondered what Arthur would think about the takeover. Good thing he had retired.

I am sitting in the mixed lounge with Margretta. We are dressed for golf except for our shoes. Through the window I can see the Poles working on the copse of trees near the fifth fairway. I can see Tadeusz talking to one of them.

Margretta follows my gaze. "They're certainly taking a lot of trees out. I'm not sure I like it. Makes the course too open. I preferred it when each fairway was completely separate, divided by the trees."

"But they're trying to get it back to how it was in 1909."

"But they're going to leave us some trees aren't they? I mean there must have been trees here in 1909."

"Not so many and anyway the extra light will be good for the heather. Unlike Sunningdale we've lost more of our heather because of the trees."

"I forgot you were so well informed. You're involved in all this of course aren't you? With that Polish chappie."

Before I can reply we are joined by three more of our ladies section. Then the room starts to fill up as others arrive. Suddenly I realise that I've missed the casual chat, the little bits of gossip. But now it seems just that – inconsequential gossip. I'm just thankful that there's no gossip about Pyotr. His absence seems not to have been announced. I wonder how long it will stay secret.

I see Elizabeth come into the lounge, deep in conversation with Judy, our captain. Judy keeps nodding and looking at me and Margretta. She comes over.

"Elizabeth tells me that you didn't manage to play your Sheringham yesterday?" She pauses for my confirmation. "Well you can play it today. That will be fine – it's only one day late after all, not a hanging offence!"

She smiles and moves off to the bar. Elizabeth scowls at us and follows.

"I think she was angling for a walkover," says Margretta.

"Yes. It's so important to her. She's nothing better to think about. Anyway why don't we get going now? Ready to do battle?"

The news about Dylans came too late to be in the morning papers and too unimportant for the breakfast news. So Arthur and Jim were unaware of the situation. They met with the contracting firm for the reservoir at 9.30. The planning application had passed all its stages and they signed the contract in the Major's office. Exploratory work would start immediately to position the borehole and the whole project would be completed before the end of the year, before 2009 the centenary of West Downs Golf Club.

Each party kept a copy of the contract which included a schedule of stage payments and penalty clauses for late completion.

Arthur and Jim co-signed the initial Dylan's Bank cheque for £100,000.

*

I look at my watch. It's just after 2. I finish my coffee and turn to Margretta. "Well good luck against Elizabeth."

"You're going?"

"Yes, I've got a lot to do so hope you don't mind. And well played."

The red light on my phone is blinking as I walk down the hall. I press play and listen to the message. It's from Constable Chandrasena and her news is not what I want to hear. Pyotr's pick-up has been found. It was in the car park at the ferry terminal in Portsmouth. There was Pyotr's heavy coat and his work boots in the car but no sign of Pyotr. The police were trying to get the passenger records on the cross-Channel ferries for the past three days to see if his name is among them."

I dial Constable Chandrasena's number but she's gone off duty. I speak to her sergeant who confirms that they are now treating the case as theft. It appears that Pyotr had taken the £20,000, driven to Portsmouth and travelled across to France. They had passed his description to Interpol.

"Forensics will take a look at the truck tomorrow. That might tell us more."

I sit down in the kitchen. The lights are on, it's dull and overcast outside. The days are short at this time of year. I try to work it out. So Pyotr, my Pyotr, has stolen my money, left his men unpaid and headed off back to Poland and Saska? I can't believe it. But why haven't I heard any more from Saska? Did she know when she phoned me? Or is she still in ignorance? Or has Pyotr concocted some story to tell her about making the money himself?

I try phoning Hugh but he's not home yet – it's still afternoon. Lettie sounds distracted but I tell her about the pick-up truck being found.

"I'm sorry about your money Maggie. Still at least that awful man has gone. I'll tell Hugh to phone you when he gets in."

I go upstairs to Pyotr's room. It looks so bare. Even the laptop has gone. There are just a few of his clothes still in the wardrobe. Beside the bed is a small picture frame with a picture of Saska and Pyotr sitting at a café-bar in the sunshine. He must have decided to leave in a hurry if he left that, I think. I try to console myself that it was not pre-planned. That he just suddenly took off with the money when he found himself at the bank without Maggie. A spur of the moment decision. Maybe he regrets it now. I like to think he does. My Pyotr.

The phone rings, I rush down to take it. It's Estelle. She's sobbing.

"Whatever's the matter dear?"

"It's Justin. It's the firm. They're going into liquidation!"

I try to calm her as she tells me the news. Justin's company has just had a creditors' meeting. Apparently its two major clients have cancelled all their contracts. New contracts in the City have been shelved or cancelled. It seems that the financial crisis is making banks and insurance companies think twice about expanding or renovating. Apparently the company's bank has withdrawn its overdraft facilities and has refused to give the firm a long-term loan.

"It's not like they were losing money, they were profitable, but they've got a lot of staff and a big liability on the lease of that new building they moved into last year. One of their customers hasn't paid them either so the cash has just run out. Even if they manage to avoid liquidation Justin has lost his job."

"Well you'll be needing some money, then? "

"I hope that we can manage and Justin gets a new job. He's worked a long time there so he will get a good redundancy package. I think we'll be alright. I just thought you'd want to know. Anyway you don't have much money now that Pole has stolen it do you?"

"We don't know he's stolen it, and anyway it was only £20,000. It's just that I can't get any money out of the account without his signature."

"There is one thing you could do, Mum. You could look after the kids for me over next week – it's half term and I have got a couple of job interviews."

"Job interviews?"

"Yes, well we were worried about Justin's firm so I thought I'd see if I could get a job – to help out while he's getting himself one. He'll be hopefully going for interviews too so the kids will need looking after."

"Of course, I will. It will be nice. Do you want them to come down and stay here?"

I make myself some tea. I cut myself some cake. It's getting darker outside so I pull the curtains. My head feels heavy still with cold. No wonder I didn't play well this morning.

38

I am woken by Mrs McGraw. The alcohol and the sleeping pills had done their trick and I was still sleeping soundly after 9.00 when Mrs McGraw let herself in.

She has a cup of tea in her hand and a worried look on her face. "Are you alright Mrs M? It's not like you to be abed."

"I'm fine. Much better thanks. My cold seems to be going. You get started, I'll be down shortly."

I'm still in the shower when she enters again. "Your son is on the phone for you – says it's urgent."

I wrap a towel round me and take the phone from her.

Lettie had obviously forgotten to tell Hugh that I'd called. Apparently it had been a very busy day at his office, he had got home late. Apparently he had finally bitten the bullet and sold a lot of his personal share portfolio at a considerable loss. There had been a small upturn in the market which had prompted him. "I needed the cash Mum, I've got a lot of expenses. I know I've made a loss but at least if I have cash I can buy back some shares when they are even lower."

I know he's due to fly off the Gstadt very soon – I bet he needs money to indulge Lettie. But I say nothing. At least he still has a job and big salary and bonuses. Poor Justin has no job at all. He tells me, with a touch of the old Hugh, that he's got a really good interest rate from an Icelandic bank in the Isle of Man.

"Is that safe dear? I mean there's a lot of talk about that Northern Rock going bust. It was on the news again last night."

"Don't worry Mum, it's totally different from Northern Rock. That was just badly run. I actually know the boss of Kaupthing – had dinner at our house recently. Anyway I wanted to tell you that apparently the police have found your man's truck – at the Portsmouth Ferry Terminal – he's skipped the country."

"I know didn't Letitia tell you? I phoned yesterday."

"No, she didn't. Must have forgot. Anyway it proves he's gone off with the money, the bastard. But the good news is that if he's stolen it then that's grounds for dismissing him from the Board and you'll be able to access the rest of the money. I've talked a to a lawyer pal of mine. It may take a few weeks, but we can do it."

"But we don't know he stole the money."

"Mother, for heaven's sake what more proof do you need? He's probably already with his wife in Poland spending it. Now let me get things moving with my lawyer friend."

"I suppose you'd better do what you think is right. I seem to have messed things up."

I pass the phone back to Mrs McGraw and realise that she has been standing there listening to me. I can see she's dying to question me. Where is Pyotr? What has he done? Why did you trust him?

I don't need anyone else telling me what a fool I've been. Before she can ask I turn back to the bathroom – "I need to dry my hair."

A few miles away Detective Constable Shami Chandrasena was twisting her fingers through her hair – a look of deep concentration on her face.

She was just 24 years old. Her father had been a policeman, rising to sergeant. She had always been fascinated by detective work. She read countless detective novels, watched crime dramas on TV and dreamed about one day solving great crimes that had defeated her male counterparts.

A degree in sociology had helped her understand some of the motives for crime, the drugs, the deprived childhood, the gang culture and just the sheer frustration of failing to compete in a market-led economy. Now, two years into her police career she was finding detective work anything but stimulating. It consisted mainly of form-filling, preparing reports for insurance companies and advising householders to take more care with their possessions.

Serious crime squads dealt with murder, rape and organised crime. Detectives like her dealt with local problems, marital violence and missing persons.

So the case of the missing Pole had come as a welcome relief. Here was a mystery, not a simple crime. On the one hand the evidence pointed to an opportunist crime, an immigrant worker being handed £20,000 in used notes and being unable to resist the temptation to take the money and run. Opportunist because she had learned from Maggie that she normally accompanied him to get the money from the bank. But this week she'd been ill. Tempting, because

£20,000 was a lot of money in sterling and a lot more in zlotys.

But there were things about the case that puzzled her. Things that didn't add up. Maggie, she realised, was so blinkered by her handsome lodger that she saw only good in him and refused to believe he would rob her. Then there was the motive itself. Yes £20,000 was a lot of money. But her enquiries at the golf club with Tom the greenkeeper had revealed that the work was progressing very well. When it was completed in a few weeks she knew from Maggie that the company she had set up with Pyotr would make a good profit, maybe enough that Pyotr's share would be more than £20,000.

On the other hand, she argued with herself, why hadn't Pyotr paid in the £50,000 cheque made out to Petmag from the Club? Unless he was going to try and open an account with it? She made a note to get Maggie to have the cheque cancelled and a new one issued.

The news she had received from the Hampshire police that they had found Pyotr's pick-up at the ferry terminal had seemed to prove that he was guilty. Pyotr had fled with the money and clearly wishing to avoid the airports, had taken the ferry to St Malo, or Cherbourg or even Spain. She expected to hear once the shipping records had been checked. Always assuming he hadn't used a false identity. (Not likely as that would have required a lot of pre-planning.)

The pick-up had been taken on a trailer to Reading. The 'crime' had been committed in Berkshire, it was their problem, not Hampshire's. She knew the forensic people at Reading. Indeed she had for a long time looked at forensics as a career path but found dealing with living people more interesting than inanimate objects and corpses.

Wednesday was a day off for her but she had nothing specifically planned. And she couldn't help turning over the case in her head. Something bothered her. Something didn't fit.

She made up her mind. Reading had a good shopping centre and she needed some more shoes. A trip there could be combined with a visit to the lab.

I finish blow-drying my hair, dress and go downstairs. Mrs McGraw is busy cleaning in the kitchen. We make some coffee. I can see that she is itching to ask me about Pyotr. I will have to tell her.

"I'm afraid Pyotr has disappeared. "

I wait for her reaction. She stops wiping the work surface and nods. "I thought as much. What you said on the phone. And he's run off with your money? That's the trouble with these immigrants. Just out for all they can get."

"We don't know he's gone off with the money. He's just disappeared. He might have had an accident or something."

"You've told the police, have you?"

"Yes. And I think I'll give the detective another call, see if anything has turned up."

I dial the number but she's not in. A couple of days off, back on Friday. No there's no more news and yes they would tell her if they heard anything. And Mr Miles who had already phoned that morning. The sergeant sounds impatient, like he has a hundred more important things to do.

I feel the need to do something. I'll go down to the Club and check on the men, see how they're getting on. Without Pyotr, I worry they will slacken off. After all it's up to me to run Petmag now.

The weather is still cloudy and damp. The course had been barely playable yesterday and very muddy. There were still puddles where last week's snow had melted. I put my thick boots on and tuck my trousers inside. I have a thick warm sweater underneath my quilted anorak. I tell Mrs McGraw I won't be out for very long and shut the front door.

A few minutes later I arrive at the Club. The car park is quite full which surprises me. I park and then set off skirting the clubhouse and heading for the fifth fairway where I know the men are working. I hear a crack as a large branch, or even a tree, comes down. There is an angry buzzing from a power saw. Then I see a group of men. Some are carrying branches to the shredding machine, others are raking up smaller branches and twigs. I see Tadeusz sitting in a kind of dumper truck. I wave and he comes across the fairway. With a mixture of sign language and English I manage to ask him how it's going. He smiles and gives me a thumbs up. He pulls a grubby piece of paper from his pocket, unfolds it and pokes it with his finger. It's one of Pyoytr's computer drawings, marking the trees to be cut down. He jabs his finger at the paper and then turns and waves his hand expansively towards what had been a thick tangled mass of trees. Now it is largely levelled, just three or four trees remaining standing. He points again to the plan and counts in English "one, two, three, four." We look at the former copse, I count "One, two, three, four." We both smile. "It's good?" "Yes, very good. Well done."

He asks about Pyotr. I shrug and say we've not heard. I don't tell him about the truck being found at Portsmouth. I couldn't anyway with his limited English. He looks concerned and mimes a telephone call to the police. I nod and then spread my hands wide to signify nothing.

We shake hands rather formally and I turn and walk back towards the clubhouse. I may get myself a coffee or pop in and see if Tom is around. I don't want to bump into the Major though.

Instead, I bump into Elizabeth. She's in the entrance hall, looking as worried as ever. She's wearing a long woollen skirt and a cashmere sweater, anchored at the waist with a gold-coloured belt. The ensemble is set off with a string of pearls. She has matching pearl earrings and has obviously spent time on her make-up and hair. Her face brightens when she sees me.

"Oh good, you remembered! I thought you'd forgotten and we'd be one short. But you were just a bit late." The last sentence carries a touch of criticism. Typical Elizabeth, she's still complaining about me playing my Sheringham a day late.

She is looking at me quizzically. Then critically. She looks at my mud-covered boots, my anorak. "I hope you've brought a change of clothes?"

I look at her blankly.

"You can hardly play bridge in those boots."

I realise that I'm not up to multi-tasking. I have completely forgotten the Captain's bridge morning and lunch. But I can't get out of it now. I retire to the ladies locker room and try and smarten up. I use the paper towels to wipe the majority of the mud from my boots.

I sit through an uncomfortably-warm two hours of bridge wishing I could remove my thick sweater but fearful that my blouse underneath was even less suitable. I use an excuse to avoid the lunch and drive home.

I am looking forward to changing out of these clothes, making myself a sandwich and sorting out the children's room for Estelle's boys. It's seemed a long day already. Or maybe I'll just put my feet up for an hour or so and watch television.

But there turns out to be no chance of that.

39

Shami Chandrasena had met the forensic man twice before. They had got on well. He took her to the canteen, seemingly glad of the excuse to stop work. They chatted over mugs of coffee.

"Of course I'll get the full report emailed over to the station when I've done it, but I'm still trying to work some things out."

"Really, like what?"

"Well it's strange. The pick-up is just as you might expect. It's pretty dirty, the Pole's work coat was on the passenger seat – it had G.D.S. across the back and there was a glove in the pocket."

"Just one glove?"

"Yes. There were a pair of wellingtons in the back of the truck. They're probably his too. He must have taken them off before catching the ferry – you don't normally sail off to France in wellies! Anyway, there were prints on them and I can match them against the ones you got from his room, but.."

"But?"

"Well that's the funny thing. Those are the only prints I've found. There were no prints anywhere inside the vehicle, or on the door handles, or anywhere. Everything else has been wiped clean."

"Perhaps he didn't want you to know it was him?"

"In which case why leave his coat and boots? Anyway he must have known the number plate would identify him."

"And what happened to his other glove?"

40

Scott Henderson got off the train at Waterloo and headed for the underground to take him to Docklands. In his position it would have been normal to take a taxi, but it would be quicker on the new Jubilee Line and he wanted to get to the meeting early. He wanted time to prepare. This could prove a very difficult meeting.

He tightened his grip on the expensive leather briefcase and felt in the pocket of his camel-coloured overcoat for change for the ticket machine.

Hugh pushed back his chair and stretched his arms above his head, intertwining his fingers. He sighed. His shoulders ached with hunching over the computer screens.

The mood in the office was once again downbeat. The main news of the morning was the collapse of the Kingdom Group, a large hotel chain. There were concerns too about Northern Rock, a Newcastle Building Society that had, a few months earlier, experienced a run on the bank. The government had stepped in to reassure customers and the smart money was on the building society being taken over by another financial institution. But no deal had been struck and there was now talk about whether the government would have to nationalise it.

The Kingdom Group had suffered when its bookings went down. It relied heavily on American businessmen and tourists. Following the collapse of Bear Stearns and the financial crisis in America the number of Americans coming to Britain drastically reduced. It was like 9/11 all over again. The Group had committed to an expensive refitting of the public parts of its flagship Mayfair hotel but had run out of money to finance it. Its loan covenants were broken and a last minute attempt to find a buyer for the hotel had fallen at the final hurdle. The directors admitted defeat and put the group into administration.

This had the effect of causing a rush to sell hotel shares which took the FTSE index down further.

"Good thing I sold my shares yesterday," thought Hugh. "I had a lot of International Hotel Group shares in my portfolio. Still it's not helping the Fund. I still had exposure in that leisure sector. Still pharma shares are up a bit so it's not too bad." But he knew there would be no bonus this year. There was no way the index could recover that much before the end of March. It was simply a matter of trying to minimise the losses and outperform his rival fund managers. That way he would at least keep his job.

"I'm going for a walk," he announced to no one in particular.

"The roof's up that way. Wave to us on the way down." Kevin's humour was black.

"Come on Hugh, it's not that bad. Let me buy you a drink." He got up and reached for his jacket.

They crossed the square and headed for the wine bar. It was on the ground floor of a typical Docklands high rise tower. They passed through the lobby towards the bar. At the elevator a man in a camel-coloured cashmere overcoat, holding a large leather briefcase, was scanning the list of companies. Novaya Zemlya Kredietbank, 8th floor. The doors opened and Scott Henderson stepped into the lift.

As soon as I arrive at the house I know something is wrong. The exit gates are open, and the entry gate. Mrs McGraw always closes them when she leaves. There is no car in front of the house so it's not one of the children arriving unexpectedly. Maybe it's Pyotr! Maybe he's come back, in a taxi!

But when I unlock the front door and enter the hall he is not there. And neither are the paintings that hung on the wall.

Hugh looked at his blackberry in annoyance. He was enjoying a second glass of Chardonnay from a bottle Kevin had bought. The screen flashed the word 'Mum'.

"What now?" He thought.

"Hugh, I've been burgled! All the pictures, they've gone, in the hall, in the lounge and the silver. What do I do?"

If Shami Chandrasena hadn't been so new to her job, she wouldn't have given up a day's shopping to visit the scene of a crime. But she couldn't leave it. The forensic examination had thrown up a lot of questions in her mind and the only way to solve them was to take another look at Pyotr's room.

She drove her Ford Fiesta to Sunningdale. She pressed the button on the now-closed security gates. She was surprised when Maggie opened the door before she even knocked and even more when she said "Thank you for coming so quickly."

Maggie was shaking and it took time before Shami gathered what had happened. The faded rectangular patches on the walls however needed no explanation.

"Phone Mrs McGraw and get her over here now. I need to speak with her."

"Oh no, it won't be her, she's not a thief, she's been working for me for years."

"I'm sure she isn't but she was the last person here that we know of, we'll need to take fingerprints, find out whether she forgot to lock the gates and so on. Please call her and get her back here."

Shami felt a surge of excitement. This was getting better and better. Firstly a missing person, then a possible theft of £20,000, then a fleeing culprit abandoning his pick-up at a port and hopping on a ferry, now a major house robbery. The job was getting more and more interesting every day.

She headed upstairs and into Pyotr's room. She opened the drawers again and looked in the wardrobe. There was no glove there. She looked in the ensuite. His razor was still there and his toothbrush. She looked at the tube of toothpaste. Colgate but with words in several foreign languages, none of them English. Obviously bought in Poland. Why hadn't he taken these items with him? It reinforced the argument that it was a spur-of-the-moment decision when he was unexpectedly left holding £20,000 in cash without Maggie being there.

She heard the crunch of gravel and returned to the bedroom and looked through the window. Two cars were coming down the driveway. The first was an old, small saloon. Behind it was the blue and white police car. She saw an elderly woman step from the small car and turn to look at the police car that had followed her. One of the policemen, the sergeant, got out and was speaking on his radio.

She hurried downstairs by which time the woman and the two policemen were being let in by Maggie. The sergeant raised an eyebrow when he saw Shami. "I thought you were off today?"

"Just checking something out. I arrived a couple of minutes ago."

Mrs McGraw was looking at the empty patches on the wall. Maggie was looking distraught.

Shami's mobile phone rang. It was Malcolm from forensics. "We've just found blood on the floor mat. We're checking the blood type now."

41

Scott Henderson was looking forward to his retirement. He'd worked his way up through Dylans although having an uncle in the bank had helped. He'd joined the board eight years ago and ran the Sunningdale branch like his own fiefdom. Outside of the City it was the Bank's most successful branch.

Business had been good. There were plenty of local homeowners who earned enough money to qualify for the discreet and privileged service the private bank offered. They didn't object to the higher fees so long as they had the smart chequebook and the black MasterCard. Few customers were active investors and were satisfied to see steady growth in their unit trusts and share portfolios. Or at least they had been. Recently the value of their portfolios had dropped dramatically.

The large deposits demanded by the bank of its personal customers were used by the bank to lend to commercial companies at higher interest rates. Loans to property developers and leisure companies in the main. Land and property made for good collateral, it was a relatively low risk investment. If a property developer ran out of money the bank believed they could recoup the loan by forcing him to sell the part-developed property which in a fast-rising property market would not be a problem. But in fact this was rarely necessary. Land and property values had been increasing rapidly since the Millennium and the bank had become almost complacent in its risk assessment. They had used not only their clients' deposits but short-term borrowing on the inter-bank market to fund their commercial lending.

Which was why, when the money markets suddenly dried up, they ran short of cash. Desperately short. They hadn't experienced a run on the bank like Northern Rock but that was because they were adroit at keeping the situation away from the press and depositors. But they couldn't keep the lid on it for much longer. It forced them into the arms of the cash rich Novaya Zemlya Kredietbank. Russian banks were bloated with cash from gas and oil revenues.

The takeover had been clinical and sudden. When Scott had learned at last month's board meeting how bad the cash situation was, he still thought that Dylans could trade out of it. He'd suggested a possible merger with Mortimers where he knew the Chairman well. (They played golf at Sunningdale together). But it turned out that Mortimers had similar problems to them. The speed of events had amazed Scott. The offer from Novaya Zemlya Kredietbank (NZK) had been generous and conditional on a quick approval. The bank's shares were not traded on the Stock Exchange so the notice period for approval was short. The tumbling FTSE and the rising interbank rate had made the decision inevitable. If the directors wanted to fund their retirement, it was roubles or nothing.

Today was the first meeting of the new board, Mortimers, Dylans and NZK. The chief executive was Ivan Berbatov, a Ukrainian who had, according to a recent article in Forbes, a short temper and a ruthless streak.

Scott tightened his grip on the handle of his briefcase as the lift doors opened. He stepped out into the marbled lobby and pressed the entry bell on the oak double doors ahead of him. These opened to reveal a close-carpeted reception area that was entirely purple. The carpet was purple, the wallpaper was flocked with purple fleurs de lys. Even the large curved desk had a plastic(!) purple illuminated panel with the words 'Novaya Zemlya Kredietbank' in Roman and Cyrillic scripts.

He was almost relieved to see that the two receptionists were not required to wear purple. The two girls were both blonde. Their hairstyles were short, sculptured around their faces. They could have been twins. Perhaps they were. They were wearing charcoal grey city suits and black blouses; he could see that much above the desk. He wondered whether they were wearing trousers or pencil skirts.

They looked up together and he wasn't sure which one addressed him. "Mr Henderson. Good afternoon. Let me show you to the boardroom."

As he passed behind the reception desk he threw a glance at the remaining girl. She was looking at a monitor. On the screen was a picture of him. Smart, he thought. Too smart by half.

His grip on the briefcase remained tight. Inside were the files with the details of the bank's lending to the Kingdom Hotel Group, until now his largest client.

Simone has arrived first. She had rung me soon after the police had left. Hugh had told her what had happened. She gives me a big hug on the doorstep. When she comes inside and takes off her coat I see that her belly is already getting rounder.

"You look well, Simone, are you feeling fine?"

"Yes Mum. I haven't felt sick at all – just a bit tired. I get tired more easily."

"Well you take it easy. Look after yourself, after all you've been through a lot for this baby."

It's almost a relief to have something else to talk about. With everything happening with Pyotr and now the burglary I've not thought about my potential new grandchild.

We sit in the lounge having tea. She looks up at the empty walls and grimaces. The room has lost its warmth. It's like someone was packing up for a removal. I half expect the chairs to be covered in dust sheets. It doesn't feel homely any more.

She is sympathetic and reassuring. She even says that it could be a coincidence and nothing to do with Pyotr at all. But it's too much of a coincidence I know.

It's after 6 when Hugh arrives. He's left work early and is about to start his week's break in Gstadt. His face is flushed and at first I think it's the cold. But I can smell the alcohol on his breath when he kisses me. "Did you drive here?" I ask. I haven't forgotten what happened to Frank. "No, train and a taxi," he replies.

"Tell me exactly what happened, everything Mum."

"Would you like a drink first, dear?"

"Yes why not, if the buggers haven't stolen that too."

Simone goes out to the kitchen and brings back a bottle of wine from the fridge. I pour three glasses.

Hugh is pacing up and down, agitated. He's looking at the empty walls, calculating.

I tell him what has happened. I tell him the police have taken statements from me and Mrs McGraw. I tell him that Mrs McGraw swears she shut the security gates.

"She says she set the house alarm too, but I'm not sure she did. She sometimes forgets."

"We'd better not mention that to the insurers," says Hugh. "Need to convince them that all our security systems were in operation. Might invalidate the insurance otherwise."

I tell him about the subsequent call from Constable Chandrasena. She had asked whether Pyotr had a remote control for the security gates. I had confirmed he kept it on his keyring, the one with the key to the pick-up. She told me there had been no keys found in the vehicle at the ferry terminal.

Hugh continues to march up and down but clearly he can do nothing. "I'd invite you back to our place but we're packing for Gstadt. Still you're welcome to come and house-sit for us for the week we're away. Might be safer."

"Or you can come and stay with us," says Simone.

I don't fancy either. I want to stay in my house. I want to protect it. I want this whole thing to be over. I wish I still had a dog.

I am still worried that someone may break in and steal something else. Shami Chandrasena has recommended I change the locks and given me the name of a locksmith.

I ring the number and get an answerphone telling me to leave my number and they'll ring me back.

A few minutes later the phone rings. But it's not the locksmith. It's Saska, phoning from Poland. She wants to know if there's any news of Pyotr. I tell her what Constable Chandrasena said, what they found at Portsmouth.

"Can you pick me up from the airport please?"

For a moment I don't understand what she means.

"I'm catching a flight tomorrow – I cannot stay in Poland when we don't know what has happened to my husband."

*

I recognise Saska from the photo in Pyotr's room. She's wearing a smart business suit (she's had to work that morning) and is pulling a small wheeled suitcase. She looks tired and worried but I'm not surprised. I'm tired, I'm worried.

"I could not sleep. I worry so much for him. I have to be here – to find out what has happened."

As we drive from Heathrow I go through everything that has happened since the fateful day. She says little, just interrupting occasionally to get me to explain when she doesn't understand the English.

I take her up to Pyotr's room. She looks at his things, picks up her photo and I can see tears on her cheeks. I cannot believe she knows anything about Pyotr and the money.

I go downstairs and wonder what I can give her for supper. I'm due another delivery soon from Waitrose but I've been too busy to do my online ordering. I go to the fridge and find a packet of sausages I'd bought for Estelle's two boys. With some frozen chips and peas I cobble together a meal. Neither of us is that hungry but we make the best of it.

We watch the TV news at ten. It's all economic doom and gloom. I switch it off and suggest we have an early night. Saska seems relieved and we climb the stairs together.

I awake to the sound of someone vomiting. Someone is being sick. For a moment I'm confused. Maybe I imagined it, or dreamt it. But no. I hear that awful retching sound again, followed by coughing. It's coming from Pyotr's room. Funny. How long is it now since it became Pyotr's room rather than Hugh's?

Saska! Yes it must be Saska. My just-woken brain finally begins to compute. Saska. She must be sick. I push back the covers, swing my legs over the edge and feel for my slippers. I'm tying the cord on my towelling bath robe as I cross the landing.

There's no response to my knock but I push the door open anyway. The door to the ensuite is ajar. Through it I can see the kneeling figure of Saska. She's holding onto the rim of the toilet bowl. her head bent over. Her raven black hair is all messed up. I see her shoulders shake and she moves her head forward and retches again.

The stone tiles in the kitchen are cold beneath my foot. In my haste to go down the stairs I lose the left slipper. I hate being sick, not ill, puking up. I couldn't bear to watch Saska so here I am in the kitchen boiling a kettle, making tea. Spooning sugar into the mug. The age-old English answer to everything – hot sweet tea.

On second thoughts I add a glass of water, put them both on the tray. I retrieve the fallen slipper on my way upstairs.

By the time I reach Pyotr's room Saska is sitting on the edge of the bed, shivering. I pass her the glass of water.

"Dziękuję Ci" Saska takes the glass in both hands. She rinses her mouth, stumbles to the bathroom and spits into the wash basin. I hand her some tissues, She blows her nose, glances at the tissue and balls it before throwing it into the toilet bowl. She splashes cold water on her face, looks up and grins at me.

"That's better," she says. Her face is ashen white.

"It's all the worry dear, I expect. And the travelling."

I return to my room. It's only seven o'clock and very dark outside. I run myself a shower. The water beats down on my head, swamping me, washing away the last vestiges of sleep and reinvigorating me. I reach for the shampoo and lather it into my hair.

Later, I sit in front of my dressing table, blow drying it. I gaze at my reflection in the mirror. I watch as my new short hair style gradually takes shape as I angle the hair dryer. With the new highlights it still looks blonde rather than grey and it frames my face better. Rather well in fact, I like it.

Not bad for nearly 60, I think. Sixty! It's less than two months until my big birthday. I haven't made any plans to celebrate it. Frank would have planned something grand. It was his style. a cruise maybe, even a big bash at the golf club. But I've been so busy with Petmag and Simone's pregnancy that I haven't given it a thought until now.

Perhaps Hugh is organising a family do, making preparations with Simone and Estelle to surprise me? The thought cheers me.

But poor Hugh. Things don't seem to be going well since Frank died. Letitia is so demanding; she seems unaware of the pressures he's under. Since Frank died, Hugh has had to become the 'alpha male' and that wasn't easy for him. And things aren't good at work I know – the stock market is really bad.

I think about the angry exchanges we've had when I insisted on taking my money out of that Icelandic bank to fund Petmag.

And now it looks as if he was right all along. Pyotr has disappeared. So has a lot of the money, and the paintings and silver. I still can't believe Pyotr is responsible. But nevertheless if I hadn't got involved, would any of this have happened?

Why did I think I could run a construction company? How could I have been so naïve? At the time it all seemed so simple. Every argument raised by Pyotr or Hugh I brushed aside. All in my enthusiasm to prove I could be independent.

And here I am, on a Thursday morning when I should be thinking of nothing more than what to wear to go shopping, to meet my friends and have coffee, nothing that's a real problem, nothing that matters.

Nothing that matters! Yes that's it. Nothing mattered before. My life was meaningless. I was the wife of Frank. Frank who no longer exists. Being the wife of a non-existent person was being nothing at all.

I think about this as I brush my hair. Yes, that's why I did it. I wanted to matter. I wanted life to be meaningful, purposeful again. And it is. Or rather it was.

Now what?

I can't carry on without Pyotr. I can't even write a company cheque! Oh yes, I've told the men to carry on under Tadeusz's guidance and they will. But now I've got to deal with the bank, that obnoxious Major Silvester as well as sort out all the wages, the paperwork, the payments.

I can't turn to Hugh – he's in Gstadt taking a break. And he would just say 'I told you so'.

"Is it alright if I make some coffee please?" Saska's voice comes from the landing.

"Yes of course Saska. Can you find everything.? I'll be down in a moment."

I put the hairdryer down and go the wardrobe. I reach for a woollen suit. Yes, that's business-like. After all I'm the boss of a construction company, like it or not. Now is the time to act as if I mean it.

Saska is a new woman. Her dark hair is shampooed and brushed, there's colour back in her cheeks and she has carefully made up her face. I notice the green eye shadow and the thin line of mascara underneath. She is drinking a cup of coffee – there is more in the cafetière for me. She seems to have got over her sickness completely.

Her first words take me by surprise. "Do you believe Pyotr could do this Maggie?" She fixes me with a fierce determined gaze. Beneath it I sense she is desperately seeking reassurance. I remember what Hugh said. It was surely no coincidence that the break-in had happened so soon after Pyotr disappeared with the money. The burglary had to be connected to Pyotr.

Then I see Pyotr's face as he gave me the book of Polish scenes at Christmas. I remember the shared vodkas, the shared hopes and dreams.

"No, I don't. Not for one minute! I don't know what has happened, why he didn't pay the men. I don't know why he drove to Portsmouth and caught a ferry. None of it makes any sense - but I don't believe he would steal from me."

"We don't know he drove to Portsmouth. We don't know he catched a ferry. Someone else can take his pick-up and leave it there." Saska looks at me for confirmation.

I want to believe that Pyotr hasn't fled to France, yet the

alternative is what? If he's innocent why hasn't he been in contact? Unless, he can't. I shiver at the thought.

But if, for some reason he is being prevented from contacting us, if he's innocent surely I owe it to him to carry on the business until he returns. And not just me. Saska can help too. I realise that for the past few days I have been toing and froing without any firm plan. It's like I can't think for myself, just react to those around me. Everyone is giving me advice, but it's not the same advice. It's time I got a grip. It's time to start taking control.

The thought pleases me. I have a purpose. Things matter.

Saska doesn't understand what I'm suggesting at first. I explain again. "All the plans for the work are on the computer next door. Pyotr was very careful to make sure he copied them to Frank's computer from his laptop. But they're in Polish. You'll have to translate for me."

*

The Polish workers are on their lunch break when we arrive at the Club. We get out two pairs of wellingtons from the boot and exchange them for our town shoes. Saska has changed back into the business suit she arrived at the airport in, her thick wool coat is buttoned up over it. She picks up the file containing the printed copies of the plans and follows me across the first fairway towards the site where the men are operating.

Tadeusz looks pleased to see us. He looks quizzically at Saska but a broad grin comes across his face as soon as she starts to speak. The men stop eating and cluster around anxious to learn who the Polish woman is and what is happening. Saska spreads some of the drawings across the bonnet of Tadeusz's pick-up.

I stand a little back and watch her as she explains. I feel a little redundant as I cannot understand the Polish. But Tadeusz keeps looking across at me and nodding and smiling. After a few minutes Saska turns to me. "Tadeusz says he is happy to have the printed plans and schedules. Normally Pyotr brought his laptop on a Friday and went through things. He did this last week before he, before he er disappeared." Her voice catches and I sense she is near to tears.

"So that's why the laptop wasn't in his room!" The realisation cheers me. It's another reason to believe he's innocent.

Saska nods. "The men are very worried about Pyotr. But they know what the work is and they will carry on. Tomorrow is pay day! Tadeusz says the men must be paid."

"Oh yes." I turn to Tadeusz and give him my most reassuringly business smile. "Oh, yes, tomorrow pay day." I mime counting out money.

"I need him to give me a list of the men and the amount of money they are due to be paid. Then I can go to the bank and get the money tomorrow. In fact we can both go tomorrow."

We set off back to the car park to change our wellingtons. It's time to confront the Major.

"The Major won't approve of us changing shoes in the car park," I tell her. It's NQW!"

"NQW?"

"Not quite West Downs." She smiles but I see she doesn't

get the humour. Difficult I suppose in a foreign language. Her English is very good though.

As we approach the secretary's office, guarded by Terri, we are accosted by Elizabeth. She comes fairly sprinting down the corridor towards us.

"Maggie, Maggie!" Her arms are flapping at her sides reminding me of a mother hen. I half expect her to start clucking. "Maggie, have you heard? Your Polish chappie has run off with all your money."

In her haste to impart the news she had barely noticed Saska. Now she looks at the elegant Pole in her smart business suit. Elizabeth has been ignoring me since the EGM and I can't help thinking that she's gloating over the news of Pyotr.

"I don't believe you've met Pyotr's wife, Saska, have you?" I pause to let my words sink in. Then I shake my head and say, "You really shouldn't go spreading malicious rumours without checking your facts."

I knock on the office door and push it open. I don't look back at Elizabeth.

"Hi Terri. Is the Major in?"

*

The Major liked his desk. It was large and made of polished oak. It had been in the clubhouse for countless years and had gained a patina that gave it 'gravitas', he liked to think. It also gave him something to sit behind. A physical barrier that signified that he was different from those who sat in the smaller, slightly lower chairs opposite. Behind the desk he was the keeper of the Club's traditions. It also made him feel more important. He wasn't a new Millennium manager who liked to have a clutter-free desk, a smart computer screen and a discreet keyboard. Oh no. He liked paperwork. Not **doing** paperwork but having files and bulging in-trays that he imagined showed how busy and essential he was.

Of course, when it came to meetings with Jim or Arthur it was different. They were important and couldn't be subjected to the lower-level chairs. No, when either of them came in to discuss the Club's affairs he would make a great show of closing some files and stand up. He would suggest a 'quiet chat in the bar' would be better 'to get away from the phone.' Invariably Jim or Arthur would stand him a drink.

With staff, however, the desk was an essential prop. It divided the commissioned from the non-commissioned. Then he could request reports to add to the growing piles on his desk. Then he could exercise his delayed decision-making, either throwing the decision back to the staff member or invoking the necessity of involving a member of the appropriate Club committee.

Members rarely entered his office. Their questions normally answered quickly and efficiently by Terri. When confronted with a request from a member he would refer them to the Club rules and more-often-than-not say that the etiquette was for them to ask the appropriate sub-committee member.

So when Maggie and Saska entered he was not sure how to act. On the one hand she was a member, and a very important one at that as she had the ear of the captain. On the other hand she was one of the trades people that he had to deal with. It was rather like finding your sergeant had been educated at Wellington – officers were gentlemen, NCOs weren't.

*

The Major stands up as Terri ushers us in. He holds out his hand, hesitantly. It occurs to me that I've never shaken hands with him before. I give it a firm grip – I read somewhere about firm handshakes.

"This is Pyotr's wife Saska." I nod in her direction. "She's helping me with the project while we ascertain Pyotyr's whereabouts."

She extends her hand to the Major who is still standing at the side of his desk.

"Ah yes. You didn't really resolve that last week when I asked. I haven't seen him around since. So where is he?" He looks at Saska, then back at me. "Does she understand English?"

"Yes, thank you, Major." Saska smiles at him. I try to stop smiling at his obvious discomfort.

"May we sit down?"

The Major looks more embarrassed and tries to make up for his poor etiquette by stepping around his desk and rearranging the two chairs. He clears his throat. "So what's the situation exactly, Mrs Miles?"

"Pyotr has been missing for several days and we are concerned that he may have had an accident and is unable to contact us."

"Most irregular, most irregular. I believe he was carrying a cheque for £50,000 made out from the Club? What has he done with that?"

"Well I'm afraid it wasn't paid into our account. He was obviously unable to pay it because of his, er, accident." I look to Saska for support. She nods her head in encouragement. "We'd like you to put a stop on that cheque and issue me with another so I can pay it into my account."

"Your account?"

"Yes, you see, in the absence of Pyotr – temporarily of course – I cannot write cheques or draw money out to pay the workers. So I am having to pay them from my own money. So if you could make it payable to me…"

"Oh, I don't think so." He sits down behind his desk. He rearranges a file.

"But why not?"

"Our contract is with Petmag Ltd. The invoice is from Petmag Ltd. We can't go writing cheques to Mrs Miles. Oh no, wouldn't be right. Against the rules."

"But the circumstances. I'm sure you understand the circumstances. It's only until Pyotr returns." I feel my confidence slipping away. It's hot in the office. My business suit feels uncomfortable. Back in the kitchen this morning I thought a straightforward approach to the Major would succeed. Now I'm not so sure. I hadn't expected such negativity. People say that the Major is indecisive, hides behind rules, but I didn't expect a flat refusal. I begin to get angry. After all I've paid the workers out of my own pocket. The men are working well, the Club is benefitting. Without a replacement cheque I'll be drawing more money from my account to fund the project. It's just not fair.

"I am sure you want the project to proceed on schedule? That is why we need the cheque from you to Maggie. We don't want to have to tell the men to stop working." Saska speaks slowly, distinctly, her heavy Polish accent making the implied threat more menacing.

"I will cancel the cheque. I will ring the bank right away ladies."

I feel the relief.

"And you will give Maggie the new one?"

"Ah well, I think the Captain and the committee will have a view on that. Of course, if it were up to me Maggie," I notice the change from Mrs Miles to Maggie, the condescension in his voice.

"Anyway, it would need to be countersigned by the Captain or Mr Balfour and he is unfortunately ill again with a cold."

"But next week we are due a further £150,000," I blurt out.

"And I'm sure that by then your partner will have returned." He rises from his chair and waves towards the door, ushering us out.

I don't know what to say. I get up and Saska follows, file in hand. She glares at the Major.

There are voices outside the office and before the Major can reach the door Jim walks in. He smiles at me and gives me a kiss on the cheek. He extends his hand to Saska. "And you must be Pyotr's wife? Major, I hope you don't mind but Terri mentioned Maggie was in with you and I know there are a few little problems to sort out."

"No, no. Not at all, Captain, but actually we had just finished." He tries to smile. Jim turns to me, "Everything sorted ok, Maggie?"

"No, not really."

"We need you to sign a cheque please." Saska directs her words to Jim

Back in the car, I say, "You were wonderful. I couldn't have got it without you."

"Yes, but it does not find Pyotr. We still don't know where he is and I think really bad things have happened to him."

42

Arthur looked at Scott Henderson sitting behind his desk. He knew him well. They were old friends. He'd even recommended him for promotion when he was still a director of the bank.

He asked again, but again the banker shook his head. "I'm sorry, Arthur. You know if it were up to me."

"But it's so sudden."

"This whole crisis has come on suddenly. No one foresaw it. And when Kingdom went down the pan, Berbatov just went ballistic."

"Nasty piece of work, that Berbatov."

"Maybe," Scott chose his words carefully, he was not convinced that Berbatov wouldn't bug his office. He was getting paranoid. But he needed three more years before he could draw his pension.

"Maybe. But he's the boss now and he's insisting on calling in the loan."

"But West Downs is a hundred years old and we've got our portfolio of investments…"

"Which are worth rather less than half your current overdraft. And Berbatov's well informed. He phoned me personally yesterday, to ask about this affair with Hamilton. He really does have his finger on the pulse."

Arthur blanched at the mention of Hamilton. He'd talked with the liquidator who held little hope of ever recovering the £500,000 sitting in the Cayman Islands.

"How long have we got?"

"Just one month."

43

I stop the car outside Terminal 1. Saska gets out and opens the rear door. She picks up her little carry-on bag. We hug, out there on the pavement. The wind is cold and there's rain in the air. Everywhere is noise. The car engines, the buses, the trundling of wheeled cases.

"Are you sure you don't want me to come in with you? I can put the car in the short term park." I don't want her to go. I don't want to be all alone again. I miss Pyotr, I'll miss Saska.

"I must get back. My job." She seems sad too but I think it is Pyotr she is thinking of leaving, not me. There's still no news. Neither of us believe he's stolen the money but we're reluctant to admit the alternative. If he didn't steal the money, who did? And what has happened to Pyotr?

I drive back slowly – I'm almost afraid to find something else has gone wrong. But the gate is closed and opens smoothly as I press the remote. Mrs McGraw's car is parked in front of the house.

"So she's gone then? Back to Poland?" Mrs McGraw is pouring the tea and helping herself to a digestive from the tin. "She hasn't found that husband then."

I can tell that she still thinks of Pyotr as untrustworthy. 'That husband'. It's not Mrs McGraw's fault, I know, the papers are all-too-quick to blame anyone else for the country's troubles and there's no amnesty for the Poles.

"I've already stripped her bed and the sheets are in the machine. Now how's Simone? How's she coping with her pregnancy? Must be showing now isn't it?"

"No, no she's only about 5 months – it's due in early June I think."

I feel guilty. I've been so wrapped up in work and finding out what's happened to Pyotr that I've not spent time thinking about my new grandchild. And Simone has waited so long for a baby. Has she had another scan yet? Does she know if it's a boy or girl yet?

Simone doesn't know the sex either. She sounds excited on the phone and pleased to hear from me. Everything is proceeding well, she says. We don't care whether it's a boy or a girl, Mum, just so long as he's healthy. (He? I wonder if she does know but isn't telling me, or maybe it's just a slip of the tongue.) Her excitement is about Tim's new job. It's more money and closer to home. He'll be on hand to help out with the new arrival.

"Why don't you both come down at the weekend and we can celebrate," I say.

"That would be nice, I'll check with Tim. Maybe Sunday lunch at the Golf Club?"

"No I'll cook for you. It will be nice. And I'm spending too much time at the Club right now."

"Oh yes, dare I ask? Is there any news of Pyotr? What's happening? Who's looking after the men?"

It's back to reality. Like it or not I'm a working woman now. I ought to keep an eye on things. Saska and I paid the men so that's settled and I'm due to get another cheque from the Club next week for around £150,00 which will be fine. I'll talk to Hugh about getting the bank mandate changed so I can sign cheques without Pyotr. But until that's done, it'll have to be my bank account the Club pays.

Mrs McGraw comes into the lounge.

"What are we going to do about those pictures?"

I look at the marks on the wall where the pictures had hung.

"You'll need to get some new ones or else we're going to have to have the room redecorated. Can't keep looking at those dirty marks."

"You don't just go out and buy half a dozen paintings," I snap. "Those were special paintings, valuable paintings, paintings we loved." The memory hits me like a physical blow. I knew how much Frank loved those Victorian pastoral paintings and then there was the one we'd bought together in Honfleur. I see Frank and me, in the gallery by the harbour deciding between the two paintings. The discussion with the gallery owner, the coffee drinking. Frank's bargaining, my embarrassment. It seems so long ago. Almost another life. A life without burglaries, and disappearances and fraudulent contractors. A nice time. A peaceful, happy time.

*

Hugh was not having a happy time in Gstadt. He found it impossible to stop thinking about work, and in particular, about the way the market was performing. He'd sold his personal portfolio – all of it – and put the money into a high interest account at Kaupthing. The interest wouldn't make up for the losses he'd incurred but at least it wouldn't go down! But the portfolio he was responsible for, his multi-million growth fund was a disaster. He just hoped that his decision to reduce certain holdings and move into safer pharmaceuticals would stop the rot and allow him to improve his performance against his rival fund managers. But he knew it would be too late to affect his bonus. There wouldn't be one. He just hoped that he would still have a job. If he lost that, what would he do?

He was thinking about that as he slalomed down behind Letitia. He saw her lean left and then right, giving the markers a wide berth. She was an effortless skier. Had skied all her life. Hugh was competitive, always had been.

He closed on Letitia, cutting the turns finely, biting into the crisp snow with his skis. The adrenalin started to pump but still his mind kept flitting back to the stock market.

It was only a little bump in the snow but the camber was wrong and he felt his left leg start to slide under him. He over-corrected, felt the tip of his right ski dig into the snow and found himself with mouthful of snow. His leg was painful.

"Thank God we've got health insurance," was all that Letitia said.

44

Marco brings me a coffee and fusses around asking if there's anything else I want. I don't know whether it's genuine concern or whether he just wants an update on Pyotr and the tree work. I've just come into the clubhouse having paid 'my' workers. I have been to the bank, withdrawn the cash and taken it home. The teller at the bank had checked first with the manager as it was a large withdrawal from my personal account. Brendan Matthews came out to see me and asked about Pyotr but I told him we still had no news. He nodded and frowned before getting one of his staff to go with me to my car with the money.

Once home I go through Tadeusz's list of workers and make up the envelopes with their wages inside and try to copy their names onto the envelopes.

The Club is quiet. It's a Friday afternoon and the weather is bad so few members are playing. There are a couple of bridge games going on in the card room. I give into Marco and order a piece of coffee cake. I realise that I've eaten very little today.

I try not to think about Pyotr. It's the week-end and I've got Simone and Tim coming down on Sunday. I'll do a nice roast. I'll have to get an order into Ocado as soon as I get back. I haven't seen Lech for a couple of weeks – it's all been so busy, with Saska staying, the burglary and everything.

I take out the invoice I've prepared for the Major. I should go in and see him now but I'm tired and he'll only procrastinate. He'll need Jim's signature on it anyway.

"Marco, can you give the Major this please, I need to get going shortly."

"Of course Mrs Miles, but he's not in this afternoon. He's gone out to a meeting with the Captain and Mr Balfour."

"Oh, he's gone with Jim and Arthur? Are they meeting someone?"

"I don't know. Mr Balfour just came in and spoke to the Captain and the next thing I know they called the Major and all three went out."

Marco looks a little embarrassed. I am being nosey and the tradition of the Club is for the staff to show due deference. He obviously knows something is amiss but he's not going to speculate.

"I'll put your letter in his office, with Terri."

*

The three men hadn't gone far. They were sitting in a coffee shop in Sunningdale. The table was in the corner, away from the other customers who were mainly young women with young children.

"So what exactly did the bank say? How long have we got until they take the overdraft away?"

Arthur continued to stir the sugar into his coffee. He kept his head down looking at the swirling liquid. "One month."

"Can they do that? Can they just demand repayment without any reason?"

"I'm afraid so. That's the nature of an overdraft – repayable on demand. Of course banks don't normally do that, they ask you to reduce it or they suggest you take a secured repayment loan or something."

"I never did like Dylan's," said the Major. "I always thought we should be with one of the big banks. If it had been up to me…"

"OK Major, that's not helping. We are with Dylans and up to now Arthur has always managed to get a really good deal from them. It's just unfortunate that the Russians have taken over the bank."

"Well then, I blame the Russians. They're not to be trusted."

"It's not the Russians – it's the Americans," said Arthur. "If they hadn't caused this financial collapse we'd still be having lots of tourists over here and Kingdom Hotels wouldn't have gone bust. Then Dylan's wouldn't be demanding money back."

"For the want of a nail a shoe was lost, for the want of a shoe a horse was lost ….. my kingdom for a horse!" Jim smiled apologetically. "But let's get back to the problem. What are our options Arthur?"

"Well we have two sources of income which we can call on to pay off the overdraft, just. We have our stocks and shares and we have the remaining members' subscriptions that have not been paid. Our investments were doing very well for years but now they've fallen through the floor. Stocks and shares should be looked on as a long term investment. We should ride out this storm and wait until they rise again."

"But we only have a month!"

"Indeed and that's the problem. If we sell them now we'll lose a lot on their value in last year's accounts and there wouldn't be enough to pay off all the overdraft anyway."

"How much are we due in late subscriptions, Major."

"Ah well, you see I'm not sure of the actual figure. Need some time to get an accurate figure. All a bit sudden."

"But roughly, Major, how many members still haven't paid?"

"I'll check, first thing on Monday."

"I think we need an emergency meeting with all the committee as soon as possible. Major, I'll need accurate figures on Sunday. We'll call the committee for a meeting at 11.00 Sunday."

*

I used to like Sundays. Frank would leave early for golf. I'd have a lie in and then catch up on a few things. Then off to the Club for Sunday lunch where we'd meet up with our friends and a few hours later stagger back home and doze in front of the telly.

Some Sundays Hugh, or Simone or Estelle would be coming for lunch and I'd be up early preparing a feast for them. But since Frank died it hasn't been the same. I don't feel like joining the other couples for lunch at the Club and

Hugh has been far too busy to come over often with his family.

So it's good this morning to know that Simone and Tim will be arriving shortly. I've got a good joint of beef ready to go in the oven, I've made an apple pie (something that I haven't done since I don't know when), and I've raided the cellar for a nice bottle of burgundy.

Lech didn't bring my order from Ocado yesterday. It was an English driver, although his Geordie accent was so strong I found him more difficult to understand than Lech. He didn't know Lech; said he had only just started with Ocado. It was a shame. I would like to talk with Lech. Perhaps I should phone him and see if he has heard anything.

But I'm silly – if he had heard anything of Pyotr he would of course have rung me.

I start to lay the table. I get the good cutlery out, the crystal wine glasses. I look up and see the empty marks on the wall. I must do something about replacing the paintings. Mrs McGraw is right – the walls look awful. I wonder if Hugh's heard back from the insurers. Maybe we could go together and look at some galleries? Oh, but he's always so busy.

I ring him. Letitia answers.

"Oh hello Maggie. Yes we got back last night. Not the sort of journey I would want to do again! Had to do all the bags myself because Hugh couldn't. It was fine for him – got put on one of those airport buggies and whisked right through security leaving me to deal with the boys and all the luggage."

"What? What's happened to Hugh?"

"Oh didn't you hear? He's torn his Achilles tendon trying to be a boy racer down the slopes! He's on crutches. Hang on I'll take the phone over to him."

I realise that we won't be going round any picture galleries soon. He sounds so morose. He seems more concerned about his job than dealing with the insurers.

"I can't drive for at least three weeks and hopping around on a crutch isn't going to go down well at work. I'll have to take taxis to and from work – it will take ages – and cost me a fortune."

"Perhaps you could all come down here next week-end? It would be good to see you."

"I can't drive and I'll have to see if Lettie has anything else on. I'll let you know."

*

Sunday morning eleven o'clock saw eleven of the Club's committee members sitting round the big table in the Card Room. Jim had phoned all committee members but some were away, holidaying abroad. He had not told them the specific purpose of the meeting, merely said something had arisen that needed to be sorted very rapidly and he needed their input.

The Major was sitting at one end of the table, alongside Jim, and had a large stack of files in front of him. He was looking tired and worried. He had worked all Saturday trying to get his papers in order, to work out how many members hadn't yet paid, and to try and list all the creditors and the amounts owed. He hadn't had the benefit of Terri as it was a Saturday. In the end he had phoned Arthur and insisted that he came in and helped.

The Lady Captain was the only lady around the table. She wasn't happy either. She had family coming for lunch at home and hoped that this meeting wouldn't drag on. She wasn't a committee person.

Jim decided it would be quicker if he outlined the problems Arthur had brought to him on Friday.

"We face a bit of a financial crisis and we will need prompt action to sort it. We don't have time to call yet another extraordinary general meeting and, in any case, it is within our remit to take the steps necessary to save the Club."

At the mention of saving the Club everyone's attention was heightened.

"Save the Club? What do you mean? What the hell has happened?" Laurence addressed his remark to Jim but looked accusingly at Arthur.

"The bank is withdrawing our overdraft facilities. We have to pay back well over one million pounds within one month."

There were gasps from several members.

Jim went on to describe the meeting between Arthur and Dylans and the conclusion that the Club would have to sell off its investments as well as get in the remaining members subscriptions in order to pay off the bank.

"What if we don't. What can the bank do?"

"It has a fixed and floating charge over all the Club's assets and income. They could take over the Club and sell it!"

"But, they can't do that – it's our Centenary next year. And anyway we own the land and that's got to be worth millions." The Lady Captain didn't often contradict the

229

Captain but she was so shocked by the news that she blurted out without thinking.

"I'm sure we would be able to raise a mortgage on the clubhouse and land but not while Dylans have their charge on it. We'd have to pay them off first and then go to another bank and try and negotiate a loan. And right now with the financial crisis, the banks are not very receptive to property-backed loans."

"But when we agreed to go ahead with the reservoir and the tree clearance you, Arthur, said we had no problems with the bank and that our investments were more than adequate." Laurence glared at Arthur.

Arthur had always felt he was a cut above many of the members when it came to things financial. After all he had been a director of a private bank. In his days gentlemen honoured their debts but also supported their friends. There was no way that in his day the bank would summarily withdraw an overdraft facility to such a prestigious customer. He suspected that the new Russians in charge, who naturally had no idea how gentlemen behaved, were trying to force the Club into liquidation at which stage they would acquire the land and make a killing.

But Arthur was under real pressure now. He had consorted with the major to pay a fraudulent contractor £500,000 and now had less than a month to find an alternative bank and pay back the overdraft.

He pulled at the lapels of his jacket, then put his long, thin-fingered hands flat on the table. He stood up. "I have always strived to do my best for this Club. I believe we can overcome this setback." He glanced down at Jim. "Yes, we will have to sell our stocks and shares and the market value is lower than it was but, with a little more effort from the Major to get in the late subscriptions we will have enough to put our account back in credit. With the value of our land I am sure I will be able to persuade Dylans to give us a fixed interest term loan to cover our running costs for the next year."

"But what about the tree work and the reservoir?" Laurence stood up too and the two men faced each other across the table.

"Well, we may have to delay that. "

"I'm not sure we can delay it Arthur," said Jim. "We have signed contracts, the work is underway. And anyway any delay would mean putting the course out of action during the summer – or at least several holes."

Jim looked at the Major. "How many members have still to pay their annual dues?"

"Around 300 I'm afraid."

"So that represents roughly £600,000. Surely with the sale of our investments that's more than enough?"

"It would be if we didn't have £500,000 of our money in some fraudster's Cayman Island account."

"Look, we have no alternative," said Jim, "We need to turn our investments into cash in the next week or so to bring down our overdraft and we need to get the remaining subscriptions in, and fast. Then we need to see if we can get a new overdraft facility with another bank, or if not a term loan."

"I'm sure I can talk Dylans into giving us a term loan." Arthur sat down and looked confidently at Jim.

"I'm not sure we want to be in hock to a Russian bank anymore," said Jim. "But I think we need to keep very quiet about the situation. If news got out about our problems we could have a lot of problems with our suppliers. If we are going to manage our way through this we will need to get extended credit terms from several of them – and there's the staff to consider. No, I think we will keep this under our hat for the moment and also see if we cannot attract some new members and get more membership fees in that way."

*

I am in the kitchen whipping up the batter for the Yorkshire puddings when I hear the gate buzzing. I dust the flour off my hands with the tea towel and walk through to the hall. Tim drives right up to the door and I see Simone get out from the passenger seat. She is noticeably heavier and looks more pregnant than she did a couple of weeks ago. But her eyes are bright and her skin looks flushed and healthy.

She takes off her coat under which she's wearing a loose-fitting flowered top and dark slacks. She follows my gaze down to her tummy. "Yes, I'm growing, getting bigger by the week," she laughs. I turn to kiss Tim and see how proud he's looking. They've waited so long.

Tim takes the coats and hangs them up as Simone and I walk back into the kitchen. The smell of the beef in the oven wafts over us. "I hope you're hungry, I've done a full roast."

"Absolutely, I can't seem to get enough these days – eating for two I suppose."

Tim comes into the kitchen to join us. He's just been into the lounge. "Such a pity about those lovely paintings, Maggie. Any news from the police?

232

Over a long and lazy lunch I hear all about their plans for the baby – sex still a mystery – and I am happy to share their excitement. I realise how much of my time and thoughts have been taken up with the problems of Petmag. It's not important. I need to think about my family – my expanding family. Grandma to a new arrival in a few months.

Simone helps me clear away while Tim dons his coat and takes a tour of the garden. "Did you ever hear from your old Italian gardener?" he asks later. "Or are you still using the Poles?"

It's been some weeks since Lech came over to help with the garden. It's not the growing season and the lawn doesn't need cutting. But soon, I realise, it'll be March, the bulbs will be up and there will be a lot for Lech and Pyotr to do. If.....

I shake my head to clear my thoughts from Pyotr. "Tell me about your new job Tim."

*

Janet, the Lady Captain, arrives back home much later than she had hoped. Her husband is cross. He's tried to prepare some of the lunch for their guests but everything is running late. Their guests arrive moments after Janet. "What was so important that you had to stay so long?"

"I can't tell you. We're not supposed to tell anyone."

Her husband looks at her quizzically? Is she joking? Seeing that she isn't he turns away as the bell rings to announce the arrival of their guests. "It must be serious if she can't even tell me. What the hell is going on? I'll have to find out tomorrow when I go to the Club."

Five miles away Arthur is still at the Club. He's sitting with the Major going through his file of the Club's investments and trying to calculate how much they will realise in the morning when he calls his stockbroker. The Major is huffing and puffing as he tries to word an email for the members who have still not paid their subscriptions. He has already scribbled on four sheets of paper and screwed them up. He doesn't type so doesn't use the computer. In the morning his final draft will be handed to Terri to type and email.

Alongside his pad is a tray stacked with post – mostly invoices from suppliers for him to check and pay. Some have been there for weeks.

4 5

Hugh lasted a week taxiing to and from work. He put up
with the office jokers and their remarks about not having
a leg to stand on. But he seemed incapable of rescuing his
portfolio. He was desperate to boost its value before the end
of March – the crucial date for bonus calculations so he
was gambling. Gambling on certain sectors recovering fast
but if anything his new stock picks dropped faster in value.
Every night the BBC newsmen reported on the deepening
financial crisis and it seemed that the investment community
was running scared.

News of serious side effects with a new drug under test
had been the final straw. The shares in the pharmaceutical
company that Hugh had backed went into freefall.

Redundancies in the City became a major talking point
and Hugh became a statistic.

Clutching his cardboard box he left the office that Friday
evening, declining his colleague's offers of a leaving drink.
He took one last look around the dealers' floor. The screens
were flickering green and red – mainly red. His colleagues

had their heads down. Sad that he was leaving, relieved that the axe hadn't fallen on them.

It was, of course, raining as he left the building. He stood on the pavement leaning on his crutch, the cardboard box with his personal possessions by his feet, already discolouring with the wet. He stood there for several minutes before he managed to hail a cab. The driver was cheery and helped him into the black cab. He started talking about the financial crisis which was the last thing Hugh needed. He needed time to think. What would he say to Lettie? How would he get another job to pay the bills? How would they manage without the bonus, a bonus that Lettie seemed to think was hers of right?

Perhaps he wouldn't tell her tonight. Perhaps he could get a new job quite quickly – and then tell her. It would be good news, not bad news. But where would he get another fund manager job at the moment? With the financial crisis, all banks and hedge funds were firing, not hiring.

He had his pay-off – three month's salary – so things would be alright for a bit as long as Lettie didn't start spending his non-existent bonus. What would he do though? All that spare time suddenly. Well he could use it to improve his handicap at golf. Yes, the weather was improving and he could fix up some games. But no, he had this wretched Achilles tendon problem. It would be weeks before he could play.

Thinking of golf made him think of Maggie. She could probably lend him some money if necessary. That's if she hadn't lost it all on that madcap adventure with the Pole. He'd meant to sort out the insurance claim for the stolen paintings and also start proceedings to remove Pyotr from the Board of Petmag so Maggie could access the money there.

The prospect of sorting out Maggie's problems pleased him and he was in a slightly better mood when he arrived back in Barnes. The house was Edwardian and detached. It had a short gravel driveway with laurel bushes on each side. There was a lot of painted wood – the fascia boards on the eves, the wooden window frames, even the garage door. All freshly-painted at great cost. He had wanted to use the Polish firm that his friend David had used but Lettie had insisted on using the painters recommended by her interior decorator. He scowled as he thought of the cheque he had written just a few months ago. These extravagances would have to stop now, until he was earning again.

He paid the cabbie and walked up to his front door. He was balancing his briefcase on the top of his cardboard box. He stopped, considered what to do with the box. It would make it obvious that he had been fired. He went around to the side of the house and opened the garage door. He deposited the box next to the lawnmower and returned to the front door.

Deep breath. He opened the door and announced he was home. There was no reply. He called again at the bottom of the stairs but there was no response. The kitchen was neat and tidy, the worktops clear and sparkling. No signs of coffee cups or lunch plates. There was no note, but why should there be. Three o'clock on a Friday afternoon, Lettie wouldn't be expecting him back for hours. She was probably out picking up the kids. Yes, that's where she must be.

Then his mind flashed back to the garage. Their Range Rover was still there, child seats fitted in the back. What time did the kids come out of school, he wondered. He had never been in a position to pick them up – he realised he had no idea.

He went back to the garage, retrieved his box and unpacked his things into his study. His study window overlooked the gravelled drive at the front of the house. He looked out and saw the taxi pull in. Lettie got out and walked to the house. She didn't pay the driver – presumably it was prepaid on her account. That's something I'll have to stop, he thought. We'll have to cut back.

She was carrying a small clutch bag but no shopping bags. That's a relief, he thought. He walked into the hall just as she pushed open the door. She stopped, looked at him for a moment in surprise. She said nothing for a moment, just shrugged off her fur jacket. Underneath she was wearing a plain but beautifully cut and very expensive dress. At her throat was a two-colour gold necklace that Hugh must have bought her but he couldn't remember. Her legs were bare, no tights despite the cold weather. Her face was flushed, the cold Hugh supposed.

"What are you doing home already?"

"Oh they let me go early," said Hugh, his mind thinking that's no lie, 'let me go' was the phrase his director had used. Let me go as in letting go of a drowning man.

"Where are the boys? What time do they get picked up?"

She pushed past him heading towards the kitchen. "Oh they're having tea with a friend today. Michael has picked them up."

"Michael?"

"Yes he's the father of one of the boys in their class, lives in Putney. I'll go and pick them up about 6."

"So you've been shopping?"

"Er yes. Why all the questions?"

Hugh shrugged, turned and walked back to his study. He wouldn't tell her today.

I awake to the sound of the telephone. I was deep asleep and fumble for the handset on my bedside table. My heart races as I worry what news can be so important as to warrant a call in the middle of the night.

It's Simone ringing to say thanks for yesterday. I look at the digital clock alongside the telephone. It's after nine! I haven't slept so long and well for weeks.

"Did I wake you? I'm sorry but you are normally up well before nine. It's just that I don't have to work today and I thought you might like to come out with me to choose some curtains for the baby's room?"

I realise that I've been so preoccupied with Petmag that I've been missing out on my old life. Shopping, lunching, girl-talk. We agree to meet for lunch in Guildford.

Spending yesterday with Simone and Tim, hearing all their plans, has made me remember my role as a grandmother. I'll give Lettie a ring and maybe see if I can have the twins down for a few days.

The second phone call comes as I'm coming out of the shower. It's Daphne, reminding me that she's signed me up for the bridge drive at the Club tomorrow. Every year the Club holds a charity bridge drive and the money goes to the Lady Captain's charity. Janet will be captain for just another month so is keen to get as many playing as possible.

Bridge is one those pastimes that goes naturally with golf. Older people, time on their hands. A desire to keep the brain ticking over as well as the body. Too many of my friends are showing signs of Alzheimers. Bridge is good exercise for the old grey matter – and it's sociable too. Frank was never that keen on it but would take part in the 'supper bridge' which I arranged with our friends. I realise that since Frank died there haven't been the invitations to supper bridge. I suppose it's because you need four people – two couples and I'm a singleton.

Of course the Club bridge drive is also an opportunity for we girls-what-lunch to doll ourselves up in our latest purchases. Maybe I can find something in Guildford today with Simone?

I decide a quick bowl of muesli will have to suffice for breakfast given the time. I know that there is a lot of unopened household post to be dealt with and I plan to spend an hour or so in Frank's study before I leave for Guildford.

I'm spooning the yoghurt onto my muesli when the third phone call comes. Suddenly it's back to reality. It's Saska. She sounds even more worried and I tell her that there is still no news of Pyotr. I try to console her by telling her the men are carrying on the work and doing well but her interest is purely on the fate of her husband. I tell her I'll ring the policewoman again and see if she has any more information. I write Saska's work number on the corner of the muesli pack.

Shami, the detective, has no more news but insists she's working hard on the case and will keep me informed. It's the not-knowing that gets to me. The longer it goes on the more I begin to believe that Pyotr has made off with the money. I don't want to believe it and I trust Saska, I don't believe she knows. But if he'd had an accident or something we would have known by now.

I put on a warm coat and comfortable shoes for my shopping trip with Simone. There could be a lot of walking around the cobbled high street of Guildford. As I go to set the alarm and leave, the phone rings again. It's Hugh. He says he's due some leave and will come down to help sort things out. I'm so surprised that I don't know what to say. Hugh never has the time to come down during the week. I tell him that tomorrow I'm out at bridge but Wednesday would be lovely assuming that Estelle doesn't need me to look after the kids. I agree to pick him up at the station as he still can't drive with his leg.

46

It was a nurse who first noticed that the man had regained consciousness. He'd been in a coma ever since he'd been admitted the week before. His eyelids fluttered and his lips moved but she could not make out the words.

She pressed the buzzer to attract the ward sister. For two weeks the mystery man had lain between the crisp white sheets. A large bandage covered his head, a small gap left over his face. Tubes ran into his arteries delivering a saline solution and a complex mixture of drugs. He had a thick stubble covering much of the unbandaged part of his face. From the colour of the bristles the nurse presumed he was blonde. She hadn't seen him until after the operation and by then his complete head was bandaged. No doubt his skull had been shaved. The head injuries were severe.

For over two weeks he had remained in a coma, constantly monitored. When the paramedics had brought him in he was barely alive and deeply unconscious. Indeed the farmer who found him thought he was dead.

He had seen the body lying underneath the hedgerow. There were still the remnants of the recent snow and the man's naked white body was hard to see. The barking of his dog had drawn him to the hedgerow.

When the police and ambulance arrived they spent a long time with the body before wrapping it in an aluminium foil blanket and carrying it to the ambulance.

The police called for back up and began to search around the hedge and the track leading from the road. They fielded the farmer's questions with measured responses. Yes he was alive, barely. Yes he appeared to have suffered a blow to the head. No they didn't know whether he'd been attacked or what had happened to his clothes. "Maybe he's a nutter escaped from somewhere. Any mental homes near here?"

Later the Surrey police would try to excuse their failure to tie up the victim with the escaped fraudster now being sought by Interpol. They had concentrated on finding the attackers of the 'mental patient'. They took casts of the tyre tracks in the wet earth, they examined the heavy shovel they found nearby and sent it to forensics to analyse the blood, tissue and hair that still adhered to it. They found an old glove and sent that to the lab too. They didn't think the victim would live.

The ward sister called the doctor and the two congregated around the man's bed. The man opened his eyes and mumbled the same two words over and over but none of the three could understand. He closed his eyes and slept.

The next morning it was the Polish ancillary worker, cleaning around his bed, who noticed he was awake and trying to say something. She listened before calling the sister. "He's saying 'the money, the money'. He's speaking Polish."

I am thrilled to hear from Hugh. This week has not been easy. After Simone and Tim left on Sunday the house again felt very empty. I wandered around from room to room. I had talked to Simone about turning one of the bedrooms into a nursery for when her baby was born. I wanted her to feel she could come down and spend time here with me.

I had gone into Pyotr's room. It was just as Saska had left it. His few work clothes were still hanging in the wardrobe. There were a couple of books. The photo of Saska was still propped up. Descending the stairs I had seen the ugly marks where the pictures had hung.

Before going to Guildford to meet Simone I had gone to the Club to check on the men. They seemed to be busy and getting on alright but I really had no way of telling if they were on schedule. I popped into the office to see if the Major had signed the cheque for me but he wasn't there. Terri looked worried. She said that something was certainly going on and she didn't know what. The Major had gone out very soon after he arrived and she hadn't seen him since. Jim and Arthur had been in looking for him too.

I am late meeting Simone. The A322 was busy and every traffic light seemed to be at red. Parking in Guildford is never that easy but I managed to find a space in the Leapale Road car park and walked across to the House of Fraser store. Simone waves across the restaurant to me. She has a coffee in front of her. I order a glass of Sauvignon Blanc. I tell her about Hugh's call and the fact that he's taking a day off to come and see me.

"I hope things are alright with Hugh," she says.

"Oh I think he's frustrated with his Achilles tendon problem but it's getting better. He just can't drive at the moment."

"No, I was thinking of his job. There have been a lot of redundancies and firings at the stockbrokers in the City. This bloody recession. I was talking with Estelle and she told me what had happened to Justin's firm. The financial companies are just not spending. They're 'hunkering down' as he puts it."

"Well I'm sure Hugh's alright – he would have told me if it wasn't. Anyway I'll find out more on Wednesday."

The afternoon's shopping is fun and we buy lots of things for the baby's room. It's dark by the time I get back to the house. Knowing that Hugh is coming over to see me on Wednesday has lifted me. I check the cupboard. What do I need to order for lunch for him? I want to make a good lunch for him, it's so seldom I have him to myself. I make out a list for Ocado and tap it into the computer. It's amazing how quickly I seem to have adapted to this new technology. When Frank was alive I would never had dreamed of ordering anything online, let alone my weekly shop. Now me and my mouse are well acquainted!

But that's the least of my achievements – if pouring money into a tree-clearing project and not getting paid can be called an achievement. Still maybe Hugh will be able to help. I have to admit that life hasn't been boring but I'm beginning to realise I'm out of my depth. When Pyotr was around I didn't have to get involved in the actual tree-clearance work, paying the men, listening to Taj. All I had had to do was transfer some money to the new company that Saska had helped to set up and then listen every evening to Pyotr's tales of his day at the golf club.

Still, I've learned to stand on my own two feet after years of leaning on Frank's shoulder. Sorting out household bills or Portuguese tax demands now seems so much easier.

I can see Hugh hobbling out of the station. He's not got a crutch but just a walking stick so hopefully that means his leg is getting better. I flash the lights and he waves and starts towards me. The commuters have long gone and now there are just a few cars in the forecourt. I get out and open the passenger door for him. He gives me a hug and I feel the knobbly handle of his walking stick dig into my back.

"Oh it's so good to see you, Hugh. So nice of you to come. Especially when you're so busy."

He smiles but says nothing and lowers himself into the car, adjusting the seat so he can stretch out his bad leg.

"How was Gstadt? Oh, sorry silly question. But the boys enjoyed it didn't they?"

He nods and smiles and tells me a little of how the boys are taking to skiing. But he is quieter than usual. Must be his leg, it's such a nuisance.

"How are you managing to go to work with that leg?"

"Taxi."

"Still it won't be long and you'll be hopping around, I suspect." I exit the station forecourt and turn onto the A30. The traffic is light and soon we are approaching the house. I press the remote control and the gate opens.

"Have you replaced the remote control?"

"No. I've had all the house locks changed but it didn't seem worth changing the gates too."

He hops up the step and we go into the hall. He eyes the marks on wall. "The bastards!"

It's over our first cup of coffee that he drops the bombshell about his job. "And you haven't told Lettie yet?"

"No. The time hasn't been right. She won't understand. I'll tell her in a few days when I've sorted out another job."

"Do you think you'll get another one quickly? I'm reading a lot in the papers about redundancies."

"Honestly, I don't know. It all came as a bit of a shock. We'd been counting on a decent bonus, or at least Lettie had. I knew it wasn't likely to be much because of the fund's performance and I tried to tell her. But you know Lettie"

"But you've always done so well. And no one foresaw this financial crisis. It's not your fault."

"Well maybe we should have foreseen it. I mean we should have known that this unlimited credit the Americans were throwing around would have to stop. We just didn't want to believe it I suppose."

"Well if you need some help with money I can do something. But things are a bit difficult at the moment as you know with Pyotr missing. I've still got to pay the men and I've been using my account for that. And Estelle's Justin's in a really bad way. He was made redundant because of this wretched financial crisis. I may have to help them out a bit."

"I think we have to face facts, Mum. Whatever you thought of Pyotr he's disappeared, along with a lot of your money. What we need to do now is to start proceedings to remove him as a signatory and then at least you can have access to the Petmag money."

"I told you that his wife Saska was here? She seems very distraught. She doesn't know what's happened to him. I can't believe he deliberately took the money and disappeared. I think something happened to him."

"If it had, the police would have found him. If he'd had an accident or something. And his car was found at the ferry terminal so I'm afraid we must face facts."

He looks at me with a mixture of affection and

condescension. Silly old moo he thinks. Taken in by this handsome young Pole. He doesn't say 'I told you so' but I know he's thinking it.

"Right, let's get started," he says. "First the insurance claim for the pictures. I've brought down the reply from Aviva. We need to fill in a lot of details."

The phone rings. "Saved by the bell" I say.

"Hello?"

He watches me, at first almost annoyed that his plan has been interrupted. Then as the conversation continues he frowns and moves closer, trying to hear what the caller is saying.

"Oh that's wonderful news! Well no, I mean it's terrible but also good. Oh I'm not making sense. Yes of course you can. I'm in all day, with my son."

"Fine, we'll see you then."

I hang up.

"That was Shami Chandrasena. You know the nice police lady that was dealing with us. They've found Pyotr! He's in hospital. He's very ill but he'll recover. She's going to come over and see us this morning and tell us more."

47

We drive down together, all three of us. In the police car. I sit in the back while Hugh sits alongside Shami Chandrasena with the seat fully back. Frimley Park hospital is not far from Sunningdale and it seems incredulous that Pyotr has been lying in bed there for weeks, so close, without us knowing it.

Hugh makes the point to Shami. "When we made our initial enquiries and contacted the hospitals they hadn't found Pyotr. Then when they did they took him to another hospital first believing him to be almost dead and also, because he was found naked, he was believed to be a mental patient who had escaped."

"That's a hell of an assumption to make," says Hugh.

"Yes it was. But remember too that after the pictures were stolen and the car was found at Portsmouth we were no longer looking for a missing person who might have met with an accident. We thought he'd fled to Europe."

Frimley Park hospital is a large complex, white, modern and low. The sign reads 'in partnership with the M.O.D.' A lot of military personnel are treated there – Aldershot and Pirbright are close and both house major army units.

Constable Chandrasena steers the car into the parking lot and collects a ticket. We walk into the main reception. The reception desk is curved and illuminated with concealed downlighters. There are two receptionists and two large vases of daffodils. The place has the feeling of a hotel more than a hospital.

Shami shows her warrant card and soon we are being led down well-polished corridors and finally into a room dominated by a large bed, with computer monitors flashing alongside and a drip feed tube hanging from a pedestal. The end of the tube is attached to the arm of the man lying in the bed. His head is still bandaged but his face is uncovered. There are dark blue marks on the left side of his forehead and his left eye is still puffy. He is clean shaven. He is smiling. It's Pyotr.

I lean forward and kiss him gently on the forehead. "Oh Pyotr. I'm so happy to see you. I thought you were gone forever."

"You can't get rid of me so easily." He smiles at his joke but I can see that it is an effort for him to talk. The nurse turns to Shami. "He's still sedated and pretty tired so don't take too long. He needs to rest."

"What on earth happened to you? What happened to the money?" Hugh is speaking over my shoulder.

"Yes, the money, the money. I'm sorry. I'm sorry Maggie."

Shami pulls up a chair for me. I sit down and take Pyotr's hand. "Take your time."

Shami finds another chair, Hugh remains standing. I introduce her to Pyotr. She explains about the abandoned car and their belief that he had fled the country with the money.

"But why would I? I wouldn't steal from Maggie – she's my partner." Pyotr looks mystified, not angry. He cannot conceive of stealing from me. I find myself dabbing at my eyes. I'm crying. I don't know whether it's relief or happiness or sadness.

Shami turns to me. "Would you mind if I just spoke to Pyotr alone? We need to find out exactly what happened?"

On the way back to Sunningdale Shami outlines what she has learned. But it is the end of the week, after she has visited him twice more that she can tell me the full story.

The men had attacked Pyotr as he went back to his pick-up parked in a small alley near the bank. There was no one around as he stepped into the alley at the back of the shops. It had been very quick. He had almost reached the truck when he remembered he hadn't paid in the Club cheque.

As he turned around he saw the first man, a hooded jacket concealing his face, approaching with a knife. He had backed away towards his pick-up truck. The man had leaped forward wielding the knife and Pyotr had used his laptop case to fend off the blow. He kicked out at his attacker and caught him in the groin. The man staggered and fell to his knees.

Pyotr turned back towards the truck just in time to see the spade come down. After that it was blank.

The next thing he remembered was waking up in hospital.

I phone Saska to tell her the news as soon as we get back. She is relieved but naturally very concerned at the extent of his injuries. I try to reassure her.

"But two weeks and he is coma? He must be very ill.?"

The doctors are not saying much, still worried that a fractured skull might not be the only problem facing Pyotr. He had been stabbed as well, possibly before he was dumped in the field. The knife had cut through an artery but missed his heart. He could well have bled to death but for the freezing temperatures and his unconsciousness which allowed the blood to congeal and prevent too much blood loss. Nevertheless the surgeon had been concerned that oxygen might have been cut off to his brain and that Pyotr might never recover. The fact that Pyotr had emerged from the induced coma with such a clear recollection of what had happened had amazed him and gave him hope that his prognosis was wrong.

Saska is fixing to fly over on the next flight she can get and I say I'll pick her up at whichever airport.

Then I phone Lech. His mobile rings for some time before he answers. I can hear the motor sound of his Ocado van. I tell him as quickly as I can. He says little but there is a relief in his voice. "Thank you Maggie, I knew he hadn't stolen from you. We all thought he was dead!"

I realise that it's not just me who has been trying to deny that dreadful thought. In my clearer moments I had concluded that either he had stolen the money and disappeared or he had met with a fatal accident. I didn't know which was worse.

It's been a long day and I'm so glad that Hugh has been with me. He has been quiet during most of the ride back.

Now he comes into the lounge carrying two tumblers. "It's been quite a day for an old girl like you! You need a stiff drink."

I nod. A hell of a day. First the news about Hugh's job, then the news that Pyotr was alive. The visit to the hospital. So much to take in.

We sit down together on the sofa. The lights are already on. The days are still short in March.

"I'll stay here tonight," says Hugh. "You need someone around and anyway we haven't sorted out the insurance thing."

I'm amazed. He's always been so busy; always had to run back to Lettie. I ask myself if he is really doing it for me or if he can't face going back to Barnes and Lettie and **his** problems.

We switch on the TV. It stops us looking at the blank squares on the wall. The news is dominated by the financial situation and worries about the banks, but the lead story is about Heather Mills winning a £24 million pay-out from Paul McCartney.

"Bloody woman. You could tell she was just after his money all along." Hugh looked bitter. He said nothing about the financial news.

I drop Hugh off the next morning to catch the train to London. He says he's going to see some head-hunters. I watch the train pull out and wonder if and when he's going to tell Lettie.

I decide to head over to the golf club rather than go straight home. I want to tell Tadeusz about Pyotr although it will be difficult using sign language.

I needn't have worried. There's an Ocado van in the car park (not the sort of vehicle the Major appreciated in his car park). I find Lech talking to the men. I'm embarrassed that they all cheer me when I approach. Perhaps it's just their way of showing relief. Maybe it's to say thank you for believing in Pyotr. I don't know but suddenly my spirits are lifted. A weak sun is casting shadows of the trees across the fairway and there is birdsong in the air.

I see that Scotty the greenkeeper is with the men and is beaming at me. He comes across. "They're really happy with the news about Peter – and so am I. Nice chap. I always thought he was a good'un. And these guys are getting on really well."

Now that we've found Pyotr the problem with the bank account is over. He can sign cheques and I can use them to pay the men on Friday. I will go over to the hospital this afternoon and see how he is.

Feeling happy and positive I walk back to clubhouse where I see several of my fellow lady members getting ready to go out.

"Are you going to play? It's a lovely day." Elizabeth was already changed, black trousers and a purple V-necked Club sweater. "We haven't seen you for ages. Ever since that man ran off with your money in fact." She turned to the other ladies. "Poor Maggie's had such a terrible time."

I tell them the news about Pyotr. I can't hide my disgust at Elizabeth. I'm heartened to see her embarrassment.

"I'd love to play this morning but I have to see the Major and then I'm going down to Frimley to check on Pyotr's progress."

But the Major isn't in. He hasn't left a cheque with Terri. I'm annoyed but too happy about Pyotr to get upset. "He's never in these days," I say.

"I think he and Arthur have got a thing going," laughs Terri. "They're inseparable at the moment and always whispering in corners. I've no idea where he's gone this morning."

He is back behind his desk on Friday when I call. He stands up as I enter and indicates to the empty chair in front of his file-laden desk.

"I'm glad to hear that your Polish chappie has turned up. Hopefully he'll be able to sort out his men and get the tree clearance back on track."

"It will be some time before he leaves hospital. I don't think we're behind schedule on the tree work. Scotty told me they were getting on really well."

"Ah yes, but that's Scotty. I wouldn't take too much notice of him."

"Anyway Major I've come about the cheque. Now Pyotr's back you can make it out to Petmag as usual."

"Ah yes,…"

"Or if you've already made it out to me that's fine too."

"Well, a bit irregular. Of course if it were up to me…. But I think the Captain needs to consider the procedure. Yes, we'll get back to you next week. I'm sure we can sort something out."

I don't know what is going on. He's fobbing me off with excuses. I protest but he's smarming his way out of it. There's obviously no cheque forthcoming. Maybe Terri's right. There is something going on that we don't know about.

I leave without a further word. The door bangs as I slam it shut. I stride through Terri's office and out to my car. Tadeusz is in the car park, driving some kind of digger. He stops and comes over and presents me with the list of names and amounts for wages to be paid. I smile and mime going to the bank to get the money.

"Watch out! Bad men!." He mimes hitting me over the head with a spade. Then laughs.

I get in the car and decide to go straight to Frimley first. The image of Tadeusz hitting me with a spade lingers with me. It's not that funny. There are still violent criminals running around with the keys to my house. OK, I've had the locks changed but the entry gates system is still the same. Maybe they have Pyotr's remote control.

Saska will probably be there. She arrived on Thursday at Stansted. She had hired a car, telling me that it was too far for me to come and pick her up. I was pleased to have her company. The house didn't seem so empty when she was there.

When I get to Pyotr's room it is empty. I find him in the small lounge at the end of the corridor. He's in a wheelchair talking to both Saska and Chami. The bandages are off his head and he has a blonde crew cut. The whole skull had been shaved for the operation but two week's later the hair is forming a closely-cut surface like the stubble of wheat fields.

He smiles when he sees me. "Join the party!". I had forgotten how infectious that smile was. Different from Lech's but very appealing.

"He's feeling much better," said Saska, "and they say he can leave the hospital in a few days."

"That's not the best news Maggie" Pyotr beams at me. "I'm going to be a Dad. Saska's pregnant!"

Detective Chandrasena was looking pleased too. "He's given us descriptions of the two men, although because of their hoodies it's not much to go on. But I've got some ideas on how we can trace them."

48

Detective work involves much that is tedious and time-consuming. With limited financial resources and burgeoning 'box-ticking' form-filling requirements from the government, it explains why so many cases remain unsolved.

Only the most important crimes get the resources required. But the brutal way Pytor's attackers had left him to die in the snowy field, not to mention the international nature of the crime, ensured that this case was given the full treatment.

For Chami this caused a problem. The case would be handled by her superiors or even the national crime squad. She would be left to find the missing paintings and little more. She might not have the resources but she had the determination.

She hypothesised about the pick-up at the dockside. If Pyotr had been stripped and dumped at Hindhead, why had the attackers driven the pick-up all the way to Portsmouth? And why was so little blood found in the truck? The severity of the wound, not just his head, but to his shoulder where he appeared to have been stabbed in the back, should have led to more than the few droplets of blood the lab in Reading had discovered.

They must have had another vehicle, she surmised. The reason for leaving the pick-up at Portsmouth was clearly to make the police believe Pyotr was trying to escape with the money to France. If they had driven it there, they must have driven another vehicle too.

She requisitioned cctv footage from the Surrey police covering parts of the A3 between Guildford and Hindhead around an hour after Pyotr had left the bank. She studied the footage from the Portsmouth car park from film provided by the Hampshire constabulary. They had already logged the truck turning into the car park but the cameras concentrated on the number plates and the driver was indistinct.

She looked for a truck on the Surrey tapes and caught glimpses from two cameras of what could be Pyotr's pick-up.

It was only after hours of viewing, video enhancement and a lot of intuition that she found the suspect vehicle. A Volvo saloon was twice spotted following Pyotr's pick-up although the number plate was unreadable.

She checked the number plates shown entering and leaving the dockside car park against the DVLA file. There it was. Maroon Volvo entering the car park three minutes after Pyotr's. More interesting still, it left the car park five minutes later. The Volvo had been reported stolen several weeks before.

So they hadn't left on the ferry. They were still in England.

The Berkshire police found the burnt-out shell of a Volvo two days later near Slough. Again Shami requisitioned cctv images from the area where the car was found. Eventually her doggedness paid off.

The two men both had previous convictions. They had been arrested after a ram raid at a golf club near Woking the previous year but the case had been dropped for lack of evidence. It appeared that they had been reconnoitring golf clubs in the Sunningdale area looking for suitable targets when they had seen Pyotr paying his men in cash.

It would take months to bring them to trial, months in which minute forensic investigation of the Volvo's burned-out boot would reveal DNA samples that matched Pyotr's and many months more before Maggie's paintings were recovered from a well-known fence. But by that time Maggie would have more things on her mind than paintings.

49

Arthur and the Major were sitting opposite each other in the saloon bar of the Running Deer, a small pub on the A30 near Bagshot.

Both were worried that news of the Club's predicament would get out.

"I know Jim had to tell the rest of the committee but a secret shared is a secret bared." Arthur sipped from his gin and tonic. "We need to get more money in fast if we are to pay off the overdraft before the end of the month. What response have you had to the email?"

"Well it's early days of course. We've had a handful of subscriptions come in, about £20,000 I suppose but there's still more than two hundred and fifty members who haven't paid up. I think we need to speak to them. After all the constitution of the Club says that membership fees have to be paid promptly at the beginning of January."

"Yes, I know, but we've always been a bit tolerant. People have a lot of expenses at Christmas. Some people are a little short."

"But not our members, surely? West Downs is a club for well-off people, people with class."

"I'm afraid the problem with Hamilton spooked a lot of the members. You remember the EGM? Very nasty. I felt that many were blaming you and me when all we were doing was our job."

The Major said nothing. They sat in silence for a while. The Major was thinking about the letter he had just received from his sister in Scotland. Maybe it was time for a move. A new posting as he liked to call it. The club up there might not have the history of West Downs but neither was it likely to have the problems. And house prices were much cheaper – he could afford a nice little place. Suit him and his wife nicely until retirement. Although on second thoughts perhaps his wife wouldn't be too happy.

"I think you need to have another word with Dylans." The Major broke the silence. "A month is just not reasonable. I'm sure you could get them to extend it. If we could get a few more months we could get the rest of the membership fees in, and with the money from the investments we could pay off the overdraft. Then we could move to another bank – a Scottish bank. I know someone at RBS."

Arthur shifted in his seat. He was acutely aware that his relationship with Dylans was no longer seen as an asset but a liability. The truth was he didn't understand the way finance today was conducted. It had been so different in his day. Simpler. It was a question of who you knew, not what you knew. Nowadays the industry was full of upstarts like Laurence with their spreadsheets and risk assessments.

Arthur enjoyed being thought of as a financial expert at the golf club. He'd grown used to spending most of his time at the Club, either on the course or in the bar. He spent as little time at home with his wife as possible. She didn't like golf and he wouldn't have been one to encourage it anyway. What she did all day he didn't know and didn't care. He'd provided her with a nice home and a respectable income and the inability to have children was no doubt down to her anyway. Children could have been a drain and a worry. Their lifestyle had been so much more comfortable without them.

He realised that the Major was right, though. He would have to bite the bullet and go and see his old friend at Dylans again.

I hear the news from Elizabeth. She was the unofficial Club gossip and the accuracy of her reports was always in doubt. I remembered how she had told everyone that Pyotr had run off with all the money.

The news that the Club was in serious financial trouble, that the bank had pulled the plug on the overdraft had everyone talking at once. The implications for the staff, the members and the contractors were all different but equally serious. I realised that was why I hadn't been paid.

I don't know how I'm going to tell Pyotr. He's at home now, recovering well and planning to come over to the Club to brief the men tomorrow. After the problem with Hamilton the prospect of not getting paid again might just be too much.

I go to find Jim, the one person I feel I can get a straight answer from. He tells me of the recent committee meeting and what Dylans had said. He tells me that they were hoping to salvage the situation by selling the Club's investments and collecting the rest of the membership fees. "I still think we can do it, Maggie, but we need time. Now the news has been leaked we may find it harder to get the membership fees paid and we will have to hold back on paying you and the Reservoir people."

"But can't you get the bank to be more reasonable?"

"I'd like to think so and Arthur and the Major are there now, but I don't hold out too much hope."

But there was more hope than he expected. When Arthur came back he was looking pleased with himself. There was much of the old Arthur back. "We've done it," he announced to Jim. "The bank has agreed to extend our overdraft until the end of September. By then we should have all the fees in and have gotten a decent price for our shares. It'll mean belt-tightening of course and we need to delay payments to the contractors until we get a new bank but the Club is saved!"

He felt so proud of his achievements that he called to Marco to serve them both doubles in the bar.

"How did you do it?"

"Well of course I did lay it on a bit thick about my time with the bank – trust and honour and all that. The Major had produced some pretty optimistic figures to give them too showing our position wasn't half as bad as they thought. I told them that we were still expecting to recoup the money from Hamilton's Cayman Island account but that it could take a little time. Of course I pointed out that our debts to the bank were secured on the Club's assets so they needn't worry about the risk."

"And they agreed to that?"

"Yes, it was surprising really. They even had a new agreement prepared. Very efficient. The Major and I were able to get the whole deal signed there and then."

Jim took a large swig of his gin and motioned to Marco to bring refills.

50

The clocks change and suddenly it's Spring. Everything is beginning to grow. It's not just the days that are growing longer, so is the grass on the fairways; the stubble that covered Pyotr's head is now like a golden cornfield, the pile of cut logs in the golf car park has grown too.

The human body is more resilient than I had imagined. Pyotr is recovering from his ordeal in a way and at a speed I couldn't have imagined. He was discharged from hospital into my care. For the first two or three days Saska stayed with me too before returning to her work in Poland. She had implored me to ring her if there should be any deterioration in him or any problems.

It wasn't just the physical injuries that were receding fast, Pyotr's spirit was ignited like never before. He wanted to know everything that had happened to the project during his recovery. He made me go and fetch Tadeusz from the Club and bring him home to talk things over with him.

As I drove Tadeusz back later that afternoon he tried to tell me something but our inability to speak each other's languages prevented me understanding more than that he was grateful for what I was doing for Pyotr and pleased to see how well he was recovering.

A few days later I take Pyotr over to the Club. He has a fleece hat over his cornfield hair and a thick blue anorak to keep out the cold. I worry that he's not ready to venture out and that the trip will tire him too much. Saska's words of caution ring in my head. But I needn't have worried.

As soon as we arrive we are welcomed by Scotty. He seems genuinely pleased to see Pyotr again and leads us across to his greenkeeper's building. It's a wooden cabin-like structure shielded from the clubhouse by a laurel hedge. There are two of the greenstaff inside having their elevenses and they, too, get up and shake Pyotr's hand vigorously.

"Now you sit down, both of you here. I'll fetch you a cuppa." Scotty fusses around like a mother hen and brings two steaming mugs of tea across. "Not the bone china you're used to in the Club" he smiles.

"Don't worry – I prefer builders to Earl Grey," I tell him.

Scotty and Pyotr talk about the work that the greenkeepers have been doing over the winter and how the tree cutting project is progressing. I can tell that Pyotr is anxious to see for himself and am relieved when Scotty suggests he drives Pyotr out to the 11th where the men are working.

I am squeezed between Scotty and Pyotr in the cab of his pick-up as we bounce along the track skirting the course. The sun is throwing shadows from the conifers across the path and dappling the fourth fairway where I see two of the ladies playing. I can't make out who they are and I'm sure they wouldn't recognise me in my current company.

There is plume of wood smoke rising from the left of the eleventh as we near. The smaller branches are being burned while the trunks are being positioned in a pile by a man in hi-vis jacket and hard hat driving a JCB.

At first I can't see Tadeusz but he materialises seconds after Scotty pulls to a halt. There is a shout as Pyotr climbs out and then the men are all running towards us, laughing and cheering. I see that shy smile broaden across his face and Pyotr grasping hands with each of the men. He's like a conquering hero returning to his troops, I think.

He looks around at the site, remarking on things to Tadeusz and pointing out this and that. I stay seated in the cab, watching. Proud. Maternal.

*

I put down the plate in front of him. Steak, oven-cut chips and peas. I am determined to feed him up and rebuild his strength. The morning at the Club has cheered him but I can tell he is tired. The food seems to revive him though and as he pushes his empty plate across the kitchen table he looks at me seriously.

"The project is nearly complete, Maggie. Tadeusz has done a great job. But …"

"But what? Aren't you pleased?"

"I am, very pleased. But the thing is what will I do now? Once this project is finished and we've got the money, what do we do? Do we look to get more business here or what?"

I haven't thought about this. I've been so wrapped up in getting him better that I haven't had time to think about the future. What had I expected when we started Petmag?

That it would go on forever? That Pyotr would remain here in England? That Saska would join him?

Then there was the money. I hadn't told him about the Club's cash-flow problems and the fact that we hadn't been paid, or even looked like getting paid for months.

"What do you want to do? Do you want to stay here in England or what?"

"Maggie, I have been so happy here. Everyone has been so nice to me – well not everyone!" He rubbed the scar on the back of his head. "And then there was that Michael who ran off with all the Club's money. But you've been so kind and I like England. But now I'm going to be a father and I need to think what Saska wants."

"Yes, I understand Pyotr but I would really miss you if you went. I'm sure we could find other contracts if I tried."

"Well yes, but I do worry if there is the money around to pay for all this work. I saw in your paper yesterday that there is something called a credit crunch. Money is tight. We're lucky we're getting the money from the Club let alone looking for other clubs to work for."

I tell him about the Club's finances. The ultimatum from Dylans. I don't want to – I'm afraid it will make him ill. But I can't bring myself to lie to him.

For a long time he is silent. He pours himself more tea, he adds milk the English way. Finally he looks up at me.

"You've put so much faith in me. You've put your own money in to pay the men. I know this. Tadeusz told me. Do you think you will ever get paid?"

"Do I think we will ever get paid, you mean. Yes, I do. It's just that we have to wait a bit. It's not like the Club is going to disappear. It's nearly 100 years old. It's here to stay – it's just a temporary blip."

"But things are bad in the country?"

"Well yes, pretty bad." I tell him about Hugh and his job. I mention Justin and his cancelled contracts. There's no denying that things aren't exactly rosy. And it all seems to have happened so quickly. One day we're all chugging along happily, no mention of financial crashes and then suddenly there are runs on building societies, talk of redundancies, no bankers' bonuses and a squeeze on lending. Didn't anyone foresee this?

"I think I have to go back to Poland when the project is finished. This financial crisis seems to be changing people's attitude towards us Poles. They're talking about us taking over their jobs. Maybe they're right." There is a sadness in his voice that I haven't heard before. He has always said that he likes the people here but I guess being hit over the head, stabbed in the back and being left naked in a snow-covered field is going to alter one's point of view. I wonder how true it is or if it is just reaction to the attack. I think back to the dinner party with the Colonel many months ago. What had he said about immigrants? *It's taking jobs from the Brits, that's what it is. God knows we have enough unemployment in this country without giving jobs to every Tom, Dick and Harry from Eastern Europe.*

The doorbell rings and interrupts our conversation. I get up and go to answer. The Ocado van is parked outside and there, on the doorstep, is a grinning Lech with the large plastic tray piled with groceries.

"Come in, Pyotr and I are just finishing our lunch. Would you like a cup of tea?"

He puts the tray down, removes his outdoor shoes and follows me down the hallway. The two Poles embrace with man-hugs. I fetch another mug.

"No milk for me please – I'm not like the English, yet!" He grins again.

I tell him about Pyotr thinking of going back to Poland and Saska. "What are your plans, Lech?"

"Oh, I'm going to stay. This pays much more than I can earn in Poland."

"Yes but you aren't about to become a father." Pyotr speaks quietly, almost as if to himself.

"Well I don't think so, no-one's told me anyway!" Lech laughs, trying to lighten the mood.

Pyotr looks down at his empty plate. I realise how tired he is. Lech, sensing the mood, stands up. "I have to go, and I think you need to get to bed!"

*

Pyotr's recovery continues to progress over the next few days and he seems to be in a more positive mood. We haven't talked again about what happens after the contract finishes. I am sure that he will go back to Poland. I will be left to sort out the bill from the Club and settle up with Pyotr when we get it.

We seem to have settled back into the familiar routine we had before his accident. He comes back from the Club towards the end of the afternoon, goes to his room for a bit and then joins me in making supper.

We've just cleared away the plates and are sitting in the lounge. The TV is on but neither of us is watching it.

"Do you mind if we switch the TV off, Maggie. I'd like to talk to you."

He tells me that he's made up his mind to return to Poland and seek a job there. He'll leave as soon as the project is complete. "I always hoped we could build a life here, Saska and me. But it is too much of a risk. Saska could probably have got a transfer to London but now she's pregnant I think she will want to be at home with the baby. I need to have a regular job."

He hoped to complete everything by the end of April, a little later than planned but in the circumstances no one was upset with that. The reservoir project was also going well and there was a possibility that some of the Poles might get work from that contractor. The only real concern was that we hadn't been paid for weeks. The money in the Petmag account was nearly exhausted and my own account was still owed money for the wages I had paid directly from it.

I tell him about my conversation with Jim that afternoon. There is to be another EGM to discuss the financial position, but the news is better. He had explained how they had at first been threatened with a one month window in which to pay off the overdraft but now had been granted until September. But he admitted that the Club was having to watch every penny and ask suppliers, like me, to wait until the shares had been sold and the membership fees came in.

There is enough in my accounts, I tell Pyotr, to cover the wages and the equipment hire so I will just have to wait, I suppose. Hugh is not happy about it but says that he understands the importance to the Club of sorting out Dylans. In fact, Hugh has become quite involved in the Club recently. He is still jobless but tells me he has several 'irons in the fire'. His leg is much better and he has been down at the Club quite often. He and Jim had lunch last week.

I worry about Hugh. I hope that everything's alright at home. I don't know that he's told Lettie yet and I'm afraid he's still pretending to go up to the office everyday. He does go to London most days but I think it's just for the odd interview with a head-hunter. More often than not he is down here, with me and Pyotr.

Pyotr looks across at me as if reading my thoughts.

"You're worried about Hugh aren't you? Everything is not good at his home. With Letitia? When I'm gone you'll have time to help him."

"Oh, Pyotr, I will miss you and I don't want you to leave. Yet I know you must be disillusioned with Britain. You came here expecting to get a job at Kew, or Wisley or somewhere that valued your forestry experience. But it didn't happen. Petmag might have been something you wanted to stay in Britain for, but not after the attack. I still can't believe how close you came to death. You've every reason to want to go home. I can't blame you."

He gets up, returning a few moments later with a bottle of vodka and two glasses. "Let's drink to Petmag then. It's been an, an experience!"

*

Major Silvester finished shaving and rubbed his hand carefully over his chin and face checking that all the stubble had been removed. He slapped on some aftershave Nicola had bought him for Christmas before walking back into the bedroom.

Nicola was still asleep. She had come back late and obviously drunk having been 'partying with friends in London.'

"I'm still young enough to enjoy partying – not an old fuddy duddy like you just happy to prop up the bar in that golf club of yours."

He went to the wardrobe and selected his dark blue suit. Very smart. Yes, appearances might be important today. The regiment tie, I think. Picking up the small overnight case he had packed last evening, he took one look at Nicola's prone form on the bed and closed the bedroom door.

He checked his watch – still ten minutes before the taxi was due. Smiling to himself he went into the kitchen and propped up the note against the kettle. She was used to him going off for a few days with his golfing buddies. Usually two or three days playing at prestigious clubs, free of course as he was a Club Secretary. Accompanied by the Captain, or Arthur or one of the other senior members, he rarely had to put his hand in his pocket.

It was just as well as his not inconsiderable salary seemed to disappear remarkably quickly in Nicola's hands. The joint American Express card might have been a mistake.

Two hours later and he watched as the suburban stations began to flash past the train window at an increasing pace. Finsbury Park, Potters Bar, Hitchin all slipped by as the train headed north. The train was nearly full but the Major had managed to get himself a window seat and was settled in with a large polystyrene cup of coffee.

It felt good to be heading home. Every station that flashed past marked his journey away from the troubles at West Downs (Founded 1909). Another four hours and he would be in Edinburgh. A further two and he would be at his destination and a meeting that he hoped would rid him of the West Downs problems once and for all.

*

Around the time the Major passed through Peterborough, Nicola stirred, rubbed her eyes and groaned. Her head hurt. Her whole body ached. She wondered if a glass of water would help or whether getting up to fetch it would bring on the nausea.

There was no sign of her husband but that was understandable. He'd be at his bloody golf club by now pontificating with the other old farts. He was so old! It had been a mistake to marry an older man. Alright to start with – apart from the sex which didn't amount to much. The money was good and since they'd moved down to London (well Berkshire) there had been a lot more to spend it on. She enjoyed going out and meeting people of her own age. Letting her hair down without getting a frown of disapproval from her staid husband.

Last night had been a great laugh, although the details were a little hazy. Annika and she had eventually left the other two and headed off to a nightclub in Battersea that Annika assured her was the 'in' place. There were certainly a lot of eligible men there and some rather lecherous dancing which she enjoyed. But it was later, much later, that Annika sprang the real surprise. Had Nicola agreed to it? Would Annika change her mind in the morning as she so often did when she sobered up?

Braving the walk to the kitchen she poured herself a large glass of orange juice from the fridge. As her head cleared she began to recall some of the details. What an opportunity! Grand Cayman. Somewhere she'd never been and somewhere her boring old husband would never take her to.

She slurped some more orange juice and tried to supress the guilt she felt. She tried to justify it to herself. "Well you're always going on jaunts to golf clubs – it's about time I had some fun too." Yes, if Annika could confirm the arrangements and they really were as good as she made out then Nicola would just tell him tonight when he got back.

It was then that she noticed the piece of paper propped against the kettle. What, away again? Two or three days with pals in Scotland? Well it would serve him right if she was gone when he got back.

When Annika phoned shortly afterwards Nicola had no hesitation. Tomorrow! Well yes, that was fine. Yes she had her American Express card. She read out her passport details to Annika so she could book the flights. Free board in a luxury villa with a friend of Annika's. Six p.m. tomorrow, Terminal 5 Heathrow. No hesitation – she'd be there!

*

Tonight it's the EGM. I will pick up Hugh from the station. I'll be interested to hear what Jim and the Committee have to say. I remember the last EGM. I remember the reaction of some of my friends. I remember my nervousness, standing in front of all those people. Tonight will be different. I'll just be in the audience. Jim will run the show.

The bar is already crowded as Hugh and I enter. It's still half-an-hour before the meeting's due to start. There's a buzz of expectancy in the room. Everyone is putting forward different versions of what they think will be announced.

"I hear they are going to double the fees."

"They say they're selling the Club to the Chinese."

"I think they'll cancel the centenary."

But when the meeting happens it is a bit of an anti-climax. Jim explains that Dylans bank made some unreasonable demands which would have given the Club some problems but that Arthur has managed to get them to see sense and the Club is now back on a firm footing. The Club is going to draw on its investment reserves to finance the great improvements to the Club, including the reservoir, but these are investments in themselves and should guarantee the Club continues to be one of the best courses in the country. There is a murmur of approval at that.

Jim continues by saying that the Club's financial position has not been helped by a significant number of members having delayed paying their fees and points out the ungentlemanly conduct that this represents. He threatens to 'name and shame'.

In the questions that follow he is asked about the missing £500,000 in the Cayman Islands. Arthur looks particularly unhappy about this but Jim says that they are hopeful the authorities will be able to recover some if not all of the money but it may take some time.

He turns to the Major and wraps up the meeting by asking if there is any other business. The Major stands up. "Just one item, I'm afraid Captain. I regret to have to inform you that I shall be resigning from my post at West Downs as I have been offered a very prestigious role at a very prestigious Scottish golf club.

The meeting breaks up as everyone starts to discuss this latest turn of affairs. Although not universally popular, particularly with the women and the staff, there are plenty of supporters of the Major. They are astounded. They want to know details of his new appointment. They try to convince him to stay. In the furore, the Club's parlous financial position is almost forgotten.

51

Terminal 1 Heathrow is busy as usual. I've parked the car in the short-stay and am watching Pyotr as he checks his bag at the BA desk. He didn't want me to come into the terminal but I insisted. I want to hang on to him as long as possible. He's going back to Poland but promises to return. But I don't know when. The contract has been finished the final bill submitted and the men paid off. There was a touching scene when the final wages were paid – bottles of vodka miraculously appeared and were passed around. There was short speech from Tadeusz and a longer reply from Pyotr. The men hugged each other and then came up to me and shook my hand warmly. Tadeusz gave me a bear hug and tried to thank me in English but the words were lost among the happy voices of his men.

Pyotr was going back to Saska. He wanted to be with her during her pregnancy. "I need to get a job quickly in Poland because she will have to stop work. But by the time the baby is born the Club will have paid our bill and we'll be rich!"

I watch him as he heads through security, his blonde hair now fully grown and covering the scars on his head. He looks back once and waves. Then he is gone.

Life returns to normal. I start to play golf again. There's a shopping trip to Bicester. Simone comes over, she's getting nearer to the birth.

But what is normal? I feel suddenly empty. The purpose that had so filled my life for the past six months is gone. I'm back to being a 59 year-old widow with too much time on her hands.

Life is not back to normal though, is it? Normal was when my family were all doing well, when Hugh was a high flyer in the City, when Justin and Estelle were celebrating the success of his business, when Tim and Simone were still hoping to become parents. All of that has changed while I've been running around with Petmag.

My biggest concern now, is Hugh.

Last week he told Lettie. He had to as she was going ahead with a new kitchen in their house. Hugh had to put a stop to her spending. He had to tell her.

If he had expected or even hoped for sympathy and support, he didn't get either. Hugh didn't tell me what she said but I gleaned that she had blamed him for not standing up to his employers, for not providing for his family as other parents did.

Now Hugh was moving in with me. Pyotr was leaving, Hugh arriving. It was only for a few days, said Hugh, while Lettie calmed down but I can't help feeling there is more to it than that. I wonder if Lettie will look elsewhere? That's an awful thing to say but I can't deny I think she is always thinking about number one. But then there's the boys, so

I'm sure she'll see sense. In the meantime I'll need to give Hugh all the support and sympathy she isn't giving him.

They say as one door closes another opens and that's how I thought about Pyotr leaving and Hugh arriving but maybe it's not the only revolving door?

We're eating in the kitchen. Hugh is unusually quiet. I guess he's thinking of Lettie. But then he surprises me. "I've been thinking, Mum. Whilst I'm looking around for another job I could offer to take over temporarily as Club Secretary. The Major has packed his bag already and has left the place in a complete mess according to Jim. I could help out there. Well just for a bit, obviously, until I get my new proper job."

We talk about the implications but the more we do, the more sense it makes. The Club definitely needs to replace the Major but isn't in a position to attract the right candidate in the current financial situation. But in a few months when everything is sorted out and Dylans is history, and with the Centenary it could be in a much better position. By that time the financial crisis would be over and Hugh would go back to the City again.

"I can make sure the Club gets a good price for their portfolio of shares, we can set up a new bank account to keep our money in until October when we have to pay off Dylans. OK we will be paying more interest to Dylans on our overdraft than we're earning in interest at the other bank but I don't trust the Russian owners at Dylans to keep to their word. If we pay back part of our overdraft they may just reduce our limit anyway. And we have bills to pay – not least yours!"

"Jim says he'll be able to pay it in September."

"I hope he's right but it depends on a lot of things. We need to get membership fees in, we need more society income, we need to cut some costs. There's a lot to be done."

"And you're the man to do it, I'm sure darling."

It's nice having Hugh around but I do worry that things are really bad between him and Lettie. It seems his demand that she cut down on spending has resulted in her spending more time around the house with friends. Last week found her having coffee with one of the dads from school. He was apparently arranging to take her and the boys to a show later.

There's still no news on any of the interviews Hugh's been going to in the City. But the good news is that Jim has asked him if he would be interested in taking the Major's position for a few months.

I can hear his car coming up the driveway. He's got the Range Rover today, another thing that hasn't gone down well with Lettie. I put the kettle on and check on the casserole. I hope he's going to stay tonight, I do like to have someone to talk to in the evenings.

"Hi Mum, something smells good. What's cooking?"

"Boeuf Bourguignonne. I see you've got the car. I hope you can stay for supper."

"Great, but I have to get back to Lettie this evening, she needs the car tomorrow."

He dumps several large files on the kitchen table and then goes back to the car, bringing more.

"What's this, homework?"

The true extent of the Major's shortcomings soon become apparent. Hugh shows me the figures the Major had prepared for the bank.

"They're hopelessly optimistic. Just wishful thinking. He's assumed all the late membership fees would be paid within a week or so, but clearly many members are not going to renew their membership at all. I found more than a dozen letters of resignation in his in-tray. I don't even know if he'd read them. Then he's just cut the expenditure on green staff and catering staff and also not counted the part-time bar staff. If we were to get rid of staff we'd be into paying redundancy money – especially for the green staff. Oh yes, in the long run we'd save money, but in the short term it would actually cost us more, and the short term is what we've got to concentrate on."

I can see that Hugh's worried by what he has found and I ask him how it is going to affect the money we're owed.

"Well that's the point. The Major assumed that he wouldn't have to pay Petmag until September or October and the same for the reservoir guys. He's assumed that the Club will have the money by then as it will have sold all its investments and cut its expenditure. But I don't think it will."

We carry on discussing the situation over supper. Suddenly I have an idea. Couldn't the Club sell off a piece of its land? There is a large field which is used for growing grass for repairing the fairways. While the tree clearance and reservoir work has been going on the field has been used as a vehicle park for the workers and their machines. It's a long way from the clubhouse and there had been talks in the past of making it into a practice area or even a driving range. It was certainly more than large enough. The field can be accessed from a small track running up from the road.

"Why doesn't the Club sell that to some developer to put some houses on? We'd get a lot of money for that."

It's a nice idea Mum but I don't think we'd get planning permission. It would take months to get it to the Council and by then it would be too late. You'd be waiting even longer for your money!"

"But if you don't manage to pay off the overdraft what will happen?"

"Well that's what I'm trying to find out. Apparently Arthur and the Major signed some form of security against the loan. But I can't find a copy of the document. I'm going to have to call Arthur and see if he has a copy. I want to know exactly what they agreed to."

I don't sleep well. I had nightmares which involved Russian troops, led by the Major, bulldozing the clubhouse. It was all mixed up with Pyotr and his men cutting down the trees to allow big lorries to enter the course with huge ready-made houses on them.

I'm glad to find everything unchanged as I arrive at the Club later for the Tuesday stableford. In fact everything seems perfect. The sun is already warm and casting deep shadows on the practice putting green, I can hear the mowers in the distance as the green-staff prepare the fairways and several of my fellow lady golfers are standing around chatting.

I go into the pro-shop. I need a new glove. There's a big notice. *New Centenary Merchandise now in.*

I look at the team sheet on the notice board. I'm down to play with Rosemary. I realise I've only played with her once since my famous hole in one. Gosh, that seems so long ago.

She is full of news about the plans for next year, our centenary year. She tells me the ladies are organising special matches with other clubs that share the same founding date. "There's going to be a big Centenary Ball too."

I wonder if there will be. I can't help thinking of what Hugh has told me. Despite the EGM and the rumours about the Club's finances Rosemary seems unconcerned. It's the same with the other ladies milling around. There's an optimism brought about by the nice weather. The course is looking beautiful although some of the areas where Pyotr did most of the tree clearing still seem a little exposed.

I realise that I am being too pessimistic. The Club has existed for 99 years. This is only a temporary blip brought on by the national financial crisis and the stupidity of the Major in paying Hamilton. Now the Major's gone and Hugh is looking after things, it's bound to get sorted.

Later, in the bar, as we discuss our round I realise that I've been missing the companionship of the ladies, the casual banter about nothing more important than the fact that Rosemary's favourite dress shop in Windsor has had to close down. It's good to not have to worry about the business. That was just a useful (if expensive) chapter in my life which helped me get over Frank's death. It certainly has given me more confidence.

I tell Rosemary all about Simone's pregnancy and how I'm looking forward to becoming a grandmother again. Not long now, I tell her.

"And not long until the Lady Captain's Day," she adds. "Do you have a partner?"

Back home I look round the smallest bedroom, it used to be Simone's. Now I am going to furnish it as a nursery for the new arrival. Simone has told me she's expecting a girl which will be nice. I will go into Guildford or Kingston to look for some wallpaper and curtains. It will be such fun. I am thinking about curtains and where to get a cot from when the doorbell rings. Looking out from the upstairs window

I see the Ocado van outside. I have forgotten I'd ordered a delivery for this afternoon.

I'm pleased to find it's Lech driving. "They gave me back my old route. The Scotsman has left. Didn't like the job." He tells me that Pyotr has found himself a job in Lodz with the Agriculture Department but it is a desk job. He's missing the outdoor life. I hope he will write or phone me. I miss him.

*

Hugh lifted his glass of Sancerre and toasted his friend Cameron from Kaupthing. He was glad to be back in the noisy, crowded atmosphere of a Docklands wine bar. The golf club was a haven of peace, green fields, clean air. But he missed the feeling of being involved in the major world of international finance. He hated the fact that he had to rely on the TV or the Financial Times for news of the latest casualty of the financial crisis. When he worked there he knew what was about to happen, not what had happened. Although he hadn't foreseen the extent of the crash caused by those toxic home loans in America.

For several weeks there had been no major surprises and the stock market had recovered a bit. In his role as acting golf club secretary Hugh had begun to sell the Club's share portfolio. The slight improvement in the market had meant he had got a better price than he originally feared although not enough to make him confident about the Club's stability.

The lunch had two objectives. City lunches are never free! He was hoping to see if there were any openings at the bank for him or, if not, whether Cameron had heard of anything that might suit him among any of the bank's clients. "I wouldn't mind working on the client side rather than the broker side. I reckon I could make a real difference to a good pension fund or even a local authority."

The other objective was to open an account for the Club with Kaupthing. He confided in Cameron the problems that the Club had been experiencing which he described as merely short term. "We don't want to stay with Dylans now they've been taken over by the Russians. There not so accommodating and quite frankly I don't trust them not to pull the rug from under us if they saw profit in it. I've advised the Club to keep the overdraft position pretty much where it is and deposit only as much into the account as we need to pay current bills. The surplus, and there's quite a lot now we're selling the shares I want to put into an instant access savings account with a high rate of interest. Then come October we can use that money to pay them off completely and close our account with Dylans."

"Well I'll drink to that," said Cameron, "and you know we offer the highest rates right now so I'll get the office to send you a mandate for the Club officers to sign and it can be up and running within days. We have loads of local councils invested with us too so I'll keep my ears open for any opportunities for you there."

It was half past four by the time Hugh got back to Barnes. The alcohol at lunchtime had relaxed him and he was feeling positive. A call from one of the head-hunters to fix up an interview had further lifted his spirits.

The Range Rover was in the driveway together with another car, a Porsche. Hugh had walked from the station, a few hundred yards, which was good for his Achilles recovery as well as clearing his head a little. The second bottle of Sancerre might have been a mistake.

Walking, now, up the path he could hear boys laughing and shouting in the small back garden. He opened the door and walked down the hall and into the kitchen. Lettie wasn't there although he could see three boys playing football in the garden. He walked back to the lounge. It too was empty but there was a wine bottle on the coffee table and two empty glasses. Lettie hasn't changed her habit of drinking with the girls, he thought.

Just then Lettie appeared at the lounge door. She glanced from Hugh to the wine glasses. Her cheeks were flushed and her hair was carelessly combed. She was barefoot.

"You're early," she said bending to pick up the glasses and the bottle. She took them through to the kitchen. "The boys are playing with Toby, from school," she said by way of explanation although she was merely stating the obvious.

"I had lunch with a friend in the City."

"Have you found a job?"

"I've got some irons in the fire. He was quite encouraging. Anyway I need to sort out things at the golf club first."

"You and that damned golf club. It's your mother talking you into it. You should have been spending your time getting a proper job so we can pay the bills."

There was a cough behind Hugh who was still standing outside the kitchen door. He turned to see a man of his own age but taller and slimmer. He had long blonde hair combed back. It looked damp like he had freshly washed it but was probably gelled. He wore dark grey suit trousers with a white shirt, open-necked.

"Hi Hugh, I'm Jason. Our boys are at the same school. They're playing football in the garden."

I'm not blind, or deaf, thought Hugh. I don't need both of you to tell me what I can see and hear for myself. What I do want to know though is what has been going on. But he didn't ask that. Years of English public school breeding had taught him politeness and etiquette. So very English. Instead, he shook Jason's hand and smiled. "Nice to meet you. What line are you in?"

The question was more direct than etiquette prescribed but Hugh was fighting an urge to ask him about the wine bottle and glasses.

"Oh I'm in property. Mather and Tomkinson in Putney. In fact," and he seemed to exhale with some relief as if he was on safer ground now, "we sell a lot of properties around here. Lettie was telling me that you might be thinking of putting this place on the market."

"Was she." Hugh looked at Lettie who was making a great show of washing the wine glasses although normally they went straight into the dishwasher.

"Yes she was just showing me the accommodation you have here. It's er, a very nice property. I'm sure it would fetch a good price."

"We're not selling!"

"Oh right, no problem of course. But if you ever change your mind.... I mean if the job at the golf club doesn't work out or you have to relocate then…"

Just how much had Lettie told this 'estate agent'. He seemed very informed.

The conversation was interrupted by William opening the garden door. "Mum, Toby has kicked the ball over the fence. Can I go and get it?"

"No dear, leave it. Toby's going home now." She looked

meaningfully at Jason. "Anyway I don't want you talking to Mrs Patel. She's not like us."

*

Simone's baby came early. Three weeks early and involved a late night dash to St Peter's. But the delivery was normal and mercifully quick so that by the time I arrive to see my little granddaughter, I find Simone sitting up in bed looking tired but very happy.

We talk about the birth, how beautiful she is, how many days it will be before they let Simone and the baby home. Tim arrives shortly afterwards with an enormous bunch of flowers. He looks proudly at Simone and his daughter.

I rush off to get the new cot blanket I've ordered for the nursery which the decorators finished only the week before. I'm glad I planned ahead. The cot is in place, the curtains hung and I am looking forward to Simone staying a few days with me.

I get home and find Hugh in the kitchen. There is a small new car outside. He's looking worried but perks up when I tell him the news about Simone. "I ought to go and see her too," he says. "I'm an uncle!"

"How are things at the golf club? Is that's where you've been today?"

"Yes. Well they're not good, although everyone else seems to be complacent. They're more interested in next year's centenary arrangements than our current problems."

"Well that's good, isn't it? We need to build confidence if we are to stop people leaving."

Hugh tells me that he has now managed to get nearly all the membership fees paid although more than thirty members have resigned. The sale of the Club's investments has also been completed and he is pleased with the amount raised. His concern, however, is the agreement that Arthur and the Major signed. They have effectively mortgaged the clubhouse and the course. It is essential that the overdraft is repaid on time.

"So they've mortgaged everything? So we can't sell off that field? "

"Well that's the good thing. Dylans obviously drew up the mortgage deed very quickly in order to get Arthur to sign it then and there. The plan of the course which was attached, doesn't actually include that field. It wasn't part of the course originally, it was purchased later. So technically, they haven't got a fixed and floating charge over all the Club's assets as they originally did. They've got a very specific charge over the clubhouse and the course itself."

"So we could sell that field?"

"Yes, but it's not worth very much unless and until we get planning permission. And we wouldn't get that by the end of September."

Hugh then goes on to explain his idea. Petmag is one of the two biggest creditors along with the reservoir contractors. Although I have agreed to wait until the end of September for the £300,000 to be paid, he doesn't believe there will be enough cash available then to pay the reservoir people let alone Petmag. The Club would have to agree with a new bank a new overdraft and the limit might not be enough.

"What I'm suggesting Mum is that you buy the field. Well, not you personally, but Petmag. I've had a valuation done, without planning permission, and it's a little more than what the Club owes you. If you were to offer to take the field instead of the £300,000 the Club's assets would immediately be £300,000 better off. The value of the field was never included in the accounts. Once the Club has got back on its feet, say the end of the year, you could offer to sell it back to them at a small profit and pay Pyotr his share. It's the only way I can see you getting paid and the Club surviving."

And so, a few weeks later, Petmag becomes the owner of a very large, very overgrown field with lots of heavy lorries and soil dumps.

52

Simone stays with me for two weeks. We are busy and short on sleep but Geraldine, my new granddaughter, is doing well and beginning to put on weight. I'm glad to be kept busy. I feel useful. I've been so busy for the past six months with Petmag that I've rather neglected my role of grandmother. I'm determined to make up for it. I'm going to help Estelle out with her boys while she and Justin go for interviews.

I need to try and help poor Hugh as well. Despite Simone and Geraldine, he has been staying here a lot, trying to sort things out at the golf club and I have tried to find out how things are with Lettie. He seems reluctant to talk. I think they are very bad.

Now that Simone and little Geraldine have gone, and there is nothing for me to do on Petmag but wait until the Autumn, life is beginning to return to as it was. I am no longer having to calculate wages, have meetings with the bank, meet with Jim or the Major. I am, once again, just another lady member of West Downs Golf Club.

I've signed up for various matches against other local clubs and of course there's a Ladies Day each Tuesday with some competition or other. Golf clubs seem to come out of their winter hibernation around Easter. Suddenly we have the longer evenings, the warmer weather and course pretties up with all the leaves on the deciduous trees. We don't have as many now of course since Pyotr and his men did the tree clearance but there's still the conifers and everything looks fresh. The heather is growing thicker and will flower later in the year. It's a hopeful time with members believing that this is the year they will get that breakthrough and a reduction in handicap.

And, of course, there's my birthday. The big Six O. I don't think Hugh's had any time to think about it what with all his problems and Justin and Estelle have had more important things to think about.

Thinking about birthdays I decide that I am going to plan my own big birthday and use it as a chance to get everyone in the family together. It's been a tumultuous time for all of us and it might do us all good to share our thoughts for the future. So! No luxury cruise, no family week-end in Venice, we'll just have a big house party here. I'll get caterers in and just invite the whole family.

I put the idea to Hugh when he comes in after working at the golf club. He looks a bit shame-faced and coughs. "I'm sorry, I should really have been organising something – a big trip to Venice maybe or a bash at the Club but what with all the problems, and Lettie ..."

"I know dear, you've had more than enough on your plate. I've decided that it would be best to have a big lunch party for the whole family, at home. After all this year has been pretty awful for all of us, ever since Frank died. The one good thing to come out of it is little Geraldine and we can all celebrate her joining the family! Families are important, Hugh, and it's much better than jetting off to some luxury hotel."

"That sounds a great idea." He sounds relieved. "But you must get caterers in."

"I've spoken to them already."

"So what day is it?"

"It's the 25th, Sunday. Do tell me you're free."

"Oh I'm free. And if Lettie is tied up I'll bring the boys on my own."

I haven't heard Hugh like this before. Things are obviously bad between him and Lettie ever since he lost his job. I do hope he gets something else soon.

*

This week it's the Lady Captain's Day.

Golf clubs in the UK and Ireland are different from those in Europe or the US. We make a big thing about being a lady captain, or more accurately, a captain of the ladies. And at West Downs we have turned it into an art form. Tuesday is a day planned totally by the Lady Captain. There's golf in the morning, golf in the afternoon, a big lunch and cakes for tea. And each year the Lady Captain gives her special prize to the best net score in the morning. She also presents many other prizes and gives every participant a little gift to remember her by.

Men do it very differently. A few shirts from the pro-shop, a few bottles of wine and they're happy. But we ladies of West Downs like, nay demand, something better. Everything needs to be coordinated – even the flowers. And the lunch menu needs to be something special too.

Margaret, our Lady Captain, is the wife of a London property developer, so we are secretly expecting a very generous gift and some exceptional prizes. I'm partnering Rosemary in the morning medal and we're with two other ladies in the afternoon foursomes. I'm trying to decide what to wear for lunch. The July weather is mild and it should be sunny so a smart skirt, blouse and jacket will do nicely. On the other hand maybe I should wear that nice blue dress?.

The car park is already half-full when I arrive and unload my trolley. I still prefer to use a trolley – electric of course, rather than a buggy. After all I'm not 60 yet. Well not quite. Rosemary joins me for a coffee and together we examine the table of 'goodies' laid out in the hall. There are little organza bags with tees and balls and a beautiful enamelled ball marker with a depiction of the clubhouse and the words '99 not out' which causes us all to smile.

Rosemary is a good partner to play with. She enjoys a good chat like the rest of us but takes her golf quite seriously. I've played so little over this eventful winter that I'm concerned that my medal score will be really bad and my handicap will even go up. But whether it is the fact that I no longer have the worries of Pyotr and the business, or the fact that the sun is shining weakly through the thin clouds, I play rather well and come in with a score of one under par.

"You could be in for the prize," says Rosemary as we are changing for lunch. "It was quite tricky out there today and I don't reckon many will have played to their handicap."

Margaret is already in the bar as we go through to get our pre-lunch drink. She is looking resplendent in a pale lilac skirt and jacket. Seeing me, she waves and comes across followed by Marco the steward. "Let me get you a drink Maggie, and you Rosemary."

Marco returns to the bar with the orders and we sit down in the window overlooking the 18th tee. Margaret turns to Rosemary and puts her hand on Rosemary's wrist. "Rosemary, I wonder if you'd be kind enough …. er I'd just like to have a word with Maggie. I won't be a moment."

Taking the hint, Rosemary gets up and joins one of the other groups gathering in the bar. I'm intrigued to learn what is so private that Margaret wants to talk to me alone. Maybe Rosemary's right, maybe I've won and she just wants to check something on my scorecard. Oh dear, I do hope I've not added it up wrong.

But Margaret has no idea of what my score is. She has something totally different to ask me. Marco brings over my drink and I clink glasses with Margaret.

"Maggie, I wonder if you might be up for doing me an enormous favour. You know I chose Yvonne as my vice captain and she will be taking over for centenary year?"

"Yes, of course, and I'm sure she'll be great in the job. She's very gregarious and a good speaker, just what the Club needs next year."

"Well there's a problem. She rang me last night to say that her husband's job has been moved. He's got to go to Frankfurt and they'll be moving as soon as they have found a house. Apparently this financial business that everyone is talking about has meant his company, a German one, is closing the London office. He's lucky to still have a job but he has to move to Germany."

"Oh dear. There's so much upheaval with the economy at the moment, I know. Look at my Hugh. He's lost his job in the City and can't find another."

"Yes, well you see, that leaves us without a captain for the Centenary Year. Poor Yvonne is devastated but there's no helping it. Which is why, Maggie, I wondered if…"

"But Margaret, why me. I'm not even on committee. I'm sure there are much better people."

"I've talked to some of the older members and a couple on the committee and they all suggested you. After what you have done to help the Club with that awful tree-clearing mess and Jim says you've really helped out the Club by not taking your payment for all the work. I think you've deserved it."

So there it is. A year after poor Frank died and I'm to be Lady Captain. What a year I've had. All starting with that hole in one, then meeting Lech and Pyotr, the Petmag business, a new granddaughter – wow it has been some year.

"Don't tell anyone yet," says Margaret, "I do have to get it approved by the men still but I'm sure there won't be a problem." I smile to myself. West Downs is 99 years old and still it's the men who rule things.

Hugh is at the house when I return, flushed with success. I won the Lady Captain's prize for the morning and Rosemary and I came runners up in the afternoon. Hugh grins when he sees me carrying in a large box and an enormous bouquet of flowers.

"Looks like someone has been playing well!"

Despite Margaret's instructions I tell Hugh about becoming Lady Captain for the Centenary.

"That's absolutely great, Mum, and it'll be good for you to have another project!"

He's right. After the work for Petmag finished there was something missing in my life, and it wasn't just Pyotr. The arrival of Geraldine had, of course, been something special and certainly filled my life for a few weeks, but here was something to look forward to. I was already thinking about how I should find out what other centenary clubs were planning – seeing what link-ups we could do with them perhaps. A lot of the arrangements were already in place. The Club's centenary merchandise had all been done and there were a Summer Ball, a big men's dinner and several other events already pencilled into the calendar.

But something special, just for the ladies. I have to think of something.

53

I'm up early on Sunday. I take time over my hair and make-up. Not bad for 60, I think, smiling at my reflection in the bedroom mirror. I've still got a lot to do before the family arrive. The caterers are due at 11 but I expect Simone and Estelle might get down here about the same time.

Hugh and Lettie and the boys will probably arrive last as usual.

The lounge is looking festive with lots of my birthday cards and several large vases of flowers. It's still a pity that the walls have the marks of the stolen pictures still showing. I really must get the decorators in.

I get myself a cup of coffee and am just buttering a slice of toast when the phone rings. To my amazement, and joy, it's Pyotr. He's remembered my birthday and is ringing to wish me well. I'm so pleased to hear from him. He tells me that Saska is getting very big and it won't be long before he will be a father. I ask him how the new job is.

"It's OK you know. Not as exciting as Petmag but not so dangerous either!" I'm glad to see he has retained his sense of humour. I tell him about the Club and how I'm going to be the centenary Lady Captain and he sounds really pleased. I ask him how he is managing financially as it won't be until the Autumn that the Club will be able to pay us for the land we took as security in lieu of what they owed us.

"Don't worry, Maggie, I get a regular salary now and Saska is earning good money at the moment and they will pay her some money after the baby arrives. We'll be fine until Christmas, anyway."

It's nice to hear his voice again and I realise how much I've been missing him. I've hardly had time to make another slice of toast before the doorbell goes.

It's Hugh. He's wearing a dark blue suit, pale pink shirt and the Club tie. He looks very smart and there's a spring in his step. He's carrying yet another huge bunch of flowers and behind him the two boys are carrying a large parcel. There's no sign of Lettie.

"You're early."

"Daddy's bought you a present and he's got some news to tell you!" William is beaming and hands across the large parcel.

Hugh smiles, gives me a hug and tells me the good news. He's landed a job with a large public sector pension fund. "It's not going to give the bonuses I've been used to but the salary's good. And anyway, I think the days of big city bonuses are over. The economy's going to take some time to recover."

"Where will you be working? In Docklands?"

"No, that's the bad bit. It's in Manchester. I'm moving up there."

"What does Lettie think about that?" I look for the boys to see if they are listening but they've already gone into the house carrying the big present.

"She's not prepared to move north. In fact I think the separation will be good. Things have been pretty bad recently between us. She's even talked of divorce."

"But surely now you've got a good job again…." I look at him and see the resignation in his eyes. There's something he's not telling me I'm sure.

"She's been spending a lot of time with one of the fathers at the boys' school. He's divorced and doing very well in the property market."

I put my arms around him and we hug. We stay like that for several seconds. It is Hugh who breaks the hold. His eyes are moist. He turns away, looking at the garden. "They're doing a good job with this garden, much better than when that Italian was here."

He clearly doesn't want to say more about Lettie. I wonder what will happen to the boys. They'll stay with her, no doubt. How serious is this 'relationship' with the property man? She has always been attracted to the big money. For the past few months she's had her husband out of work and I suppose she has seen me spending her inheritance on the Petmag venture. Not that I'm about to drop dead. In fact I feel more alive now than I have for months or years. The Petmag project took my mind off growing old, being widowed and now little Geraldine has been keeping me fully occupied.

We find the boys in the lounge. They are waiting for me to open my present. It turns out to be two large framed pictures. They are lovely pictures of our villa in Portugal.

"I thought they'd cover up some of the spaces on the wall," says Hugh. They remind me of the many holidays Frank and I spent there. I must see if I can't get over for a week or two with one of the ladies from the golf club.

I send Hugh down to the cellar to choose some nice wine from Frank's dwindling collection and turn to let in the caterers who arrive bearing large trays and polystyrene boxes.

The caterers serve up the main course and retire to the kitchen. I look around the table at the family. Everyone who matters is there. Only Lettie is absent and no one seems concerned. In fact everyone is very happy and the room is resounding to the chatter and the clatter of cutlery on crockery.

Hugh is sitting to my right. He gets to his feet, tapping his wine glass with a spoon. The room hushes.

"This is a very special day for a very special person. Mum, Grandma, is 60 today and we are all here to celebrate." He clears his throat.

"We are all very proud of you Mum and how you've coped with life after," he paused again, "what happened to Dad. I have to admit we thought that maybe you would struggle to cope without him. But far from it. You've not only carried on but become a real entrepreneur – forming international alliances with handsome Polish men" there is laughter from the adults round the table, "and becoming the saviour of my beloved golf club! And the future looks even busier as Mum will soon become the Lady Captain in the Club's Centenary Year."

I look around at the family as Hugh continues. It has indeed been an eventful year and a stressful year. But in the end everything has worked out very well and I certainly have never been at a loose end.

The day turns out to be perfect. Everyone makes a fuss of me and of little Geraldine. Justin, Hugh and Tim seem to get on better than normal, in fact seem to be really enjoying themselves. I'm sorry when around 6pm Simone says she needs to be heading back with a now-sleeping Geraldine and the others start packing up.

Hugh and the boys are the last to go. Hugh says he will be down tomorrow and we can talk about his new job then.

I switch on the television. There's nothing interesting so I decide to turn in early. After all I'm 60 now and it's been a long day. I gaze at the two pictures before I switch the light off and head upstairs.

*

It's mid-afternoon before Hugh and I drive over to the Club. The days are shortening again but it's still warm and we sit outside on the terrace with Jim. We watch as a fourball comes down the eighteenth. The shadows of the tall pines are spreading across the green like huge fingers pointing to the clubhouse. The fairways are lush and green thanks to the reservoir supply of water for the sprinklers. We can see across to the first and the practice ground beyond. The tree clearance has made such a difference. The fairways are still delineated, there are some specimen trees among the pines. But the thinning of the trees has let the sun and air through to the greens and promoted their growth.

I sigh. This really is a special place. And next year it will have been enjoyed by members for a hundred years.

Hugh tells Jim about his new job and that he can no longer help out with the secretary's job.

"Well you've done a sterling job, steadying the ship and I for one really appreciate what you've done. There was a time when I seriously doubted we'd be celebrating next year." Jim looks across to the eighteenth as the players remove their caps and shake hands.

"We're not out of the woods yet Jim. We've got to keep a tight rein on costs and make sure we keep enough in the kitty to pay back those bastards at Dylans next month. "

"Yes, I know, and it's going to be tight. But your help Maggie, taking that field in payment of the amount we owed you has certainly helped. Now we just need to settle with the reservoir guys."

"Who will you get to take over the secretary's job?" said Maggie.

"Arthur's keen to make amends. I think he'll be only too happy to hold the fort until we can afford to get a full-time secretary."

54

The news, when it came, was sudden. It was a shock. In fact it was a double shock. It was so unexpected. It was, ultimately so tragic.

In the last week of September I had gone out to Portugal with Daphne. It was a year since I'd been out to our house there and a year since I'd had a holiday. The villa overlooked the 6th hole at San Lorenzo facing across the salt flats to the ocean. The temperature was hot during the day and warm in the evenings. We played our golf and took walks in the Ria Formosa nature reserve observing the birds. It was peaceful, relaxing, invigorating.

The first signs of trouble came at the end of the first week. We watched the Sky News report that some Icelandic bank, Glitnir, was being nationalised. But this seemed a million miles away and not something to worry us on holiday.

It was as we were flying back the following week that we caught sight of the Portuguese news at Faro airport. We couldn't understand the words but the pictures told their own story. The Icelandic government had taken control of the banks.

By the time we got back to England the full extent of the crisis was clear. Kaupthing, Landsbanki and Glitnir, Iceland's major banks were in liquidation.

The message light on my phone in the hall is flashing as the taxi driver puts my bags down. I pay him and take my coat off. I make myself a cup of tea and bring the mug into the hall, sit down and press the messages button.

There are six messages but it is the last two, today's messages, that grab my attention. One is from Hugh. He wants me to ring him as soon as possible. It's about Lettie. It's very urgent. The second is from Jim. He also wants me to ring him.

"Oh dear. Back to reality."

I decide to phone Hugh first. He tells me that that Lettie is filing for divorce. She wants to sell their house and is moving in with Michael. He seems resigned. I ask him what he will do. "Well you know Manchester's not so bad. In fact it's quite a happening city. I'll get myself a nice apartment in the centre. And I'm really enjoying the new job."

"I'm glad the job's ok," I say. "The news seems very bad for the economy. I was just hearing something about the Icelandic banks closing down. We've got some money in those haven't we? What will happen to it?"

He tells me not to worry. After transferring the funds to Petmag I had only a few hundred pounds left in the account. He had been warned about the problems by his friend at Kaupthing some weeks ago and closed his account, moving it to one of the major British banks.

"I told Jim to get the Club's money out of Kaupthing too, last week. Told him to get Arthur to pay off Dylans quickly."

Hugh says he will be back to sort out things with Lettie at the weekend and asks if he can stay with me. I say goodbye and think about the two boys. How will they react to the divorce?

I am still thinking about this when the phone rings. I think it must be Hugh having forgotten something. But it's Jim.

"I'm so glad you're back Maggie. I need Hugh's work number. I need to speak with him urgently about this Icelandic thing. Have you got his number?"

*

Whenever you arrive at the Club you glance at the flagpole. If a member has died the Club flag is lowered to half mast. It was like that when Hugh and I arrive on Saturday morning. Jim is already there. There are two men erecting a sign by the front gate. I can't see what the sign says as it is lying on the ground.

The car park is full with members' vehicles. It's a warm sunny October day and people are already out on the course.

Jim takes us into the secretary's office. His face is grim. There are bags under his eyes. He looks like he's not been sleeping.

"The flag's at half mast. Who's died?" I ask.

"Arthur."

"Arthur?"

"Yes tragic really. He just blamed himself. I suppose he just couldn't face the fact that he'd destroyed the Club."

Hugh and I look at him in amazement. Our amazement turns to sorrow and then to anger as he outlines the goings-on of the past few days."

Hugh already knew from Jim's mid-week phone call that Arthur had not taken his advice to move the money out of Kaupthings. Arthur had maintained that withdrawing it before the following week would incur an interest penalty. The Club needed every penny. And Dylans didn't need the overdraft cleared before next Friday. In the meantime the reservoir contractors were threatening to sue the Club if they didn't receive their money immediately. Arthur had written them a cheque, counter-signed by Jim. The cheque, on their Dylan's account had taken them over the agreed overdraft limit. Not by much, but nevertheless it was over the limit. Arthur had miscalculated and forgotten about certain direct debits.

Dylans had honoured the cheque and paid the contractors. But the next day they served notice that they were taking over all the assets of the Club immediately.

"But they can't do that, surely?" I said. "Can't we just pay the overdraft off? Even if we have to get a loan from some of our richer members?"

"I'm afraid not. We can't get any of our money out of the Kaupthing's account and even if we got the money from somewhere else, Dylans won't take it. It appears that the agreement Arthur and the Major signed had a codicil that said that in the event the Club exceeded its overdraft the bank would be entitled to ownership of the Club. Not like a mortgage where they could sell it, recoup their debt, and give the rest to the Club. No, it was a cynical ruse to get the entire Club for little more than £1 million."

"Is that legal," asked Hugh.

"Well we will of course dispute it, but I'm not hopeful. They've got some pretty sharp lawyers."

"I feel bad," said Hugh. "I should have noticed that in the agreement when I got it from Arthur."

"It was added as a codicil. I don't think Arthur gave you that."

"But what happened to Arthur? How did he die?" I can see the flagpole through the window of the office.

"An overdose, last night. He left a note for his wife saying sorry."

*

The lake is still. There's no wind. The cloud-speckled November sky is reflected on its surface. I place my ball on a tee. So this is the last time I'll ever play this hole. The course will be finally closed tomorrow, 99 years after it was opened. The new owners have applied for planning permission for 260 houses. The council is looking at it sympathetically, there is a requirement for them to build more houses. There's no money to fight the takeover, and no real will from members either. There are other clubs in the area anxious to accept new members. There's been too much mismanagement at West Downs.

I think back to last year when my life changed with that hole in one. I think about everything that's happened since, the highs, the lows.

I swing back my club and it connects with the little white ball. But the ball doesn't rise into the sky. It skids off the club and bounces once on the surface of the water before sinking into the still, dark water.

EPILOGUE

It's a week before Christmas. The snow lies thick and piled up against the perimeter fence as the Boeing 737 of LOT airlines touches down on the runway.

I peer out of the small cabin window. So this is Poland. This is Pyotr's home. It doesn't look like the pictures in the book he gave me last Christmas. Last Christmas! Just a year ago.

As Pyotr drives me through the frozen countryside towards Lodz, I glimpse the brightly-coloured cottages from the book, their snow-capped roofs looking like icing sugar on a gingerbread house.

I think back to how my life has changed in the past year or so. I've lost a husband, and nearly a stone in weight. But I've gained something too; self-confidence and two really good friends. And something else. A sense of purpose to life.

Saska is looking really well and is so proud to introduce me to little Pyotr. Motherhood suits her although she confesses to missing her work. I give her the presents and watch as she opens them.

It's good to see them both so happy at home and to see Pyotr so clearly recovered. He'll have to come over to

England in March for the trial and hopefully will get a good amount of compensation from the Criminal Injuries Board. I hope Saska and little Pyotr will come too.

We talk about his job in Lodz. "He does not mind it and it is secure," says Saska, "but he misses the outside work, like he had in England."

I tell him about the Club. He wants to know what has happened since the Russians took it over.

"They've got the planning permission," I say. "Of course the local residents are appealing but the council seems impressed by the amount of money the Russians have."

"And the amount of money they can pay to the councillors, no doubt." Pyotr is no fan of the Russians. Not after what they did to Poland in the war.

"But how is the course?"

I tell him about the bulldozers. I tell him about the demolition of the clubhouse.

"It's all happening so quickly. And what about the Club's money in the Icelandic bank. Will they ever get it?"

"Maybe but it will be a long time I expect and then it will be shared among the members."

"So we won't get our £300,000 bill paid," said Pyotr. "That's gone."

"Well not exactly, Pyotr. You remember I agreed to take the old practice field instead? Well we were going to sell it back to the golfclub when they had the money. Petmag still owns that large field."

"So we can sell it and get some money? Pay the money you put in and split anything that's left over." Hope shows in his eyes as he glances at Saska.

"Indeed. Hugh says that with planning permission it would be worth over a million."

"That's great, we'll apply for planning!"

"Well we could, but I've been thinking. With 260 houses being built next door, and the way everyone is talking about wanting organic vegetables, and knowing how you love growing things, Pyotr, I just wondered if we three might turn it into a market garden for organic vegetables."

Pyotr looks at me and I see his face break into that special grin. He gives me that look that says "Maggie you're incorrigible."